The Hollidaysburg Christmas Miracle

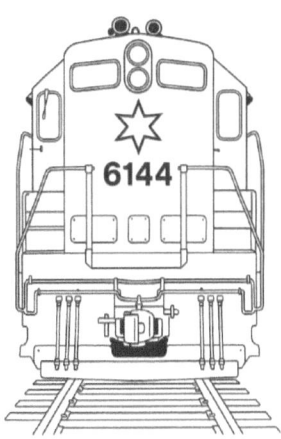

THE HOLLIDAYSBURG CHRISTMAS MIRACLE

Bruce Bracken

Latte Press

This is a work of fiction. Names, characters, places, and incidents are products of the author's imagination or are used fictitiously. Any resemblance to actual persons, living or dead, events, or locales is entirely coincidental.

Published by Latte Press

Cover design by Bruce Bracken, Jr.

ISBN: 979-8-9936654-0-5

First edition published 2013
Revised edition 2025

Printed in the United States of America

CHAPTER 1

Chris stepped onto one of the ties protruding beyond the iron rails and faced Pleasant Valley. Just after the roiling stream and not too far from the base of the trestle, icy water pooled serene and quiet, free of the upstream eddies and whirlpools. Chris lifted his face toward heaven, stretched his arms outward, and contemplated the outcome of jumping from this height—the crushing blow to his body, the crushing blow to his family.

Though it is human nature when standing near a precipice to have thoughts of leaping, few people act on the impulse. And so it was with Chris, at least for now. After leaving his eighth-grade class at the end of the school day, he'd walked more than an hour to get to where he now stood, and he'd be content to sit for a while and think. Chris drew his hands from the pockets of his lightweight jacket, steadied himself, and lowered his bottom onto the frigid rail. His buttocks felt the bite of cold iron through his corduroys. Despite the sting, he pulled his knees toward his chest, his shoes rested on the creosote tie and his heels pressed against the spike binding the rail to the trestle. He laid his hatless, curly red-haired head onto his knees and closed his eyes.

A foreboding winter front was approaching, and a harsh

1

northerly wind bore both the sweet scent of the advancing squall and the caw of a lone crow hurrying across the valley to avoid the storm. As if in response to the crow's warning, the breeze changed from damp and frosty to something sharper — a fine, wintery sleet with harsh crystalline edges that sliced the tips of Chris's ears like miniature razors. Nevertheless, the young man was oblivious to the deteriorating weather, insulated as he was within his personal blanket of despair.

Chris sat with his eyes closed for a long while, contemplating how his life had once been and what it had become. To the one person who mattered most but who was present only in spirit, he implored, "Why did you have to die? Why, Grandpa? I don't understand. Knowing I'll never see you again makes me ache so much I can barely stand it. Dad said that God took you. If that's true, then I hate God; God didn't love you and He doesn't love me. I'm done with Him! I've done the best I can, Grandpa—really, I have. But I can't ...."

"Hey! Hey, kid! Watch out!"

Rex, an out-of-context cowboy, hadn't noticed the young man sitting mid-trestle until his attention was drawn upward by three short blasts from an approaching locomotive. The rumble of the train's diesel engines and the lead locomotive's blaring horn drew Rex's eyes to the boy. Backlit by the brilliance of the engine's headlight was the silhouette of a curly-haired kid who looked no older than thirteen or fourteen. The boy leapt to his feet from the rail where he sat and stood uncertain like a fawn on newborn legs. The horn must have startled the kid, because at first he scrambled through a swirl of fine, wind-blown snow toward the intense light. Then, just as suddenly, he reversed his steps and tried to run away.

Rex let the empty water jugs he'd been carrying fall from his calloused hands; the plastic bottles bounced aimlessly downhill in the general direction of the pond. He cupped his hands along either side of his unshaven chin and hollered a warning through cracked lips. Despite his efforts, his yelling and waving had no effect; Rex

2

was below the bridge, in the dark. He couldn't be seen from the trestle, and he couldn't be heard over the din of the locomotive. Rex swore and tugged at the threadbare hem of his mustard-colored range coat, intuitively knowing there was no way he'd make it to the top of the ravine in time to save the kid. All the same, he turned and sprinted up the trail.

The creosote-timbered bridge, still erect after more than a century, spanned more than one hundred and eighty feet from entrance to egress. The boy, standing in the middle of the span, some five stories above the rocks and stream below, would have to cross at least ninety feet of treacherous track in either direction if he was to get off the trestle alive. After overcoming his panicked false start, the young teen appeared to have gathered his wits and assessed his chances of escape as more favorable if he ran away from the engine than toward it. While the boy headed for the far end of the bridge ahead of the locomotive, Rex did the same. He hoped the kid would make it of course, but he really wanted to hear why the boy was on Cresson Trestle in the dark just a few days before Christmas.

Rex stumbled uphill over exposed tree roots and the eroded ruts that scored the trail. Jolted by a deep, burning pain in his right calf, Rex went face forward into thick, gooey mud. The Texan cussed as he wiped his grimy hands across the thighs of his worn jeans and then desperately tried to massage the cramp from his aching calf. If the pained muscle cooperated, Rex hoped to use his lanky six-foot-one-inch frame and long arms to haul the boy to safety. But fate was not cooperating; Rex's calf cramped again, and the boy faltered with the train gaining on him. Seeing that the locomotive was getting the better of the kid, Rex feared he would be of no more assistance to the boy than to collect his scattered body parts after the engine passed.

Rex had seen the gruesome result of men killed by heavy equipment, but nothing had prepared him for what was unfolding before his eyes. He had never gathered the mangled body of someone so young, or, for that matter, anyone torn apart by two back-to-back diesel engines pulling sixty or more cars through rugged mountains. At the precise moment Rex accepted the bleak outcome of this race between boy and train, the teen stopped running and turned to face the glare of the locomotive's headlight. His head and shoulders sagged, and his languid arms dangled at his sides, offering not even a pretense of defense.

The cowboy couldn't turn his gaze away; his eyes were riveted to the impending disaster. He gasped and held his breath as the train rumbled forward, and his body tensed just before impact. The instant the train reached the young man, Rex blinked. When his eyes fluttered open, the boy was gone from the bridge. At the very last moment before being struck, the young man, gambling on the vagaries of chance, had sidestepped the train and hurled himself off the trestle, into the rocky chasm.

"My God!" Rex muttered. He reached for a nearby oak to steady himself as he tried to comprehend the surreal ending to the unfolding horror. The cowboy's eyes pierced the darkness, anticipating the boy's trajectory through the ravine, estimating whether the kid's choice would make a difference in outcome or whether he had simply decided to end his life one way rather than another. Rex stood still and alert, straining to detect the telltale report from below; would he hear the boy hitting the pond or striking the rocks that surround it?

With eyes closed and one ear turned toward the pond, Rex again held his breath, listening for the faintest clue, but he heard nothing except the drum of diesel engines and the squeal of rattling railcars. Impatient to know whether the boy had hit rock or water, Rex hobbled down the trail as quickly as his cramped muscle allowed.

Rex's friend Leo, a heavyset, bald-headed Black man, had been walking down the rugged trail well ahead of him paying no attention to this particular passing train—the men were used to trains passing by their camp in the woods. Only when he glanced over his shoulder did Leo observe his friend's peculiar role in the tragedy developing in the mountains overlooking the small western

Pennsylvania town of Hollidaysburg. Perplexed at the sight of Rex bolting up the trail, Leo hollered after his friend, "Hey, man, where you goin'?"

Without answering, Rex suddenly stopped, stared upward, and after a moment sprinted downhill in Leo's direction. As Rex hobble-dashed past Leo, the toe of his right boot snagged the root of a mountain laurel, plunging him headlong down the trail. He tumbled out of control through mud and snow, sliding downhill on wet leaves, grasping for anything that would hold him, until his shoulder careened off the trunk of a sapling. The sturdy young maple stopped him cold, leaving his chest sucking air as futile as torn bellows. The collision shook the sapling too, forcing it to release its tentative grip on the handful of leaves it held captive into early winter. With Rex on his back moaning and looking heavenward into a black sky, liberated orange and red leaves and fluffy snowflakes fluttered down, settling on and around the cowboy's spread-eagle body.

Just as old and nearly as tall as the wiry Texan, Leo cast a broader shadow than his companion. Because of his greater bulk, Leo generally struggled to keep up when the two men walked together, and often the large Black man took the lead to set a more relaxed pace for the pair. Right now, though, he found himself lumbering well behind Rex, trying to close the gap as he navigated the dark trail toward the pond.

Befuddled by why Rex lay on the ground, Leo stopped and stood over his friend. He stared down at the pitiful man and shook his head. Like a minister, arms spread wide and his hands facing upward, Leo explained apologetically to the shaken maple in Rex's terms, "The *hombre* is *un poco loco.*" Looking at his pal, he asked, "What's with you, man? Ya got a bee in your bonnet? Cain't be that. Ain't no bees out here, lest they be Snow Bees!"

Rex didn't have enough breath to respond to his friend's humor, and as Leo leaned forward, offering support, Rex grasped the helping hand, bounded to his feet, and hopped in place a few times favoring his bum leg. In an effort to secure his balance, he collided

5

with Leo, sending the big man reeling backward and onto his bottom, jolting the knit stocking cap from his head into the mud.

Now Leo was the one who looked a bit crazy as he sat partially submerged in muck. He plucked his dirty, frayed cap from the mire and pulled it down snug over his balding head. Glaring at his gloved hands, which were now wet and muddy, he considered them and the water oozing through the seat of his bib overalls. Too irked to get up but too miserable to stay put, Leo sat temporarily transfixed. His personal dilemma was short-lived, however, because as Rex had resumed his hobble-dash down the trail without so much as an offer of a helping hand, he yelled over his shoulder as he departed, "Come on, Leo. Don't just sit there!"

Leo gripped the stout sapling that Rex had attacked and heaved himself off the muddy ground. Once afoot, he brushed snow and leaves from his overalls, separated the wet seat of his pants from his bottom, and hastily strode down the trail in pursuit of his addled friend. Leo found Rex balancing on one leg at the water's edge, rubbing his sore calf with one hand and his chest with the other, all the while scanning the surface of the pond. Striding up to his buddy, Leo blasted, "What in tarnation you doin', man?"

As if searching for wranglers on the open range, Rex squinted in resolute silence into the deep shadows. Taking a cue from Rex, Leo glanced over his shoulder at the rippled pond, trying to see what the Texan sought so intently. The two grubby men stood side by side on the bank, panting, seeking something vague in the nighttime shadows.

Rex bent forward peering deeper into the snowy obscurity, oblivious to Leo's presence. The Black man shook his head and slapped at the mud on his overalls. Looking away from the filth that covered him, he tried once more, "What is it, man? What you lookin' for?"

Still, Rex said nothing, while concentrating on the ripples that radiated across the pond's surface. Leo stepped in front of his friend to block his view and gain his attention. Before Leo could press him further, Rex sidestepped the big man, pointed toward the center of the pond, and yelled, "There!"

Leo turned toward the water and looked through the falling snow in the direction of where Rex pointed. In the inky water, he saw what appeared to be a curly-haired head bobbing about forty yards out, near the center of the pond. Without a second thought, Leo ripped loose his laces and kicked off his boots. He tossed his cap and brown oilcloth coat to the ground and bounded three quick steps through the shallows before plunging headlong into the icy but not-yet-frozen water. He sank beneath the surface, the icy water gripping his chest like a vice. As soon as his feet touched the rocky bottom, Leo straightened his knees and thrust upward, gulping air as his face broke the water's surface. With arms flailing, Leo splashed toward the epicenter of the ripples where the inert body floated face down. The floating head rose and fell with each passing wave like an apple bobbing in a galvanized washtub.

Leo's inexperience in deep water was immediately evident to Rex, who, unlike Leo, had second thoughts about the wisdom of his friend's heroic act. Rex stood on his tiptoes bawling into the swirling snow, "Come on back, Leo. The kid's gotta be dead. I don't want you dead too, man. Get back here before I come in after ya."

Leo hollered back, "Stay put, Rex. I'm okay. I've almost got him."

Confident in his ability to keep his head above water, Leo gave little consideration for his own safety. He figured the water was shallow enough for him to touch bottom just about anywhere in the pond. When Leo reached the body, he tested his assumption and to his relief found himself standing on his tiptoes in chin-deep water.

After rolling the body onto its back, Leo could see he was holding onto a young teen. He bellowed toward shore, "I got him, Rex. I'ma comin' back. Stay put now! You hear me?"

"Yeah, I hear ya. Just keep comin' or I'm gonna be comin' in there with ya."

Snatching the collar of the boy's shirt, Leo towed the lifeless body behind him as he side-kicked toward shore. After just ten minutes in the icy water, Leo was anesthetized almost to the point of paralysis; his movements became sluggish, and his thoughts garbled.

Rex cupped his hands around his mouth and yelled into the darkness, "How ya makin' it, Leo?"

Getting no response from his friend except the sounds of panting and groaning, he sensed Leo's physical and mental deterioration. Preparing to enter the water, Rex paced the muddy bank, coaxing his friend forward. "Come on, Leo. You can do it. Come on, man. Keep swimming; you've almost made it!"

Leo concentrated on inching ahead, but his heart and breathing were slowing in response to the freezing water temperature. Despite his initial awareness of the cold, Leo felt deceptively warm. He wanted to linger in the pond's warmth and emulate the passivity of the young man he towed. *Why struggle any further?* About ten yards from the shore, Leo could hardly move through the shallows; he hunched shoulder deep in ice-water, mesmerized by each fallen snowflake as it melted upon contact with the pond surface and merged with the ripples embracing him.

"I n-n-need t'stop a minute, Rex," he whispered after lowering himself onto the rocky pond bottom, his chin just above the water's surface.

Placid as the pond, Leo observed Rex striding into the knee-deep water, not understanding the man's urgency as he yelled, "No, you ain't! Listen to me you fool. Get up and keep going!" Cringing as the freezing water pricked his legs, Rex waded toward the two inert bodies. With all the voice of authority he could muster, he shouted, "Come on, Leo. Git off your butt. Now!"

Leo was barely able to stand, but he did as Rex demanded. Cradling the boy in his arms, as if holding a newborn that had not yet caught its first breath, Leo stumbled toward the shore. Rex met him in the shallows and received the boy's limp body. He placed the young man onto the semi-frozen ground, then grasped Leo's wrist and pulled his friend ashore. Leo collapsed nearby, out of breath, in a sodden heap.

Relieved his buddy was out of the water, Rex diverted his

attention to the young man. He put two fingers into the boy's mouth to remove any debris and afterward pinched snot from the boy's nostrils. Pulling his shirttail loose from his jeans, Rex dried the young man's face with the soft flannel. As he laid his ear against the kid's nose, he heard the rattling, gurgling sounds of air being forced through a watery passageway.

"Yes! He's breathing!"

"Th- tha-that's g-good," Leo stuttered.

Burdened by the weight of his cold, soaked clothing, Leo pulled himself to his hands and knees and crawled toward the boy. He knelt beside the young body and slapped his hands together, trying to rally himself. He had to be sharp if he was to save the young man's life.

Rex, now standing over his pal, released a torrent of emotion. "Durn you, Leo! You scared the dickens outa me! You swim like a three-legged kitten in a bucket of molasses. What was you thinkin' when you up and dove into that freezing slush? I won't be surprised at all if you come down with a case'a pneumonia. I knowed if you didn't out and out drown yourself in that pond, you'd end up havin' a heart attack! You scared me, man. Don't never do nothin' stupid like that again. You hear me?"

Leo warmed to the attack as he leaned over the unresponsive body. He glanced up at his friend and weighed in, "D-D-Don't be talkin' like that to me, old man. There you was ba-bouncing down the trail like you was in some kinda pinball machine. You was rackin' up points, ba-bing, bing, bing! Down the hill you went ricochetin' from tree to tree 'til that scrawny maple done tilted yo' game. I knew you couldna or wouldna done any better in that freezin' mess than me, bein' the shape you was in. So, I jumped in. That's that. Now, g-get over it."

He paused, numb and dumb from the cold, and mumbled, "I'm a-freezin', Rex."

"I know ya are, buddy. We gotta hurry up an' get you back to camp."

"First, I gotta ch-check the kid to make sure we can move him."

9

"Aw'right…aw'right, but hurry! We ain't none of us gonna last very long in this freezin' weather, 'specially, bein' wet like we are."

Leo's deft hands defied the cold and maneuvered methodically from the boy's bleeding head to his shoeless right foot. The kid's left foot was still clad in its scuffed black leather shoe. Leo checked every inch of the teen's chilled flesh. As a former Special Forces medic, Leo had conducted similar exams during or after attacks under comparably adverse conditions. Despite the onset of hypothermia, he executed this exam, assessing the immediate needs of his patient, in total darkness and freezing temperatures, as only a well-trained and experienced medic could.

Leo dictated a report aloud as he examined the youth, "He's breathin' okay, but he's . . . ah . . . got some facial injuries . . . maybe bad head trauma . . . a concussion, and maybe some cracked ribs. An' his hands, legs, and chest—um, they all scraped up pretty good. I need to check his eyes and reflexes when we get back to camp." After his brief examination, Leo spoke up, "Rex, we gotta git or we all gonna freeze to death right here. I don't like it, but we gotta take a chance of movin' the kid with him havin' a neck or back injury. We gotta carry this boy back to camp, now. He's soaked and in these temps, I'm thinkin' 'bout him dyin' of pneumonia even if he survives us draggin' him back to camp—'specially with chest injuries and water rattlin' about in them lungs."

"Don't you think we should take him straight into town?"

"We'd freeze to death before we got halfway down the mountain, Rex. Besides, it's gonna be hard enough on the boy to get him back to camp in this snow that's a-fallin', let alone drag him down the tracks in the dark." Leo lifted himself to his feet and commanded, "C-come on, Rex. We gotta go!"

With nighttime winter temperatures quickly diminishing the strength of the sodden three, Rex knew the only hope for their survival was for him to lead Leo, with the injured boy across his own shoulder, out of the dark craggy ravine before they all succumbed to their injuries and hypothermia.

CHAPTER 2

Leo's clothes had stiffened against his body and his internal temperature descended toward life-threatening hypothermia. Rex was wet only from his knees down and compared to either Leo or the boy he was warm. Nevertheless, he was banged up from his freefall down the ravine, and his cramped calf still nagged him. He winced as he picked Leo's coat and cap off the ground and helped the gentle giant pull his coat on over wet clothes.

Leo sat down again on the muddy ground, shook the accumulated snow off his cap, and put it on, and forced his feet into stiff boots. His rigid fingers wouldn't work the slippery, wet laces, so he left the boots untied. He tipped forward, his head bowed low, soon motionless.

Rex hefted the young man over his good shoulder, then grimaced as he tugged upward with his injured arm on Leo's coat sleeve, trying to get his friend back onto his feet. "Come on, buckaroo. Let's get outta here before I have to come back with an ice pick an' chip you out of your frozen duds."

"I don't think I can make it, T-Tex. You go on with the boy. I'm g-gonna rest here a while. Go on, now. I'll be along."

"No doin', *compadre*. I ain't leavin' ya here. Now, get up!"

11

Leo remained as stationary as a rusted-out, abandoned car. He stared at the ground, the whites of his eyes resembling two dimly lit headlights.

Suddenly, he began shaking and talking gibberish, mumbling something about milking the cows. Rex yelled, concern in his voice. "Get up, Leo! Now!"

In response to Rex's command, Leo lifted his head and looked at him through glazed eyes. He hefted his unwilling body off the ground with Rex's help, and once afoot, he stumbled forward. The Texan grabbed the confused man and spun him hard to the left. "Not that way, *hombre*. You're staggerin' to the wrong bunkhouse. I'd suggest we all go to our camp, up the hill. This way, remember?"

As the men stepped off in the direction of their camp, Leo's muddled mind revisited the days just before he'd left his home in Georgia for this odd and uncertain trip to the Pennsylvania mountains.

Two days before leaving, Leo sat with his sister Brenda at the hickory kitchen table that had once belonged to their parents. Almost midnight, everyone else had gone to bed. Leo was tired, weary and torn really. His bulk rested on the tabletop; his hands folded before him. Brenda sat opposite her brother, having just dried the few coffee cups and saucers stacked on the drain board of the yellowed porcelain sink. Leo sensed Brenda studying him. He knew he owed her an explanation for his silence, but before he could begin to unload his burden, she wiped a few random bread-crumbs from the tabletop and asked, "What is it, baby? What's got my big brother's forehead all wrinkled?" Brenda leaned forward in the ladder-back chair, looking at her brother with concern. When Leo failed to make eye contact or speak, she laid the thin dishcloth aside and held out her hands. In return, Leo put his big hands over hers. She squeezed.

Peering deep into his sister's soul, he whispered, "Sis, I gotta go."

12

Brenda's dreamy gaze shot from their joined hands to her brother's sorrowful eyes.

"What do you mean, you gotta go? Are we too much for you, Leo? Tell me if we are. If so, then we gotta go . . . not you."

"It's a lil' crowded with you, Melvin, and the kids I admit, but no, that ain't it. We family. I love havin' y'all with me."

Fingering a missed breadcrumb on the tabletop, Brenda pressed, "What is it then, Leo? Tell me."

"I ain't sure . . . I cain't really explain how I'm feelin.' I prayed with Reverend Powell about it a long while yesterday, an' he said I should follow my heart an' do what I gotta do."

With tears welling in her own dark brown eyes, Brenda asked, "What is it yo heart tellin' you gotta do, big brother?"

"My heart is a'tellin' me to pack up some things an' go north for a bit. I don't know why, sis, but I know I'm supposed to do it as well as I know you my sister."

"But where up north . . . an' why? This don't make no sense, Leo!"

Leo shuffled his stocking feet across the oiled, wide-plank floor beneath the table, "I know it don't make no sense. But truth is, I jus' don't know where I'm goin' or why. I thought I'd just tell folk around here I'm gonna take a lil' vacation to Washington D.C. Never been there before, an' I always wanted to see the Lincoln Memorial…I jus' know I gotta go, an' I guess I'll figure it all out along the way."

"That ain't no good reason for you leavin', Leo. What is it, baby? You'd tell me if we was too much trouble for you, wouldn't you?"

"Darlin', you ain't never'd be too much. You my sister, an' you an' Melvin need to stay right here with me 'til y'all can get back on yo' feet. I was a-thinkin' about goin' away for a while an' when I come home, I'd ask Melvin an' some of the men an' women from the church that's been help buildin' them Habitat houses to maybe help me build a new place."

Brenda slammed her hand palm down on the tabletop, startling Leo first with the resonating sound and then stinging with the words that followed, "Leo Regis, you own this farm! You don't need to be buildin' a new place. That's foolish talk. Melvin an' I need to move on, not you!"

Seeking to placate his sister, Leo went on, "No, now hear me out, sis. I like havin' family nearby an' I was thinkin' you an' Melvin could have this ole place an' I'd build me a new house yonder down the road, on the other side of the barn. I got seventy-some acres, an ol' unpainted leanin' barn, an' this rickety house that needs paint more than the barn does. I figure Melvin an' I could farm the land together an' share the tractor an' stuff, an'..." Leo's eyes lit up with excitement, "... I'd build me a new house ... maybe put up a brand new crib for some corn, a coop, an' a new pole barn, an'...." Love radiated from the man's bright eyes, "we could live next door to each other, neighbor-like. Wouldn't that be nice?"

"Leo, that sounds nice. *Real* nice. But why do you have to give everything up jus' for us? That ain't right. You got a beautiful house. With a little scrapin' an' a new coat'a paint, it'll look like new. You don't need to be givin' it up 'cause of us."

"It ain't all for you, sis. It's for me too, an' I was thinkin' maybe Sister Powell might like a new house too."

With a napkin over her mouth, restraining a smile, Brenda slapped Leo's hand as it lay on the tabletop, "Leo! You cain't shack up with Reverend Powell's daughter. She the choir director, everybody would know. Jus' think of the talk!"

Grinning, Leo rubbed his hand over his shiny bald scalp, "Brenda, you know me better 'n that. Sister Powell fusses over my baritone voice at church all the time, an' that's all ... 'cept lately she been getting' kinda friendly. An' I'm a-feelin' she might like more about me than my voice."

With a coy grin, Brenda asked, "You been whisperin' in Edna's ear?"

Leo's eyes twinkled with sneaky pleasure. In response to the question, he replied, "Naw, but I been sweet talkin'' a bit, and she been respondin'."

"Leo, you ol' dog! I shoulda knowed all about this by how

14

happy you is when you go off to choir practice. Do she know you thinkin' about goin' away?"

Leo regarded the 30-year-old single-door refrigerator humming in the corner, avoiding his sister's probing stare. "Yeah, she know, an' I'm 'fraid I ain't her favorite fella right now. But her daddy talked with her and she agreed that I gotta follow my heart. Problem is she's a-thinkin' my heart oughta keep me right here on the farm, close by hers."

With both of her slender hands held high above her head, Brenda looked heavenward and offered her testimony, "Amen! I agree with Edna about that. Brother, you need to listen to that girl an' stay at home an' take care of yo' farm." Putting her hands back on Leo's, she added, "But I guess that ain't none a' my bidness, now, is it? When you figurin' to come home? Did you tell her that?"

"No, I ain't tol' her that 'cause, I don' know. I really don.' I jus' know I gotta go, an' I gotta go now."

"Is you runnin' away from love, brother? Is you afraid to court Sister Powell? You don't need to be, you know. Edna ain't all that special, 'cept in your heart."

"Now listen here, little sister. I ain't runnin' from her, or you, or nobody or nothin' else. I just gotta go. I cain't explain why. I'll work out what I can with her when I come home. But I want you an' Melvin to come to the bank with me t'marra to put your names on my accounts an' to deed the house over. That's somethin' I definitely gotta do 'fore I leave."

Brenda pushed away from the table and took to her pacing path in front of the sink. Wringing her hands on the dishtowel, she turned and leveled her eyes with his, and pointed at her brother, "We ain't gonna spend your money, Leo!" And then, considering her brother with knitted brow, she asked, "Are you sure you plannin' on comin' home?"

With his hands raised in defense, Leo pleaded with his sister, "Come on, Brenda. Yeah, I'm comin' home. I promise. I jus' don' know when, Sis. You can ask all ya want, but I ain't got no better answers than what I tol' you already."

15

With a wide-eyed questioning face, Brenda put her hands on her hips and pressed, "An' Sister Powell okay with that uncertainty, huh? I cain't believe Edna gonna be all right with that!"

Leo dropped his forehead into his open palms, sighed, and whispered toward the tabletop, "No, she ain't okay at all with that. She warned me there are other men in the church with deep voices who can sing nearly good as me. So, if I don't get home soon, I might jus' lose my place in the choir."

"Leo! That ain't what I meant, an' you know it!"

"Look, child. We ain' nowhere near where she can tell me when or where I can go, an' she ain't that kinda lady anyway. She an' I both know things can change. She said she'll wait an' see, an' so will I. She trust me, an' you gotta trust me too."

Brenda shivered as the cool nighttime breeze blew through the curtains. She pulled the kitchen window a little lower and tried one more tack. "Leo, it's already November, baby. You ain't got clothes for livin' in the north. Cain't this wait least 'til spring come?" She pleaded, "This is crazy talk. Why don' you jus' stay home an' court Edna Powell like yo' heart be tellin' you to do?"

Resolved not to budge, Leo looked at his sister with determination and replied, "No, I cain't stay home an' I cain't wait but just a day or two more before I gotta go. I been feelin' this comin' on for the past month or so, and I jus' know it's what I gotta do. I'm a-leavin' Friday. That's all there is." He held his hands up, palms forward to end the conversation, but Brenda ignored the gesture.

"What? You made crazy plans like this already? Without even talkin' with me?"

"I made plans *an'* I'm talkin' with you right now, baby girl. An' I'll talk with Melvin t'marra. I know this sounds crazy to you, an' me too if I'm honest 'bout it, but you a big part of my life, lil' sister, and I ain' running you off and I ain't runnin' off on you, and I ain't runnin' from nobody or nothin', no matter what you might think. I'll be back when I come back, an' when I'm home I want you an' Melvin an' the kids close by so we can be together on holidays an' weekends an' for church events an' stuff like that. An' I wanna see if Reverend Powell will let me court his girl."

"Oh, Leo, I ain't tryin' to give you a hard time. I jus' worried 'bout you, baby. Cain't you see that?"

Leo joined his sister at the sink as she stared out the kitchen window into the void. He squeezed her thin shoulders from behind, "No reason to worry, hon. I'm doin' fine, and since you got your job at Bangles and Bubbles—"

Brenda corrected him for at least the twentieth time since taking the job, "Bangles, Baubles, and Beads."

Turning his sister toward him, he pointed with an accompanying grin and continued, "Yeah, since you been a stylist at that salon an' Melvin got himself the maintenance job at the University, you both doin' real good, too. I don't want you goin' back to Atlanta. I want you right here with me." Leo reached out to his sister and implored, "I jus' want you to put me on the train in Athens come Friday, pay the bills from my checkin' account, and keep the farm up while I'm away. It's winter an' there ain't much need to be done. Would you do that for me?"

"You know I'd do anythin' for you, Leo . . . Melvin too. We love you an' we both know we'd be on the street if you didn't take us in like you did."

"You my sister; what else would you think I'd do?"

"I know we family, but I also know you'd take in a stranger to help 'im out, just like you did us. You a good man, Leo Regis."

Leo took his sister in his arms and hugged her the way their momma and daddy once did. Brenda swayed side to side in his embrace, and then, unable to handle any longer the intensity of the love she felt for her brother, she shoved him away. Simultaneously laughing and crying while covering her face to hide her tears, she stamped her foot and then stood childlike in the soft glow of the lamp on the oak sideboard. Leo pulled his sister back against his chest with one hand and pressed the side of his face against hers. He wiped her tears with his own cheek and kissed her forehead. Uncertain how to end such a tender moment, Brenda looked up at her big brother through weepy eyes and whispered, "How about

17

that last piece of lemon meringue pie?"

At arm's length, Leo asked, "I thought that pie was for Melvin's lunch?"

"Melvin would want you to have it. I'll fix him somethin' else nice. He won' miss it, I promise."

"Aw'right then, let's share the pie and then get ourselves to bed. I got a lot to do 'fore I leave, includin' makin' sure Melvin is okay with handlin' the farm while I'm away."

Leo's memory of his sister that November night kept him going, when all he really wanted to do was collapse and fall asleep on the frozen Pennsylvania ground. He promised Brenda he'd return to Georgia as soon as he could, and he meant to keep his promise. He put his hand into his overall pocket and rubbed between his finger and thumb the good luck twenty-dollar gold piece his grandfather had given him years before. Afterward, he willed his chin off his chest and concentrated on placing one foot in front of the other.

Leo and Rex slipped and tripped up the snow- and mud-slick incline. With the boy's body flung over his good shoulder, Rex used his injured arm to prod Leo forward. By the time they'd surmounted the ridge, Rex's shoulder and gut ached under the strain of carrying the limp body up the hill and over uneven terrain. Finally reaching level ground, the two men forced their deadened bodies another quarter of a mile or so down the snaking path toward their camp. As soon as they were within vocal range, the Texan yelled out, "Hank! Hank! Come help a couple of old friends, will ya?"

Sandy-haired Hank, at thirty-three, was the youngest and fittest of the three living in the makeshift camp. He yelled back from within the pines, "What? You two can't carry a couple of jugs of water? You sissies are such a pain! Let me set my coffee pot down, and I'll herd you two ladies into camp."

As Rex and Leo shuffled forward, Hank pushed through the pine boughs to exit the camp. He was stopped short by the sight of the approaching apparition, a hovering, slow-moving mist with three ghoulish figures imprisoned within. The frosty, snowy night air and the men's wet clothes created a steamy haze that drifted above and behind them. Hank ran to Rex, lifted the battered youth from the beleaguered man's shoulder, and heaved the boy over his own like a sack of potatoes.

Making light of their emergency and downplaying the urgency of the situation, the cowboy asked, "Hank, we found that stray you're totin' — ya think we can keep him?"

Hank bent forward under the weight of the youth and shook his head as he pressed the other men toward their camp.

With downcast eyes and chin against his chest, Rex fussed, "Does that mean we can't keep him? I was gonna name 'im an' everything."

"It means I can't believe you. I send you two out to get some water to cook and clean with, and you come back soaking wet, hauling a 125-pound throwaway you want to keep for a pet."

Hank bore the boy's weight while shepherding both of his friends forward. Rex did his best to support the bigger man as he and Leo staggered toward the spruces like drunken cowboys returning to the bunkhouse after a night on the town. Once inside the camp, Hank laid the unconscious lad on the old wooden door that served as their table. Turning to his wet companions, he asked, "Does your stray have a name? More important, is he housebroke?"

Leo and Rex collapsed into tattered aluminum lawn chairs near the fire, looked at each other, and shrugged. Hank threw a frayed electric blanket over the boy's nearly frozen body as he crossed the camp. Within minutes the men would carefully remove the boy's wet clothing and attend to his injuries, but first, they had to pull themselves together.

Approaching Leo, Hank stopped to heave two oversized logs onto the fire burning near the table that held the boy, then chided, "Dude! You're supposed to take your clothes off before you go surfing! Come on, let's get those sopping togs off you."

Leo chuckled at his companion's affected surfer jabber, but his mind was too dull to appreciate the younger man's attempted humor. With Hank's assistance, Leo disrobed and stood as close to the fire as he could tolerate, wearing nothing but jockey shorts.

Hank feared that Leo might collapse into the fire, so before turning his attention to the boy's motionless body, he nudged him back into the lawn chair, saying, "Sit! Stay!" Leo mumbled, "W-w-woof!"

"I'll get you two some coffee. Hang tight."

The younger man poured coffee into two porcelain-glazed metal mugs and handed the stout, black brew to each of the "old-timers." He returned to the mysterious boy lying on the tabletop and studied the passive face for any sign of recognition or identification. The boy did not look familiar to Hank from any of his previous forays into Hollidaysburg, but then again, his face was battered nearly beyond recognition. Hank removed the boy's wet clothes with care and swaddled him again in the worn electric blanket to await Leo's medical attention. He searched through the schoolboy's pockets but found only a punched lunch ticket and 65 cents.

"Hey, Tex, would you plug the blanket in for me? This fella's so cold his skin's turned nasty shades of blue!"

"Yeah right, L.A. If you've got an extension cord that'll reach town, I'll do it for ya. Didn't I tell you we was gonna need some juice for that thang to do ya any good? An', you paid *mucho dinero* for it too!"

Gazing skyward, Hank pressed his hands together in prayer, "Becky, darling, please tell the man it was a good buy at two dollars."

Absorbing the warmth of the fire and the coffee, Leo gradually returned to a sense of normalcy and mental clarity. Once his bluish-black skin warmed to reveal its natural burnt umber, Leo hefted his mass from the chair, leaving the comforting warmth of the fire behind. Waddling barefoot through the camp's thick mat of pine straw to his bunk, he retrieved dry skivvies, bib overalls, a heavy turtleneck sweater, wool hunting socks, and a small plastic

20

flashlight. He dressed and approached his patient lying unconscious on the tabletop. The former medic removed the powder-blue blanket, handing it to Hank, who draped it over Leo's chair to warm near the fire.

Leo struck a wooden match and lit both mantels on the Coleman gas lantern. Under its glow, he studied the body from head to toe, appraising the extent of the boy's injuries. All he said at this first peek was, "Unh!"

Separating the boy's eyelids with the finger and thumb of his left hand, Leo shone a beam into unseeing green eyes. The targeted pupils dilated in response.

"Now that's what I wanted to see! If he don't have a subdural hematoma, he might jus' make it. His eyes are respondin' like I hoped they would, but I'm still worryin' about a hematoma."

Standing beside Leo, stretching his cramped leg, and trying to rub away the soreness in his shoulder, Rex looked perplexed, "A what?"

"The boy suffered some whoppin' head trauma an' I cain't see inside his head. He could be havin' bleedin' inside his skull, and with all that blood poolin' up and causin' pressure on his brain it could kill him. We'll likely know soon what's gonna happen, and ain't nothin' we can do but wait."

"Shouldn't we all just get dressed in something dry and take him down to Hollidaysburg right now?"

"Like I said earlier, we cain't be movin' him down the mountain in the dark. That'd be too dangerous for him an' us. Besides, I jus' don' feel safe movin' him 'til he's conscious."

"What if he dies? Ain't someone gonna accuse us of killin' him or somethin'?"

"Maybe they will, maybe they won't, but I think we all a lot safer keepin' him warm an' treatin' his injuries right here. At least for now. When he's awake we can see if he can be moved an' then heft him down the mountain. Somebody not gonna be too happy if we up and drop the boy off the trestle when we be tryin' to get him across in the dark, now would they?"

21

Rex didn't have a comeback to Leo's reasoned challenge, so Leo followed up by saying, "Now, go take some aspirin and sit your skinny butt down by the fire. An' git away from me while I'm doin' my doctorin' stuff."

Leo began his "doctoring stuff" by further inspecting the boy's body for contusions, abrasions, lacerations, and fractures. "This cut above the kid's left eye is gonna need some stitches," Leo said aloud, but mostly to himself. The former medic retrieved his small suture kit from his medical bag, and after washing his hands with soap and water and then cleansing his hands and the wound with a medical disinfectant, he closed the laceration with four tight stitches. As professional as a plastic surgeon operating in a hospital surgery suite, Leo neatly tied off and trimmed the excess nylon suture beyond the knot with a small pair of scissors. Next, he examined the boy's mouth and teeth, wiggling each tooth, top to bottom. Satisfied that all of the boy's teeth were intact, Leo pressed the young man's tongue down with a depressor from the old, faded medical bag and peered inside the boy's mouth. The only injury he could see was a laceration caused by the boy's top teeth cutting into his lower lip.

With the curved, stainless-steel suture needle lying across the sterile gauze, Leo disinfected the wound and then added two stitches to the boy's lower lip. "I'm thinkin' if the boy makes it, he's gonna be mumblin' through some pretty thick lips for a few days."

Smirking, Rex leaned forward toward the warmth of the fire with his coffee cup in hand, "I don't know what you're talkin' about, doc. His lips don't look any different from yours, and you don't mumble all that much."

Hank laughed aloud at Rex's comparison, and Leo stared back at the two of them, "Now, don't be pullin' that race crap on me or you'll both be needin' some stitches in yo' own lips." After a moment, Leo winked and returned his attention to his patient.

Hank smiled to himself as he prepared to hang Leo's wet clothes on the line. Rex sat back in the lawn chair with hands as strong as oak folded over his belly, grinning like a kid who'd just driven a long ball over the centerfield fence.

Leo continued his exam, palpating ribs on both sides of the boy's chest. Upon hearing the rasp of aspirated water in the kid's lungs, Leo said, "I ain't sure whether this rattle I'm a-hearin' is pond water or blood from a punctured lung. I don't like it neither way. I wish I wasn't hearin' none of that at all!"

After cleaning and bandaging the boy's abrasions, Leo covered the body again with the powerless electric blanket recently warmed by the fire. Hank approached Leo and the young man, "What do you think? Is he going to make it?"

"I don' know. I really don', Hank. He might die any time from a hematoma. In a couple hours, he might could drown in the blood that's maybe gatherin' in his lungs, or he might die t'marra from pneumonia. I don' have no way to tell what's goin' on with him . . . an' if he lives, he might have a messed up brain. I jus' don' know. We gonna have to wait an' see. But no matter, it's all serious stuff!"

"Are you sure we shouldn't try to get him down the mountain?"

Leo scratched his chin whiskers, "What're we gonna do if we out there in the dark and cold, and he stop breathin'? At least here we can see what we doin'. No, we need to stay put 'til we got a better idea of how bad his injuries are."

Hank nodded and continued hanging the corpsman's wet clothes on the clothesline.

Leo turned to Rex who was sitting quietly, sipping his coffee like a patient in an ER waiting room contemplating the event that had caused his injuries. Leo put the boy out of his mind and pointed at his patient in waiting.

"Next!"

"What do you mean, 'Next'?"

"Let's look at that shoulder of yours, that's what I'm talkin' 'bout. You been sittin' yonder all to yo'self, like I told you to do. An' if you be mindin' me, I know you gotta be hurtin'. Otherwise, you'd be a-standin' right here buggin' the b'jeebers out of me, tryin' to tell me how to fix the boy up. Now, come over here into the light where

I can get a look at you."

Rex strained to lift himself out of the aluminum chair with his right arm, while his injured arm hung at his side. Lifting Rex's tee shirt, Leo examined the man's shoulder and chest, noting Rex's left shoulder and most of his back and chest had already turned an ugly shade of purple.

"Unh-unh-unh! Does that hurt half as bad as it looks?"

"Naw! Not quite *half* as bad."

"You sure?"

"Yeah. No need to mess with me, doc. I'll be back in the saddle, ropin' and brandin' doggies when the sun comes up."

Incredulous, Leo pulled the shirt back down over Rex's belly. "Let's check yo range of motion, cowpoke. Lift that ropin' arm as high as you can."

"Tarnation! Why don't you just ask me to hogtie and brand a frisky calf or somethin' easy like that!"

"I thought so, you stubborn mule. I knowed that shoulder was a-hurtin'. Let me have a feel of it."

With his chin jutted ahead of his puffed-up chest, Rex leveled, "No way, man! You just wanna see if you can make it hurt worse than it does already. You just tryin' t'get back at me for givin' you a hard time 'bout the boy's lips. Am I right or am I right?" Rex asked with wide, challenging eyes.

"Look, it don't matter t'me. We need to be gettin' the kid down to Hollidaysburg. You can come too, and you can get a real doctor to look at ya. Either I'm gonna get the satisfaction of makin' you hurt some or one of the docs down the valley gonna have the fun. Like I said, it don't make no matter to me."

"Aw, dang, Leo. You know I hate hospitals more 'n classical music. Don't even like the smell of 'em. You're probably the best trauma doc in these parts anyway. Go ahead and take a look-see but be darned gentle. My shoulder hurts like the dickens. And don't be tryin' to take advantage of me 'cause I'm hurtin' a little. Remember, nobody messes with ole Tex-Mex Rex!"

Leo beamed his famous broad, disarming smile and said,

"Yeah, I'm 'fraid of you and yo' Jim Bowie, for sure!" referring to Rex's cherished knife. "I promise to be as gentle with you as any of the kid goats on my farm, mister rough and tough."

Rex inched forward, and as soon as he was within reach, Leo grabbed onto his arm with the talons of an eagle snatching a salmon from a stream. He began kneading the injured man's arm and shoulder relentlessly. Rex fussed and tried to squirm free, but Leo scowled and held tight. With a well-practiced schoolyard feint, Leo slid his hand to Rex's collarbone. Before Rex could counter Leo's move, the former medic had his hand on the man's wrist, lifting the pained arm forward, backward, and sideways. After bending the arm at the elbow, Leo announced, "Well, nothing is broke."

"What are you talkin' 'bout? You darn near broke it your own-self once you got a holt of it an' turned it every which way but loose."

"Relax, *amigo. You* banged yourself up all on your own. I didn't do it. Be happy, nothin's broke. If you wasn't so durn clumsy you wouldn't be cryin' right now."

"I ain't cryin'!"

"Uh-huh. I'm hearin' ya. You gonna need to sling that arm up an' keep it stable a few days. Problem is, I don't got nothing to keep you stable 'cept some aspirin. Good news is you won't be fetchin' no water for a while. Besides, if I remember rightly, yo' water jugs are out there somewhere by the pond. Yo' momma wouldn't be too prouda yo' water fetchin', so you might just as well sit here scratchin' and complainin' an' let Hank and me tote water fo' awhile."

"That's all right by me, an' if I'm rememberin' rightly, your jugs are down by that pond too. But whatever, you best be leavin' my momma outta this."

Laughing as he continued doctoring, Leo folded a tattered rag diagonally and made a triangular sling, which he tied behind Rex's neck. Rex continued muttering veiled threats of revenge long after he slinked away from Leo. As a final parting shot when Leo was out of reach, Rex yelled a warning to Hank, "A word of advice, *compadre*. With that ole sawbones around, you and me best be getting some health insurance."

CHAPTER 3

Friday afternoon passed to evening and evening to night. The young man, lying unconscious on the wooden door near the fire pit, resembled a human sacrifice placed upon some ancient altar. Throughout the evening, the three men paid homage to the altar and its offering by checking on the boy's well-being. Periodically, Leo assessed the boy's vital signs and shined light into his eyes, seeking assurance that there was no cerebral swelling or bleeding. Hank and Rex interrupted their chores from time to time and stood by the edge of the table to study the boy's lifeless face.

Given the unanticipated activities earlier in the day at the trestle and then tonight within their camp, the trio had been too preoccupied to think about how late it had become. Hank was first to notice the lateness of the hour and, more importantly, that they had not yet eaten dinner. Massaging his growling stomach through an oversized UC Berkeley sweatshirt, Hank broke the sleepy silence that had settled over the camp. "I don't know about you guys, but I'm getting a little hungry."

Until Hank made mention of it, Rex hadn't noticed how long it had been since he'd eaten last, which was odd because when Rex missed a meal, he generally made everyone aware. A hungry Rex was prone to developing a "serious case of the grumps," as Leo described the condition in medical terms. Tonight, however, Rex's mood remained light and there were no "hissy fits" from the cantankerous cowboy. "Hank, ole buddy, when I'm just a tad bit hungry I can eat one of them little 32-ounce Texas Porterhouses. 'Bout now, I believe I could eat half a Fort Worth stockyard. Why don't you just get the ole chuck wagon a-rollin'?"

Hank was the most creative and talented cook among the three. He had been a chef for several restaurants over the years, including the struggling restaurant he co-owned with his longtime friend Stan. He enjoyed transforming basic ingredients into gratifying meals, and he often said cooking was his therapy. In preparation for dinner, Hank cleared off a section of the tabletop around the boy's feet, converting it from emergency room gurney to a food preparation space. He gathered up a wooden tongue depressor, bandage wrappings, and scraps of paper from the table and tossed it all into the fire. He stowed Leo's medical bag inside his sleeping compartment and put away the clutter that had accumulated in the cooking area, then gathered the utensils necessary to prepare their late-night dinner and placed them all around the static body.

After retrieving a scorched and sooty Dutch oven from beneath the green nylon tarp protecting their belongings from the weather, Hank set the pot on a glowing bed of embers. He dribbled vegetable oil into the hot oven, which immediately began to sizzle, and then scraped in a couple of pounds of sirloin beef tips. Leo had rescued the gray-brown, out-of-date beef tips from a dumpster behind the A&P grocery store Thursday afternoon.

He chopped and added one of Leo's Vidalia onions and the few potatoes and carrots left in the camp pantry, a lidless liquor box holding some canned goods and root-cellar vegetables. The smell of hot oil and braised beef permeated the campsite until Hank poured spring water into the pot, which enveloped the seared beef's tantalizing fragrance. As a final touch, Hank tossed the contents of a can of succotash into the grizzled pot along with a pinch or two of salt and pepper. With the heavy iron lid on the Dutch oven, he left the ingredients to simmer.

Rex hollered to Hank from across the camp, "Now, don't be forgettin' the hot sauce, *amigo*."

"No sir." Hank replied. He had planned to add Rex's spicy pepper sauce a little later in the cooking process, but for the Texan's benefit he uncovered the pot and tapped the bottom of the upended Tabasco bottle several times, sending the last of the fiery red pepper juice into the stew. Next, he twisted the brass lid off a quart Mason jar and set aside a couple of tablespoons of flour. He'd add the flour near the end of the cooking process after the ingredients had "integrated soulfully," as Leo described the process.

The wood smoke smelled sweet and inviting. Leo, eyes nearly closed, enjoying the smell and warmth of the crackling fire, stared into the embers, his thoughts elsewhere. He bore a peaceful, reminiscent smile. Rex sat beside him wringing water out of the boy's socks, waiting for an end to his friend's distant associations. Yawning, Leo broke free from his meditation, leaned forward, and turned the face of his wristwatch into view. Rubbing fatigue from his bristled face, he said mostly to himself, "Man, oh man. What a day!"

Rex looked at the worn man sitting beside him, "You did a fine job with that kid today. You're a darn good trauma doc, my friend."

"Thanks, that means a lot coming from you, Rex."

Shaking his head from side-to-side, the Texan, quipped, "Now, don't be gettin' a big head. I have to warn ya, my arm has been cryin' malpractice and it's a-lookin' for an ambulance-chasing attorney to make its case ag'in ya."

Chuckling into the licking flames before him but speaking sideways at the former cowboy sitting next to him, Leo replied, "Tell your contrarian arm to be takin' some aspirin. It'll be hushin' up in no time. Yo' arm ain't got no case 'gainst me. Now, some social worker might be makin' a case against you for self-abuse. I could see that a-happenin'!"

"Un-huh, I hear ya," Rex grumbled, turning his gaze back to the fire.

Holding his hands toward the heat, Leo again was in deep

thought. Rex leaned back, intending not to bother the man further. As he reclined, Leo did the same, his hands folded in his lap. Supper steamed on the hot coals with a delicious fragrance bubbling from beneath the iron lid.

Glancing sideways, Leo withdrew from his private fire-lit dreams and asked, "What happened out there today, Rex? You figure it out?"

"Yeah, I been thinkin' 'bout the kid. I figure he's a runner."

"You mean, like in track?"

"No, man. He's a runaway."

Turning toward his friend, Leo countered, "Naw, he ain't runnin'. He jus' a boy dressed for school . . . jus' gotta lightweight jacket and street shoes on. He'd be changin' his clothes b'fore he'd run away to the woods, don' you think?"

"Then what was he doin' sittin' high up on the bridge like he was, with it gettin' dark an' all?"

"Maybe he gonna kill himself."

"Maybe he was a-thinkin' 'bout it, but I don't think he was gonna jump, not the way the train scared him and set him to scramblin'."

"Maybe he plannin' to jump off the bridge when he was ready, an' just didn't want to get squashed by that big ole train."

"Maybe," Rex nodded.

"Maybe," Leo echoed as he scratched his shoulder and looked deep into the flames.

While Leo and Rex bantered, Hank stirred the thickening stew one last time. He tried to recall Becky's face. He didn't want to forget her smile, her eyes, her hair, or any of her delicate features. Though she had died at a very young age, early in their marriage, she'd held onto Hank on that sterile hospital deathbed as if they'd been married for decades. She'd assured her husband that as long as it was within her power, she would never leave him. But she did leave him. She died just five hours after her promise and, through two hard years of depression since her death, Hank's only consolation was the daily recollection of her beautiful face and the feeling that her guiding spirit was with him still.

It had been three months to the day since Hank called Stan, his business partner and the co-owner of their restaurant in Monterey and told him that he would not be coming to work that day or any day soon. Hank replayed in his mind his conversation with Stan, still a painful memory.

He'd climbed down from the train that had taken him across the desert from California to Casa Grande, Arizona. The morning sun had not yet risen, and the eastern horizon just began to reveal the pre-dawn rays. None of the local stores Hank passed was open as he walked the littered streets in search of a pay phone. He pulled on the fob of his silver pocket watch, opened the ornate case, and considered the early hour. He pocketed the watch and stepped inside a dusty booth with glass walls smudged by body oils and its floor littered with discarded candy bar wrappings and crushed cigarette packs. Hank lifted the telephone receiver from its cradle, dropped a quarter into the coin slot, dialed O, and wedged himself backward into the corner of the booth. His nose wrinkled at the smell of the sour, accumulated dirt and sweat on the receiver as he asked the operator to place his call. Hank wasn't sure what he'd say after Stan accepted the collect call.

In response to the operator's question, Stan stammered, "Umm, uh... yeah, sure I'll accept the call," just as Hank knew he would. Stan was confused, wondering why Hank called so early, why he hadn't called from his cell phone, and where was he that he had called long distance. Stan answered warily as he yawned into the phone, "What's up buddy . . . where are you . . . are you okay?"

Hank didn't answer any of Stan's questions; he didn't want to explain himself. Frankly, he couldn't explain himself. Instead of answering, Hank launched into an emotional confession of anguished feelings, "Stan, I need to get away for a while — umm, I should say I am away, and I . . . ah . . . won't be back for . . . some time. I don't know how long. . . ." His voice trailed off with uncertainty.

Stan's sheets and bed cover rustled as Hank's friend bolted up in bed. "What are you talking about? Where are you going? What's up?"

Kicking the phone booth door closed with his right foot, trying to shut out some of the noise from the dusty red semi idling at the traffic light, its wood slat trailer crowded with drowsy pigs, Hank replied, "I haven't been able to pull it together since Becky died, Stan. You know that, and I just need to get away for a while. I need to find...I need some purpose in my life."

Hank could hear Stan's clock being scraped along the top of his nightstand. "Hank, it's five o'clock in the morning. What do you mean you're looking for purpose? Where are you and why are you calling me at this hour? We have a business to run...we have to, or I mean, you are supposed to open up the restaurant in two hours. Isn't that enough purpose for you? Do you expect me to get up and open the place this morning after working the late shift last night? How long am I supposed to run a restaurant from seven to ten, six days a week, by myself? We're barely making it as it is—help me out here, buddy. Tell me what's going on."

With his forehead against the opposing cool glass wall, Hank sighed, "I'm sorry, Stan. If you need to hire a chef to replace me, go ahead and take it out of my side of the revenue. . .."

What revenue, Stan wondered, but he kept quiet.

"I just can't come back to work until I'm ready. I'm sorry to be putting this on you; you don't deserve it. But I've got no choice."

"Hank, I know you're hurting. I'm with you there...you know that. I can forgive your absence from the kitchen for as long as you need to be gone, but you know the business won't forgive you—it can't. What am I supposed to do?"

Reconsidering the wisdom—or folly—of leaving California or calling Stan, Hank replied, "Let me think a minute...I have enough money to catch a bus back... I could be back by...No! I can't. I don't mean to sound heartless, Stan, but you can close the restaurant doors for all I care right now. My heart is not in Monterey and I can't fake it any longer. Do what you must. I'm sorry, but I can't come home right now, and I don't know when I'll be back."

32

Stan sounded panicky as he pleaded with his friend, "Okay, forget the business for a minute — the dream of your life just two and a half years ago — what about you? Are you okay? You aren't going to kill yourself or do anything stupid, are you? About the restaurant...I'll make it happen somehow. We'll survive. But you gotta get better, man. Do that for me...do that for you...heck man, do it for Becky. You know she doesn't want you suffering like you are. Get better, okay? And come home."

"Okay...I'm trying to get better, Stan...I'm trying."

"I know. Hang in there, buddy. Okay? Where can I call to check on you?"

Laughing at how ridiculous what he was about to say would sound, Hank responded, "I don't know where I'm going, Stan. If I did, I'd tell you.... But I don't. I'll call you...."

"Call me every week and anytime in between if you need to talk. I don't want to push you any more than that, but I want to know if you're okay or how I can help you. Promise you'll call me every week."

"I can't do that, Stan. I'll call when I can. I'll call when I feel up to it. But don't worry about me. I'll be coming home, and when I do, I'll be better. I promise you that much. There's nothing more to say, Stan, except, thank you. Thank you for bailing me out and for being a stand-up guy."

"We go back a long way, Hank.... I was your best man. I'm here for you no matter what. Stay safe, that's all I ask."

"I will. Keep your eyes peeled, I'll be walking through that restaurant door some morning bright and early. Until then..."

"Hank? Hank?"

Hank hung up the phone, fearing Stan would talk him out of going on. He walked around Casa Grande feeling as if a load had been lifted from his heart. He was determined to keep going, searching for what he felt fate led him toward, but uncertain of his destination or purpose. After the businesses opened, he went into a dry goods store and bought enough food, bottled water, clothes, and equipment for an indeterminate period of living a rugged existence on the rails. Afterward, he climbed aboard an open box-car, crawled to a corner, and curled up. With his few possessions in an over-the-shoulder canvas grip and using a jacket for his pillow, he slept soundly, not waking until the train was somewhere deep in Texas.

Reflecting on how his cross-country trip, influenced by Becky's guiding presence, had brought him to these Pennsylvania moun-tains and to the men who were now his best friends, Hank looked at Leo and Rex sitting peacefully by the fire. "How about you two detectives setting your case aside and getting over here for some-thing to eat. If you boys don't hustle it up, I'll be eating by myself."

"Not likely," Rex said, as he struggled to get up. It wasn't so easy for the two exhausted rescuers to extricate themselves from their chairs now — stiff and sore as they were — not as easy as it had been earlier in the day before they'd set off to haul water. When they did manage to stand, the two worn men shambled toward the table edge where Hank had placed the stew.

Rex scooped a hero's helping onto a tin plate and handed it to Leo.

"Ummh! Now, that's remindin' me of a Wednesday night church potluck back home." Leo reached into a bread bag and pulled out a couple of slices.

Rex patted the man's shoulder. "Well, eat up, Deacon Regis. Af-ter your heroics today, you deserve the blessin's of a fine meal!"

Rex ladled his own large portion over two pieces of bread. Hank spooned a smaller amount onto his own plate, having sam-pled the dish several times while it simmered.

Although each man was hungry, none had much of an appetite. One by one, the men dug into the cellophane-wrapped loaf of bread near the boy's head and studied the young man's bruised face. Without mouthing his concern, each wondered whether the boy would live to eat another meal. While they sat near the fire and picked at their bread and stew, the men conjectured what the boy had been doing on the desolate railway bridge, the Hollidaysburg

Cresson Trestle.

Cresson Trestle, near their encampment, was never as celebrated as Altoona's Horseshoe Curve about ten miles northwest on
the opposite side of the valley. The Curve and Trestle were famous
because they had opened the Allegheny Mountains to coast-to-
coast rail travel more than a hundred and fifty years ago. Earlier,
Hollidaysburg had been the transfer point between the Pennsylvania Canal and the Portage Railroad. The Portage Railroad lifted canal barges loaded with freight over the mountains, dispatching the
cargo westward. Since the mid-1800s, however, with the construc-
tion of the Curve and Trestle, a continuous span of track traversed
the mountains, forever altering the transport of man and material
cross-country.

Although the Cresson Trestle was an impressive structure, the
Horseshoe Curve was truly spectacular. Early railroaders saw outside Altoona the opportunity to lay track across the Allegheny
Mountains. Irish and Italian Gandy Dancers reshaped the mountains and laid track in a stunning 220-degree horseshoe shape.
Completed in 1854, the Curve made it possible for the American
industrialists' mighty steam engines, with billowing black smoke
and plumes of steam, to chug up the gradient and thunder around
the curve. With whistles blowing, the cargo- and passenger-laden
trains would then descend into Altoona and the massive Juniata
railroad shops in Pleasant Valley. Although people and freight continue to pass by rail through Altoona and Hollidaysburg today,
they do so with much less notice and far less frequency than during
America's glorious railroading years.

There were no obvious answers to the men's questions about
what the young man was doing on Cresson Trestle two days before
Christmas. No one, except the person who had been perched so
high above Blair County that he sat near the threshold of heaven's
door, knew what he was doing there. And that someone wasn't
providing any answers as he lay unconscious on the bare tabletop,
warmed by a roaring campfire deep within the mountains. Just as

curious to any outsider who might be looking in at these men was why *they* were living in the woods near Cresson Trestle.

Some unseen guide had led each of the men to five towering, blue spruce spires, situated just over the ridge and down a slight hill from the trestle. Within the sheltering confines of the star-shaped blue-green conifers, the men had made their camp and lived spartanly for the past six weeks in an area of about twenty-five feet in diameter. Inside the site, the campers had assembled a creative, if crude, living space. They'd laid a discarded interior house door across two empty 55-gallon drums as a surface for cleaning game, preparing food, and eating. Inside one drum they stored perishables, keeping the staples away from scavenging animals. In the other, they stored anything else they wanted to keep dry. Today the door doubled as an emergency room gurney; tonight, it would be either a recovery room bed or a mortuary slab.

Rather than sleeping in tents, the three had constructed compartments out of heavy-gauge cardboard boxes salvaged from behind Hansen's appliance store in Hollidaysburg. Each box had at one time held either a refrigerator or a freezer and was set off the ground across wooden shipping pallets, protecting the boxes and their sleeping inhabitants from the cold, damp ground. Nylon tarps lay under and then draped over the three boxes, at a slope to run precipitation away from the interior of the camp, insulating the men from blowing wind, rain, and snow. Hank referred to his box as his "apartment"; Leo, the "rack"; Rex, the "bunkhouse."

Using Rex's Bowie knife, the men had hacked a long oval opening into each box along the front-facing side to provide easy access to the sleeping chamber. Being the largest of the three men, Leo had claimed the sole freezer box for himself, joking, "the biggest man should get the king-sized bed." Within their respective boxes, the men had layered a bed of six or so inches of pine straw and laid a down-filled, mummy-style sleeping bag atop the straw, and then stuffed more pine needles into the voids of the pallets to block cold drafts from creeping along the ground and into camp. The additional insulation beneath the tarp provided unintended nesting material for a community of field mice who lived within the pallets. Rex found the mice and their cute antics endearing; Hank hated rodents of all sizes and was unnerved by the multitude of mice scurrying around the camp. Encouraged by the tidbits Rex left throughout the campsite, the mice were omnipresent, much to Hank's edgy and frequently vocalized displeasure.

The trio arranged their boxes within their camp end-to-end at acute angles, with one box facing north, the second facing northwest, and the third container placed perpendicular to due west, like three sides of a hexagon. In this configuration, the three sleeping compartments blocked the brutal northern or westward winter winds and absorbed the scant rays of sunlight emanating from the south, keeping the camp warm and cozy at all times. Equidistant from the openings of the three boxes, Leo dug a large fire pit such that their nighttime fires would radiate warmth to each of them while they slept.

Each man kept the few personal possessions he owned in a small cardboard box stored at the head of his compartment. At the foot of their boxes, they placed hot bricks wrapped in burlap in the bottom of their sleeping bags before turning in each evening. The bricks, heated in the embers of the evening's waning campfire, kept the men as warm throughout the night as three peanuts in a Georgia roaster. As winter approached and nighttime temperatures began to drop, the men appreciated their heated bricks during the nights as much as their hot coffee first thing in the morning.

Between the protective pine boughs, low-burning, nighttime wood and coal fires; thick, pine straw beds; foot warmers; and their protective cover overhead, the trio stayed warm and dry, even on the coldest or wettest days. Defying foul weather, the men slept throughout the nights as soundly as any black bear hibernating within the multitude of crags and crannies dotting the mountainside.

Although the three were prepared to survive the most severe winter weather in relative comfort, they were not prepared for visitors. They were short on food and had no "guest room" to accommodate company. The campers discussed how best to provide for their unexpected visitor and determined for now he was best placed where he lay, off the ground, close to the fire. To keep him warm and dry, only an additional blanket covered by a stiff plastic sheet was needed to protect him from the damp night air and the morning dew.

The men agreed at least one of them would stay awake throughout the night in case their silent guest woke up or took a turn for the worse. It was obvious the kid needed more thorough medical treatment than they could provide, but Leo remained adamant that it was not safe to move the boy until he was conscious and stable. This was the dilemma they faced: they risked having the boy die either on the way down the mountain while seeking medical care or in the camp for want of professional medical attention. It was clear the men could do nothing more for him that evening than what they'd done already; whatever additional intensive care they might give their young patient would have to be provided during daylight hours when they could see more clearly.

Leo crawled into his Amana wide-body freezer box, and Rex announced in a haggard tone, "I'm headin' to the bunkhouse. I feel like I been rode hard and put up wet." With that pronouncement, Rex scooted into his Frigidaire frost-free double-door. His shoulder had throbbed all evening, and he doubted whether he'd be able to sleep. He'd already rid himself of the pesky sling that kept catching on protruding tree branches, the tabletop, and just about everything else. The tough-talking Texan swallowed a couple of aspirin and stoically pulled his mummy bag up and around his head. He prayed for the boy and asked too that the pills soon take effect. In the camp, all was still.

Hank stood first watch. While the others found sleep, he sat close to the fire and began reading Steinbeck's *Cannery Row* by the soft glow of lantern light. He'd purchased the used book at the Hollidaysburg Saint Vincent De Paul thrift store. After a few pages, it was clear to Hank how strongly he identified with Steinbeck's characters—good-hearted souls who played out their lives near his

38

home in Monterey, southwest of the Salinas Valley Steinbeck often wrote about. He sat hunched forward in his webbed chair warmed by the glowing embers, with his sleeping bag snug around his shoulders. Late into the night, he alternately read and reminisced about his own former, idyllic life in Monterey.

At one point, Hank dog-eared the last page he'd read and stared into the fire with a heavy heart. After several moments of self-indulgence, he wiped his eyes on his sweatshirt sleeve and exhaled a long, slow breath to rid himself of self-pity. To encourage his mind to venture elsewhere, he stood and peeled back the blanket and plastic sheet covering the boy's face. He felt for the lad's pulse and was relieved to detect a weak but steady beat. So far, their patient, this unnamed youngster who had sat on the trestle, it seemed, with the weight of the world on his shoulders, continued to evade death by will, by chance, or possibly despite his own desire.

CHAPTER 4

About three miles down the track from the trestle, in the small town of Hollidaysburg, population 5,300, Friday afternoon and evening had unfolded differently than it had for the campers up in the mountains. In town, children sledded after their last day of school before the Christmas holidays until they were too cold and too hungry to continue. Afterward, they scattered for warm houses and hot dinners.

In one typical Hollidaysburg household, Mary Ballentine prepared dinner for her family, expecting the entire clan to be home soon. She'd spent much of the day decorating for Christmas and readying the house for the family's traditional evening of tree trimming.

She had wrenched the collapsible stairway down from the second floor-hall ceiling and climbed into the dusty attic, where she retrieved an assortment of old, older still, and ancient boxes filled with generations of ornaments and decorations. She stacked the boxes, fragile with age, in the downstairs family room. Mary also brought down her deceased father's green, stenciled metal tree stand, a substantive, thrice-repainted basin representing an odd but sentimental memorial to Mary's childhood and her father. To Mary, the tree stand represented her father's strength of character, an

40

underlying moral fiber that advocated for "getting things right" and "leaving no job unfinished." The tree stand had grown in significance to Mary since her father died after the Christmas holidays two years ago.

The family's long-needle white pine, picked out several days before from a lot near Lakemont Park, stood outside the back door in a bucket of ice. Mary's husband, Joe, meant to free the tree from its ice-encrusted confinement that evening, when he would also obsessively prune its already exquisite shape. If he could enlist the disinterested assistance of his son, Chris, they would haul the eight-foot beauty into the family room and position it in the corner, by the doublewide patio door and the adjacent knotty pine paneled wall. As in years past, once the tree was in its stand, Joe would fiddle with the three adjustment screws, just as Mary's father had for more than thirty years, until the tree stood as tall and proud as a nutcracker soldier.

Once the tree branches had relaxed after an hour or so inside the warm house, the Ballentines would adorn the pine with an assortment of circa 1950, oversized colored lights, schmaltzy handmade decorations, multicolored and multigenerational baubles, and metallic icicles, all of which would cause the tree to sag as gloriously as the medaled chest of a "tin pot" dictator. Warmed by tradition and the family room fireplace, the Ballentines would trim their tree while sipping mulled cider and singing along with the eclectic collection of Christmas songs broadcast on the local radio station.

Ten-year-old Maggie Ballentine came home after school and, after commenting on how good dinner smelled, changed out of her school uniform into warm clothes and a bright red snowsuit that zipped diagonally from her right shoulder to just above her left knee. As soon as she put it on and devoured a reindeer-shaped sugar cookie, washing the treat down with a quick glass of milk, she joined her neighborhood girlfriends outside. The girls began rolling snowballs through the deep snow, directing the growing spheres toward the side yard, where they would struggle to stack

41

one ball upon another to create a snowwoman. The girls had gathered a brown scarf, a purple felt hat, and a matching purple purse from attic wardrobes to accessorize their snow dame.

Grace, the Ballentines' frisky, young golden retriever, lay whining on an oval, weaved rag-rug at the kitchen door. Grace's ears perked up each time she heard laughing or yelling outdoors before she lowered her head to the rug with sad eyes and a heartbreaking sigh of abandonment. Mary could see that the despondent dog couldn't stand being in the house with all of the cheerful sounds beckoning from outside. When Mary couldn't tolerate Grace's plaintive whimpers any longer, she wiped soap suds from her hands onto a dishtowel, opened the utility room door, and yelled, "Maggie, here comes Grace. Keep an eye on her."

Maggie replied, "Aw Mom, Grace will be all over the place!"

"I know, but she's been in the house all day and she's dying to be outside with you. Run her through the snow a bit and then bring her in. She needs some exercise, and I need some peace."

Mary smiled as Maggie and her friends called Grace out to join them, and watched the rambunctious dog slide out of sight as she dashed toward the bunch. From the kitchen window, Mary watched as Grace, in her enthusiasm, ran into Maggie, sending the young girl sprawling to the ground. As Maggie rolled onto her belly in an attempt to stand, Grace bit into the hem of her red nylon snowsuit and jerked. Each time Maggie attempted to get up, Grace tugged her feet from under her. Whenever Maggie managed to raise herself to her hands and knees, Grace growled and shook ferociously, and Maggie found herself back on her abdomen. Roberta and Annie, Maggie's friends, laughed so hard that tears left frozen tracks on their ruddy cheeks.

Realizing Grace was too exuberant to allow her to stand, Maggie tried another tack. She scolded Grace with her best imitation of a stern, adult voice. Grace took heed of the serious-sounding admonition and released Maggie's pant leg, but she wasn't repentant. She darted in front of Maggie as she approached, remaining a step or two away, thereby avoiding capture and rebuke.

Roberta and Annie joined Maggie in pursuit of the playful dog, and in both large and small circles the girls and dog ran throughout the front yard until no casual observer could be certain whether the girls were chasing Grace or Grace was pursuing the girls. After everyone collapsed in an exhausted heap in the front yard, the girls reassembled to catch their breath on the gray concrete and field-stone steps; Grace lay nearby, belly to the snow with her legs sprawled outward, eavesdropping as girls gossiped about class-mates.

The sky turned black, more from the approaching storm than the onset of evening. Taking note of the darkness, Roberta and Annie returned to their homes, leaving Maggie in the yard patting Grace. Maggie once more examined "Snow Girl," as the girls decided to call her, entered the garage, and pushed the electric button to close the heavy wooden garage door. Grace followed Maggie through the electronic safety beam, causing the garage door to reopen. Barging through the kitchen door ahead of Maggie, Grace shook wet snow and ice from her thick golden coat, before dripping icy water across the room to see whether her food dish had been filled. Finding nothing to eat, she lapped a long drink from her water dish and settled on the kitchen rug, again looking woeful.

Mary directed, "Maggie, get a towel from the utility room and wipe Grace down. She's a mess! She's going to smell like a wet wool blanket all night."

Maggie smiled, knowing her mother was right about how musty Grace smelled when her fur was wet. She pulled a thin towel from the shelf in the utility room and began to clean up the mess Grace had tracked through the kitchen. She patted the dog as dry as possible and broke clumps of snow from Grace's feathered hind legs. Finally, Maggie wiped snow and water from the floor, exterior door, and the fronts of the kitchen cabinets.

Grace, named after Chris and Maggie's departed paternal grandmother, gobbled her dinner as soon as Mary filled her dish. Within minutes of eating, she was back to sleeping under the kitchen table, where the Ballentines' dinner would soon be set and a second opportunity for food would be availed.

Mary stirred a dollop of butter into the green peas simmering on the stove. "Maggie, did you see Chris this afternoon?"

"Nope. But a bunch of eighth-grade boys were off to the cemetery with their sleds after school. I think Chris might have gone with them."

"Then he should be home soon. It's getting late," Mary said with little conviction. She put a half-loaf of garlic bread under the broiler but kept a watchful eye on the clock above the sink. It was already much later than Chris typically came home from school, even when he went sledding.

A red Jeep Grand Cherokee turned into the Ballentines' driveway, but before it could advance all the way to the two-story fieldstone house, the vehicle was pummeled by a barrage of snowballs from the shadows of a distant hedge. Joe Ballentine flung open the driver's door and bound out, yelling threats at the marauders lurking in the shadows. Using the Jeep as a shield, he threw together a half-dozen snowballs with his bare hands and charged the privet hedge, throwing fast and furiously. His attack was absorbed without enemy losses and immediately countered. Joe retreated toward the safety of the Jeep, with snowballs flying harmlessly past. Thinking he was out of his attackers' range, he lurched as a rock-solid snowball exploded between his shoulder blades.

"Yeow! That hurt! All right, you hooligans, you better watch out."

Joe packed another half-dozen snowballs and picked up a few lying on the ground and charged the aggressors hiding behind the hedge; he ducked and weaved in his advance, trying to dodge the incoming fusillade. Although his aim should have been more accurate at such close proximity, he was out of shape and heaved his entire armament, missing his targets with every snowball.

Before the assailants initiated their next counterattack, Joe threw his hands in the air and yelled, "I surrender."

The opposing attackers approached Joe laughing. "You've got

44

a pretty good arm for an old man, Mr. Ballentine," one said with feigned sincerity while patting Joe on the shoulder.

"Hey, I'm not that old," Joe wheezed, as he bent over with his hands resting on his knees, trying to control his breathing. His back and chest hurt from the exertion and the last snowball that tagged him. His suit jacket was unbuttoned and askew. His white dress shirt was half-tucked into his slacks, and his charcoal-gray wool topcoat hung open, with the wild paisley tie protruding over his middle-aged potbelly. His black wingtips were soaked.

An independent insurance agent for the past twenty-two years, Joe had done little to keep in shape or to prepare for these annual winter battles, or for shoveling snow for that matter. He was out of shape, and his pounding heart reminded him why he had bought the heavy-duty snow blower—and why now he even delegated its operation to his son.

For the duration of the snowball fight Joe had figured Chris was in alliance with the attackers. With the garage door open as it was, he assumed Chris was preparing to clear the snow off the driveway and had been drawn into the snowball fight. When he noticed Chris was not a participant in the fracas, he guessed his son must be in the house, probably reading in his room, where he seemed to spend most of his time. Joe wondered why Chris hadn't closed the door or blown the driveway this evening, especially with the impending snowstorm, which was expected to deliver another twelve to four-teen inches overnight. *Do I have to tell him everything? Why can't he just take the initiative to do what he knows has to be done?* If Chris wouldn't assume his responsibilities on his own, and if Mary wouldn't ensure Chris would do what needed to be done, then Joe would see to it that Chris would do his chores. He'd get the boy outside right after dinner to clear the sidewalks and driveway and get a head start on the approaching storm.

Joe climbed stiffly back into the warm Jeep still idling in the driveway. With the four-wheel drive engaged, he drove the re-mainder of the unplowed driveway and into the open garage. He gathered his leather briefcase full of actuarial reports and sneaked through the cluttered passage leading to the utility room and into the house. He slid his shoes off without untying them, hung his wet coat on a wall hook, and tiptoed into the kitchen, preparing to wrap his icy hands around his wife's neck.

Alerted to his presence by Grace's tail thumping on the kitchen floor, Mary turned toward her husband. "Not so fast, fella. I wasn't born yesterday!"

Joe, still panting from the recent snowball fight, said, "Me neither. That's my problem!"

He kissed his wife and in return got a somewhat distracted mini-hug. Sidestepping Mary, who appeared preoccupied with dinner, Joe peeked under the lid of the casserole that had been in the oven and was now resting on the stovetop. It was Friday, which meant something meatless. The scent of tuna noodle casserole met his nose before his eyes took in his favorite dish. The last time they had tuna noodle casserole for dinner Joe hadn't been able to eat it hot because Grace had gotten loose and the family had ended up searching the neighborhood for her while their dinner cooled on the table. By the time they'd found Grace and brought her home, Joe had been too hungry to microwave his plate of food and ate the casserole cold. Tonight, he was determined to eat it hot.

"Where's Chris? Why hasn't he cleared the snow off the driveway? Didn't you know another storm is coming? He needs to get going before the next storm arrives."

Mary stood with her hands on her hips, "Whoa, first of all, I don't know where Chris is. He hasn't come home from school. Maggie thought he went sledding with some of the eighth graders, but he should have been home by now. . . .." Mary wrung the dishtowel she held in her hands and couldn't bring herself to answer Joe's other accusatory questions.

Ignoring his wife's bruised feelings, Joe responded, "Well, he *should* be home by now. I don't know what's gotten into him."

Ever the peacemaker, Mary set aside her own hurt and worry, and pleaded, "Honey, can't you be a little patient with him? I don't know what he's feeling, but he needs our encouragement. Why don't you drive past the cemetery and round him up? Let's try to have a nice dinner together, and then he can blow the snow from the driveway. Just try to be nice to him, okay?"

"Ok, ok, ok, I hear you. I'll head out to see if I can find him and bring him home. But he *needs* to get a start on the driveway before the next storm blows in."

Seeking more empathy from her husband, Mary responded, "Thanks, honey, for looking for him. I appreciate that. But what about being more patient with him? Can't the driveway shoveling wait until tomorrow when it's light outside?"

Sensing his wife was not going to budge, Joe replied, "All right, I'll try to be more patient too, but he can shovel the drive by the light of the garage and streetlights. This approaching storm is going to be bad!"

"Alright, I understand, and thanks. Your promise means a lot to me. We'll have dinner as soon as you guys come in. Then Chris can start on the drive."

"Sounds good. I'm starved. And, honey, why don't you call a couple of Chris's buddies just in case he stopped at someone's house on the way home?"

Mary looked at Joe with sad eyes, "Chris hasn't had many close friends lately. I wouldn't know who to call."

Unsure of what to say to allay her apprehension, Joe walked into the utility room rubbing his left shoulder, sore from the snow-ball fight. He put on his wet shoes and wool coat, which seemed to have gained the additional weight of sorrow he and Mary felt about Chris's recent unhappiness. He stepped back into the garage and tugged open the driver's door on the Jeep, wondering how this sad, sullen teenager, so different from himself, could be his own. Joe stooped forward, feeling twenty years his senior. Even before he backed out of the garage, he had a feeling he would not find Chris at the cemetery.

Joe approached the cemetery, where for years kids had sledded down a portion of the steep lawn that was yet without graves. The snow was packed to an icy crust on the crest of the hill, having been trampled beneath children's feet and then packed hard by sleds, saucers, and toboggans. To out-of-towners and some "proper" folks in town, it seemed irreverent to allow sledding in the cemetery, but most of the Hollidaysburg community had thought it appropriate that the cemetery be a place where they could celebrate life and death together in a respectful, joyous manner. Few residents seemed to think twice about the matter. After all, Lutherans had situated the Cemetery high on the hillside at the northern edge of town back in 1803. It had long ago become a natural part of the town's landscape and, importantly, it had an awesome slope that ran a full city block.

The leading edge of the forecast snowstorm had begun to blow with a fury. Joe drove through town in near whiteout conditions as he looked for his son. Hollidaysburg was rapidly turning into a modern day Pompeii: the town folk above and belowground were becoming a civilization buried under dense snow falling from the sky like ash from Mount Vesuvius. The sky was thick with air-puffed snowflakes, which mostly concealed the community's softly glowing streetlamps and porch lights. Although Hollidaysburg wore its oily, coal-contaminated past on the surface of its older buildings, a pristine façade of new snow refreshed and concealed everything dreary within moments.

At the rate the snow was falling, Joe knew there would soon be no demarcation between streets and sidewalks, and he'd better get home while he could still tell the difference. Hoping to intercept Chris along the way, Joe took a circuitous route, passing landmarks from which Chris might be traveling. He drove down Allegheny Street, past his office, the town square, the theater, and the closed shops and businesses along main street. Chris was nowhere in sight.

Although the classic Capitol Hotel and its restaurant in the square were still open, its few employees sat in a booth near the front window, talking and drinking mugs of what appeared to be coffee or hot chocolate. Joe peered hard through the blowing snow and examined the faces of the young people sitting inside to see if any were his son; none were Chris. Outside the hotel, not a single set of fresh footprints was visible in the deepening, drifting snow. It was clear Chris hadn't walked this way. Thinking he'd better get off the streets before the snow was too much even for his four-wheel drive vehicle, Joe navigated the Jeep toward home, driving through the borough on ever more perilous streets. With nagging guilt about his strained relationship with Chris, Joe prayed his son would be home waiting for him.

Fresh footprints leading to the garage door through the still falling snow raised Joe's spirits, and his guilt reverted to peevishness. After parking the Jeep, he rushed into the house through the utility room, and queried, "Okay, I've driven all over town in this lousy weather looking for him! Where has he been? Where is he, I want to talk with him. Now!" Joe's confidence in Chris's safe return was dashed seconds later when he saw Roberta standing in the kitchen with a plate of fresh-baked cookies her mother had asked her to deliver to the Ballentines.

Mary pushed Joe back into the utility room wagging an angry finger in front of his face. "Joe, that's no way to talk. I thought you were going to be more patient." She touched his coat sleeve and, with an anxious tone, whispered, "I've called everyone Chris has been friends with during the past two years, and not one of them has seen him since he left school." Mary gasped, "Joe, I don't know what could have happened to him."

Joe hung his coat on the hook. He winced as he put his arm around his wife's tense shoulder and said with resignation, "I'm sorry, honey. I was just relieved, thinking he was home, and angry he was being thoughtless to cause us to worry and require me to go out looking for him."

Mary looked at her husband through distraught eyes. "I too felt a flush of anger when I heard Roberta come into the garage. But we have to be patient when he returns, Joe. Okay? I don't know what's wrong with him, but something is. I can tell."

"Okay, you're right. Let's wait to see what unfolds when he comes home. For now, I say let's eat dinner." Joe continued with a hint of invented optimism, "We can reheat Chris's meal when he comes in. He should be home soon and then we'll get to the bottom of where he's been."

Mary knew the family had to eat, but her uneasiness grew each time she looked at Chris's empty place setting. She didn't feel like eating but there was nothing else to be done, at least for now. It was too dangerous to go out looking for him again, and they had no idea where to begin their search anyway.

The Ballentines picked at their food without talking, each glancing out the kitchen bay window on occasion at the snow rapidly accumulating and shifting directions, sculpted by the wind's capricious eddies. As Grace laid her head on Maggie's leg, subtly begging a morsel of food, Maggie pushed Grace aside and blurted, "I miss Chris!"

"Oh, honey. Chris is all right. He'll be home soon. We're all a little concerned about him because of the weather, but there's no need to be upset. I'm sure he's okay." Mary tried to present a confident face to back her assertion, but Maggie knew her mother too well and could read her false hope.

"I'm telling you, I miss Chris . . . he's never coming home. Never! I know it." Maggie bolted from the kitchen and ran up the stairs to her room. She threw herself on her bed, sobbing.

Mary searched her husband's eyes for refutation. Sensing no reassurance, she laid her fork on her plate alongside the uneaten tuna noodle casserole and looked out the window. Joe shoved his own plate mid-table. His gut told him Maggie was right about Chris not coming home tonight. A wave of angst swept over him like a tsunami; he too worried that Chris might never again come home.

Mary leaned over the table and confided, "Maggie idolizes her brother. She's the only one who seems to get through to him anymore. They have an almost psychic connection . . . Joe, she's wrong. I know it. She has to be, but it terrifies me she would say such a thing."

Unable to sit helplessly any longer, Mary stood and began transferring dishes from the table to the sink and placing leftover food into the refrigerator. She reflected aloud, "I'm going to call Father Byrne. Maybe he knows something we don't."

Joe pushed away from the table and stood alongside his wife. "Good idea, hon. I'm going back out to see if I can find Chris."

Mary stopped scraping casserole from the baking dish into the storage container. "No, Joe! You are not going out. The weather is far too bad to go looking for him, especially in this storm. I don't want to worry about you being outside in this mess too. Please stay home. At least, let me call Father Byrne first to see if he knows anything helpful before we do anything else. Okay?"

Scratching the stubble on his cheek, Joe consented. "All right, I'll check on Maggie while you call Father. I'm sure there's nothing to what she said; she's just worn out from playing so long and hard in the yard. But I'll make sure she's okay."

"I hope that's all it is," Mary said as she walked into the living room carrying the cordless phone.

Father Byrne was their parish priest, as well as the principal of Immaculate Conception Parochial School, where Chris and Maggie attended. Mary dialed the priest's number, uncertain what she would say when he answered.

Father Byrne had retired for the evening and was relaxing before the rectory fireplace, sipping a fragrant cup of Earl Grey, immersed in the soft crackle of a slow-burning fire and relishing the anticipated holiday break from the school's students and their parents.

As a true Irishman, Father Byrne preferred tea to coffee and ale to tea. This frosty evening, however, Father had his favorite white porcelain teapot adorned with green shamrocks sitting on the serving table beside his leather wingback chair. He sipped the stout amber liquid from the delicate matching teacup, when the phone rang in the rectory office. Father Byrne stood and rested his cup on its saucer, brushing the wrinkles from his black flannel slacks and pulling his black cashmere sweater taut over his portly belly. In times past, such a distended abdomen might have caused parishioners to whisper, "Father is looking scandalously prosperous."

51

Today, it seemed all priests were portly. He stamped his feet to ensure adequate circulation and strode across the carpeted room to his desk where the phone rested on its corner.

Reaching the telephone on its third ring, Father picked up the receiver and answered, "Hello?" Father decided long ago when someone called him at the rectory, he need not identify himself as "Father Byrne." Most often, the caller was a friend, a relative, or a brother or sister in faith calling him at his residence. There was no need for formalities among friends or family.

"Good evening, Father, this is Mary Ballentine."

Father heard her strained voice and sigh. With almost forty years in priesthood, he had become remarkably perceptive, even on the telephone. He knew his parishioners well and could detect even the slightest hint of their anxieties, fears, worries, or anger.

"What is it, dear?"

"Father, did you see Chris today?

"I passed him in the hall at the close of the school day, but there was nothing remarkable in that. Why?"

"He's not home, Father. He's not at the cemetery sledding and . . ." Mary's voice broke, and she held back a sob. "Father, the weather is terrible and it's not like Chris to stay out this late, especially with a storm blowing as bad as this one is."

"I see," Father said with genuine concern. "Mary, I share your apprehension, this doesn't sound like Chris. And I don't know where in town he might be at this hour either. He might have gone to the home of one of his friends, but I'd suggest you err on the side of safety and call the police department. Don't wait any longer, Mary."

Mary's stomach churned. She had no way of knowing or expecting that Chris's growing unhappiness would lead to his disappearance and who knows what else? She wanted to mention what Maggie had said, but she couldn't bring herself to do so. "Father, you've talked with Chris. Is he okay?"

The priest paused before responding, and then on a sigh he said, "I don't know, Mary. I have no way of knowing anything for sure..."

Mary didn't let the man finish his thought. "I know," she blurted, "but . . . um, do you think Chris would run away . . . or hurt himself? Joe and I don't understand him . . . he's become so unhappy lately, especially this last month."

Father Byrne confided, "Mary, I am not a psychologist, but I can tell you I've worried about him too. Chris has confided that he is disillusioned with the world, including church and school. Because his father attended Immaculate Conception, albeit nearly thirty years ago, Chris now resents the feeling of walking the halls in his father's shoes. Knowing how much you and Joe have given of yourselves to the Church, Chris finds his father's shoes a bit too large and uncomfortable at times — especially given Joe's influence as Parish President."

Mary tightened her grip on the receiver as she listened to her son's principal and her parish priest share what she knew was true and what she had feared for so long.

"Mary, Chris is angry and seems driven to disprove God's existence for some reason. I am not sure where that's coming from, but he said a loving God would not be so heartless as to let cruel things happen, like allowing good people to die."

At the mention of death and dying, Mary's heart sank.

Father continued. "I trust in time, Chris will turn out fine, but I am afraid he is depressed right now. That's my best guess. What he needs most tonight is to be home with his family."

Mary asked, "Depressed? About what...why? I don't understand, Father. What does Chris have to be depressed about? He has a good home...parents and a sister who love him...he used to be so funny and had so many friends. Father, I don't get it."

In his most compassionate tone, Father Byrne confided, "Mary, I don't know what's causing Chris's depression, but I would add somewhat cautiously, he seems to be very angry with Joe. I had hoped all of this was a temporary adolescent mood or a passing 'existential crisis.' I was going to talk with you and Joe after the holidays if Chris returned to school still acting glum. Let's find him first and then figure out what's going on with him. You need to make your phone call to the police."

Now in tears, Mary beseeched, "Father, I'm worried sick. I'll call Police Chief Jamison, and Joe and I will pray. Would you pray for him too?"

Father cleared the emotion from his throat before speaking, and then assured, "Better than that, Mary, I will ask the sisters to join me in prayer this evening. Now, get going and see if Chief Jamison's office has any information. And Mary . . ." he paused.

"Yes, Father?"

She could hear the priest shifting in his leather chair.

"Mary...you might also call the hospital to see whether any young men were admitted today."

CHAPTER 5

The boy needed to be in a bed in the Hollidaysburg Regional Hospital, but instead he lay on a wooden door, within the protective confines of a pine-encircled camp, near the top of Cresson Mountain. The three men had done what they could for the injured youth but had resigned themselves to the fact that the boy's fate rested in God's hands.

The men felt impotent, unable to do any more for the young man during the night than observe him. Hank had tried to stay alert during his watch by reading his novel by lamp light, but he interrupted his reading regularly to rub his bleary eyes and check on the boy. It was now 2:00 a.m., Saturday: time for Leo's shift. Hank shook Leo awake and kneeled outside the rack while he gave a succinct briefing on the boy's condition. There was little to report; the kid had not stirred, and his breathing and pulse continued steady, but weak. After the debriefing, Hank drew the mummy bag from around his shoulders, shambled to his apartment, threw the bag in, and crawled in after it. Within minutes, the exhausted man's snoring alternated with Rex's, creating the resonating cadence of a crosscut saw rasping in both directions.

Although the substantial blue spruces sheltered the campers from the severe winter winds and made living conditions tolerable inside the circle of trees, Leo rued how cold their camp had become in the few hours since he'd retired for the night. As Hank had done before him, he pulled his sleeping bag from his rack and wore the bag around his shoulders as a cape. He didn't have a book to read and, after poking through a few pages of Hank's book, he decided he wasn't interested in life along Cannery Row. Leo converted his worry into something useful. He'd spend his three-hour shift decorating the campsite for Christmas, hoping the boy would live to see what he'd accomplished.

Before decking the boughs, Leo brought the gas lantern to the table and examined the boy, who continued to lie motionless on the tabletop. Pulling the plastic sheet and blanket off his patient's face and torso, Leo laid the stethoscope against a bruised chest and listened. The rattle had largely dissipated, and his lungs appeared not to be punctured. Encouraged by the minor improvement, Leo shone his small flashlight into the young man's unconscious green eyes. Both pupils responded by narrowing to a pinpoint, and again Leo was thankful to note subtle improvement. After replacing a couple of bandages and wiping some crusted blood from facial wounds, Leo worried that with the lack of antibiotics, the boy's injuries might soon become infected. He covered the lad again and stood contemplating possible medical scenarios he might face. Although hopeful his patient's vital signs would remain stable, Leo grew increasingly anxious for the boy's condition to improve. His lack of consciousness concerned the former medic. If the kid had suffered a head injury no more serious than a mild concussion, he should have woken up by now.

Leo threw himself into decorating the camp as festively as possible during the remainder of his shift. To its credit, the campsite had not one majestic Christmas tree to decorate but five. To its detriment, the men didn't have a single ornament with which to decorate even a small, sparse "Charlie Brown" tree.

In the warmth of the fire and insulating nature of the surrounding trees, Leo wore only bib overalls and a sweatshirt. He gathered every small, colorful, or metallic object he could find that was not

56

in use and hung or placed the pieces on branches from just above the ground to as high as he could reach. The flat steel bottle opener hung on a branch near the table, three tin coffee cups also hung by their looped handles, apples and oranges were positioned high and away from Rex's growing community of mice, and the few remaining canned goods were arrayed here and there for visual appeal. He cut colored pictures out of *Time* and *Newsweek* magazines and poked branch tips through the pictures to hold them in place. Leo did his best to assemble possibly the gaudiest, tackiest Christmas decorations ever, in hopes the boy would regain consciousness to see and appreciate what he'd done. When he finally ran out of adornments, the campsite resembled a poorly stocked, one-room, rural grocery store. Undeterred, Leo kept at it, rearranging items to get the look just right and avoid sitting worried about the young man who, hour after hour, refused to awaken.

From the storage box in his rack, Leo selected three heavy-duty, gray wool socks with red toes and three-inch red top borders to hang on the clothesline. He turned back and picked up the lone sock remaining in his sleeping compartment, for the boy. Before attaching the socks to the line with standard wooden pinch-styled clothespins, he made duct-tape nametags and stuck a nametag on each sock. For the first three socks, he printed in black ink *Rex*, *Leo*, and *Hank* on the respective gray tape tags, and then paused, wondering whether the boy with no name would awaken. At last, he printed a large question mark as a moniker for the youngster, chuckling aloud as he recalled the old sixties song "96 Tears" by Question Mark and the Mysterians. How appropriate, he thought. The unconscious young man held the answers for many of the men's questions, and Leo was certain someone somewhere cried over this lost and possibly fatally injured soul.

A few minutes before five on Saturday morning, Leo was still humming the organ portion of "96 Tears" as he withdrew a frying pan from the crate near the table and set the pan on a side of coals. He scraped the bottom of a five-pound cloth sack and collected a handful of green coffee beans. He scattered the beans around the bottom of the pan and stirred them with Rex's 15-inch Bowie knife. Rex asserted his Texas heritage with flair. That Jim Bowie and his legendary knife helped defend the Alamo was reason enough for Rex to carry a replica of the celebrated Texan's knife with pride.

Hank was very particular about his coffee. He liked it freshly roasted and ground and then perked and poured. He'd taught his companions how to roast green beans to a consistent "City Roast," which yielded a chestnut-colored bean, perfect for a rich, mellow cup of coffee. Leo mixed the beans with the tip of the knife's long blade. After the beans turned a pleasant dark hue and their husks cracked and flaked off, Leo held the pan away from the heat of the coals and blew the loose debris from the pan. The beans' natural oils had sweated from their core to the surface, leaving a swirl of glistening paths around the bottom of the fry pan, like a figure skater's trailing imprint on an icy pond.

Switching ends of the knife, Leo held the blade in his gloved hand and crushed the small, brittle beans with the knife's round-butted brass handle. He swept some of the coarsely ground coffee into the tin percolator basket, closed the hinged lid, and set the water-filled, navy blue and white porcelain coffeepot on the grill above glowing coals. Leo reserved the remaining grounds for breakfast and possibly another pot sometime later in the day. Within a few minutes, the coffee bubbled, sending a billowing stream of steam skyward where it dissipated along with the campfire's light smoke. The robust aroma of percolated coffee engulfed the campsite, causing Hank to stick his head out of his bunk to ask, "Man! That smells good. Is there enough in that perkin' pot for me?"

With the coffeepot in his gloved hand, Leo asked, "Are you plannin' on gettin' it yo'self or you lookin' to be gettin' yo' coffee in bed?"

Hank wiped the sleep from his eyes. "Coffee in bed sounds great. When I finish with the coffee, I could catch another couple of winks before getting up to make breakfast. How's the boy?"

"The boy hasn't changed, which has me worried, but at least

he's still with us! Hold on an' I'll bring a cup of brew to ya."

With a hot mug of coffee in each hand, Leo handed one off to Hank and, setting the other on top of the bunkhouse, he rousted Rex from his slumber with his deep cavernous voice. Sounding like the stereotypical public radio announcer, Leo intoned, "Rise and shine, Tex. Room service is here with some coffee for ya an' a couple of aspirin. Come on, m'boy. Open them peepers."

Normally a slow riser, Rex made a concerted effort to open his eyes. Squinting through tight slits, as if searching for a lost heifer on a western plain at sunset, he focused on Leo's face and asked, "Are the eggs over easy, like I ordered 'em?"

"No, man. I jus' got some coffee for ya. You gonna have to rustle up yo' own grub this mornin'."

Rex reached out of the bunkhouse and accepted the coffee and aspirin with appreciation just the same. His shoulder ached from deep within; the pain was intense enough that his breathing had become difficult. Before attempting to dress, Rex swallowed the aspirin tablets and sipped his coffee while leaning on his good elbow and appreciating the warm fire from the bunkhouse. Once fully awake and dressed, he push-pulled himself out of his sleeping compartment and handed Leo back the empty mug. Without commenting on the feebly decorated camp, Rex stood at the table and slathered peanut butter onto a slice of bread, over which he sprinkled sugar from a fast-food restaurant packet. He washed the dry sandwich down with a second mug of mouth-blistering coffee. Before Leo could stop him, Rex plucked two oranges from a nearby branch and then quickly peeled and devoured them.

"Oh, man! What are you doin'? Those was my decorations. I was tryin' to make the place look nice for the boy."

"Leo, I hate to remind you, but the boy hasn't stirred since we laid him on that table. Those oranges mighta rotted 'fore the kid laid eyes on 'em"

"I know, but if he does wake up, I want him to see my decorations."

Rex laughed, "Decorations? I thought you was just advertisin' what we had to eat — like some kinda livin' menu or somethin'. Toss me one of them apples, will ya?"

"No! Now, get outta here. I need the red in them apples to stand out against the green in the pine trees. Cain't you see that?" Leo asked with his hands on the hips of his bib overalls.

"Okay, Martha. I'm leavin' ya to your *decorations*. I've got something more important to do this mornin' than play house-keepin' in the woods."

"Well, Mister bigshot, you just run along and go catch yo' Saturday mornin' train to town and have yo'self a big ole hot breakfast in one of them diners."

Dropping his almost non-stop humor for a moment, Rex looked at his friend of nearly two-months and asked something he had asked both Hank and Leo several times in the recent past, "What are we doing here, Leo?"

"Whataya mean?"

"I mean, you know . . . it's just a couple days 'til Christmas and here we are livin' in the woods like a bunch of nature lovers. I just closed up my house back in Texas, jumped on a train, an' rode one after another all the way to Pennsylvania — I mean, what's that all about anyway? I've done some odd jobs and weird things in my life, but I ain't never just run away from home for no good reason. What's the explanation for why all three of us did the same durn thing...and then ended up together right here in this hobo camp? Is there some kinda cosmic, intergalactic conspiracy goin' on someone forgot to tell us about?"

"Yeah, it really do seem like that, don't it?"

"Well, I got grass to mow, some machines that need fixin', an' I'm a hopin' we don't get a freeze down in McAllen an' have all my pipes burst. You know my Aunt Ruth just laughed when I called from Branson an' told her I was out ridin' trains around the country. She said, 'Now, don't that sound fun! See if you cain't get me some big shot's autograph while you're in Branson. You have a good time boy and be careful and get yourself back here in time to clean up your momma and daddy's graves for Memorial Day.'"

"Unh, now I see where you get your sense o' humor!"

"Yeah, my family never took life too seriously. In fact, that's what's got my drawers all pulled tight; it ain't like me to be somebody's foot soldier marching off as soon as orders is given. But that's exactly what I did—just up and dropped everything, grabbed some gear, and climbed aboard some durned-fool diesel and rode trains day and night to get here...an' for what?"

"Like I said before, Rex, I don't know."

Fiddling with the ruby ring he wore on his finger, Rex warned, "Well, I'm about to put my foot down and get my hide out'a here. I got grass to mow! We coulda at least stayed at a hotel or motel and had real room service, know what I mean?"

"If we'd done that, we wouldn't been here when the fool kid went off the rails."

"Yeah, yeah, yeah...I know that's right, but I still don't know what it's all about. And I'm getting' more than a little tired livin' in these woods. Ain't you tirin' of this primitive livin' and dumpster divin'?"

"Come on man, it ain't so primitive. We got us a nice camp. Warm, dry beds, good coffee. An', yeah, we could buy more of our food at the store, but why do that when perfectly good stuff is bein' thrown away at the A&P?"

Hank set his empty coffee mug in the fragrant bed of pine outside his apartment, and before rolling over to go back to sleep, he contributed to the conversation, "Rex, if you're grumbling about the grub, you can take over the cooking for a while, you know? And pipe down about your ranch. You know darn well your pipes aren't going to freeze, and your grass isn't growing worth a hoot down in south Texas in late December. You're just like Leo and me; we don't have anything better to do right now. That's why we're here. The good Lord looked around and said, 'Now there are three guys with a little extra time on their hands. Let me find something for them to do—maybe take a little train ride just for the fun of it and go camping in the Pennsylvania woods for a couple months.' I have a feeling we're going to be on our way real soon. But for now, we've got to

61

take care of the kid over there. Now, get going man and do your part."

"Aw'right, aw'right, yer point's a-taken. I'll suck it up and do my part, so's we can figure out why we're here and finally skedaddle."

Leo laughed at the grumbling ole blowhard, knowing Rex would do whatever it took to save the boy's life, including what he was getting ready to do right now — trying to hitch a ride down the mountain in the worst possible weather and return to their camp with emergency medical care.

Rex bundled into his three-quarter-length range coat and pulled on heavy leather gloves with wool inserts. After wrapping a burgundy-colored wool scarf around his neck and mouth, he pocketed another apple from a nearby branch and strode out of the encampment, entering the bleached-white world beyond. He stretched his stocking cap down over his ears and marveled at the contrasting black and white landscape that lay before him. Nature's bright white freshly laid carpet and matching horizon-to-horizon wallpaper contrasted with her dull gray-black deciduous furnishings, making everything look starkly nouveau. To Rex, however, it was like the rest of his life, simply black and white.

Twenty-two inches of fallen and still-blowing snow covered everything in sight. Low spots were waist deep; some drifts were chest high. Rex goose-stepped, plowing through the snow while following the deer trail that led up hill to the trestle. When he arrived at the bridge, breathing hard and wincing in pain with every deep breath, he kicked aside as much snow as he could from beneath the tracks and slid under the support beams to evade the biting wind. He sat upright on the frozen ground as stiff as death and tried all the while to turn his face away from the badgering gusts that seemed to slap both reddened cheeks at once. Still hungry and worried about his own well-being, he ate the apple from his pocket before it froze solid and tossed aside the core, hoping some scavenging animal would come by and enjoy it later.

As sometimes happens after a Pennsylvania snowstorm, this

early-winter blizzard was followed by an arctic blast from the north that sealed the region in a deep freeze often referred to as an Alberta Clipper. Aware that exposed skin would become frost bit within five minutes in temperatures this cold, Rex covered his face as best he could with the scarf. He shivered and stomped his feet trying to keep them from freezing. He wiggled his toes and pulled his fingers into the palms of his gloves. With his head buried deep inside his coat, he breathed the air circulating inside, warmed a little by his own body heat. No matter what he did though, nothing helped. Given the life-threatening subzero conditions, Rex hoped beyond hope the Pittsburgh train would arrive on time, though he was uncertain whether he'd be spry enough or able to get a solid enough footing to leap aboard if it did pass.

Sitting under the bridge on snow-covered crushed limestone and cinders as he was, Rex gave free rein to his imagination. His thoughts wandered to days past. He contemplated the cinders and oily soot from the old coal-burning steam engines that once wended through Altoona, around the Horseshoe Curve and beyond. That carbon residue, present on buildings throughout the region, was a constant reminder of the earlier railroad days, days when the Horseshoe Curve and the Cresson Trestle were known throughout the world.

By 7:30, Rex couldn't tolerate the deadly temperatures and worsening wind chill any longer. He tried to picture his now nearly frozen feet dangling outside an open car while rounding the Curve on a sunny summer Sunday, glimpsing the blue-green reservoir below. As attractive as the imagined scene was, sunny summer thoughts were not keeping him warm.

The smell of a campfire and breakfast cooking in the relative warmth of the campsite below further tested his resolve. He longed for the corned beef hash and eggs he smelled taunting him from down the hill. He knew Hank would have doctored the canned hash with sautéed Vidalia onion, Leo's favorite, and a generous dose of black pepper. Rex could not ignore the smell of onion sautéing. He was freezing and hungry, desperate for the hash he could envision simmering within the distant ring of spruces.

Though Rex felt guilty about not braving the weather any longer, no man could stand such unforgiving weather for long without adequate clothing and protection. He was a patient man, as far as Texans go, but his patience and tolerance for the bitter cold had expired. He concluded the snow was simply too deep for the morning train to pass. He stood to stretch his legs and back and their contracted muscles, and worried about the loss of feeling in his toes. Looking like a ninety-year-old, bent over and finding it difficult to maintain his balance on numb feet, Rex took one last look down the Pittsburgh-bound track. There was nothing to see in the desolate, arctic setting except one long trailing mound of snow coursing through the mountains. He gave up his vigil about eight o'clock and forced his way back the way he came, through the deep snow, pursuing the warmth of the campfire and the lingering scents of coffee and breakfast whipping around in the stiff breeze.

Concealing his frustration and sense of failure, Rex barked as he approached the camp, "Hey, can a man get a meal around here?" As if stepping into a saloon in the old west, he pushed open two overlapping pine boughs and surveyed the camp interior looking for the potbelly stove. Later, after he warmed up, he might join a good poker game and get a hot meal, but now he was looking for refuge from the storm. He swaggered into the camp's cavernous interior, allowing the boughs to swing back into place as he sallied forth. Thursday's newspaper lay across Chris's knees in a disheveled pile. Hank and Leo sat opposite each other at the table, dressed warmly in wool shirts, sweatshirts, and scarves wrapped around their necks. Their breakfasts had been finished, and they sat jawing over a cup of coffee. Between them, the boy's feet protruded surrealistically from beneath the electric blanket like salt- and pepper-shakers, covered only by the plastic drop cloth.

Hank looked up from his coffee cup as Rex approached the table and said, "I thought you'd be sitting in some warm diner eating pancakes and sausages by now. What happened?"

Shaking off the cold and taking off his outerwear and boots, Rex

64

confessed, "I'm afraid I failed y'all. I couldn't get to town. The train never made it, and I don't 'spect any trains are gonna be coming through here very soon! I like'd to freeze to death out there, an' here you was a-torturin' me with the smoky smell of a warm fire, corned beef hash, and coffee a-cookin. So, you gonna serve this freezin' ranch hand some breakfast, or are ya gonna continue the torture?"

Leo heard his frustration, "Don't worry none about not gettin' off the mountain this mornin'. Come on in where it's warm and we'll figure something else out."

Relieved at being forgiven, Rex sparred, "So, what about breakfast. Ain't anyone gonna answer me?"

"Sorry, cowpoke, kitchen's closed. Come back around noon for lunch," Hank quipped.

"Don't be tossin' me chips, sodbuster. I'm here to tell you I'm *hungry!*"

After a cruel pause, Hank responded, "I guess you could scrape up what's left in the skillet over there, as long as you wash it up afterward." Hank pointed offhandedly toward the frying pan sitting covered at the edge of the fire.

Rex trundled stocking-footed through the deep pine straw floor over to the fire, lifted the pan's cast-iron lid, and laid his eyes upon a mouth-watering mound of crusted, heavily peppered hash with translucent onions shimmering throughout. There were also a couple of large spoonfuls of scrambled eggs left in the pan, though dry and stiff. Texture didn't matter to Rex this morning. He was "powerful hungry." He sat in a lawn chair savoring the warmth of the pine-insulated camp, his deadened feet warming by the flickering flames, and dug into the victuals.

After cleaning his plate, Rex joined the men sitting at his imagined saloon counter near the kid's feet and listened to Hank and Leo discuss the weather and their concerns about what they might be accused of if the boy didn't live. Would anyone believe their rescue story, or would the authorities suspect they had harmed the boy? Even if their story was believed, would they be blamed for not risking their lives in an effort to travel the three long miles down the mountain in the dark and through impassable snow to seek assistance? It seemed no matter what they did, they were in jeopardy if the boy died. They'd just have to be patient and wait for the weather to improve, and as soon as conditions permitted and the boy was conscious, they would set out.

The three talked over the boy's feet and ankles as if body parts were common fixtures on a dining table. After about twenty minutes of conversation and with his stomach still growling, Rex finished the crusty eggs and hash in the pan. Hank would cook breakfast for the kid when he woke up—if he ever woke up—and Rex was too hungry to let perfectly good chow go to waste, waiting on the comatose young man to open his eyes.

Looking at the boy's feet under the sheet of plastic for the first time this morning, Rex said to the others, "Somebody needs to trim this youngun's toenails. He's gettin' close to some serious ingrowns startin' on that left foot."

Even though inside the camp the temperature was nearly sixty degrees, Leo cautioned as he picked up the empty plates, "We might wanna see whether he makes it through the day before we worry 'bout his nails. But y'all might could cover the boy's feet with a blanket. His toes be turnin' as blue as those bruises on his face. An' it's cooling off in here steady-like. I'm thinkin' we all might catch the chills if the temps keep going down like they are, 'specially if we run out of firewood."

Rex chimed in, "Leo, the thick pines surrounding us are going to keep the wind out, just as they have been doing all along. We got our bunks and we ain't gonna run out'a wood. There's a forest full dry wood for the having, and we've still got a lot of coal we foraged from the tracks. Don't be getting' yourself all jacked up."

Despite the truthfulness of Rex's come back, the men left the table one by one, each tending to his solitary business. It wasn't necessary to do so, but Hank covered the boy's feet and threw several more logs onto the fire before he began heating water to wash dishes and bodies. While Rex straightened the camp, Leo used some of the remaining roasted beans to brew one last pot of coffee.

None of the men ventured more than a few feet from the fire pit, unless they absolutely had to. To make things worse, it was clear they were out of green coffee beans and from this point on would have to drink tea, at least until they could get to town. The thought of drinking tea worried Hank, a self-professed, unapologetic coffee snob. The three men spent the remainder of the morning taking "bird baths" near the fire, and all the while treasuring what little coffee remained in the pot.

After filtering the final bitter swig through his teeth, Leo dashed the dregs to the ground and washed his cup. He put on his outerwear and prepared to set out and retrace his steps from yesterday. He was determined to locate and fill the two empty milk jugs that had tumbled down the hill, but he was not looking forward to putting any part of his body back into the frigid water. The pond had likely frozen overnight, leaving the convulsive stream as their only source of water. Like it or not, Leo knew he was going to get wet filling water jugs this morning.

Fearful Leo might be attempting something else heroic, Rex asked, "Where do you think you're going, pardner?"

Leo responded, "We 'bout out'a water, Rex. I figured I'd see if I could fetch us some to get us through."

Hank chimed in. "No, you're not! It's too dangerous for you to climb down that ravine in these conditions. Rex could barely make it to the tracks earlier. No way, dude. Now take off your coat and go sit yourself down. We have to stay smart, or one or another or all of us isn't going to make it off this mountain alive. We have enough water to get us through if we're careful. We can melt snow if we must, but we all have to stay close by this camp today."

Knowing his friends were right, Leo unzipped his coat and slid one arm then the other out of its respective sleeve. "You right. I just wanted to do somethin' to help. I'm gettin' real restless jus' sittin' in this icebox. You know, feelin' a little helpless?"

Hank agreed. "I'm getting cabin fever too, but we don't have any choice but to mind our safety. You know that. So, let's just sit tight for the next couple of days. Then we can make our break."

As Leo joined Rex sitting by the fire, Hank scrubbed the aluminum stockpot they'd used for bathing. From one of the barrels, he pulled out a black garbage bag and reached inside. He withdrew a package containing a frozen roasting chicken. Like the beef tips, the chicken had "liberated" from the A&P dumpster. Hank tore the cellophane wrap off the chicken, stuck his nose close to the bird's yellow skin, and sniffed. The bird didn't smell any too fresh; however, satisfied the chicken wasn't spoiled, he pulled the giblets and neck out of its chest cavity and dropped the carcass into the pot with a hollow *kaplunk*.

To accompany the chicken, Hank added water, salt and pepper, and the remaining onion from breakfast. He set about boiling the daylights out of the bird, reducing the liquid to a rich, greasy broth. Later, he'd set aside the meat and remove the bones. He beat together half-dozen eggs with lots of pepper and a little salt and gradually added handfuls of flour until he had pliable dough. After rolling out the dough to a thickness of about a quarter inch with an empty wine bottle, he cut the floury sheet into two- to three-inch squares. Later, after removing the meat and bones, he brought the broth back to a boil and stirred the doughy squares into the stockpot one piece at a time. Careful not to waste anything edible, Hank scooped up and sprinkled into the pot the flour remaining on the tabletop. When the meal was finished, the cold and hungry men would feast on huge bowls of chicken and dumplings.

The camp's supply of ready-cut firewood dwindled. Rex crossed the camp to an unkempt brush pile and, with his good arm and a rusty brush saw, cut branches into eighteen-inch lengths. He stacked branches and logs onto the wood pile, periodically adding an armful to the fire. By tending the wood pile and cleaning up the branches dragged into camp after forays into the woods, Rex had tidied up a sizable portion of the camp and ensured another evening of warmth. The task also distracted him from his pain and assuaged his guilt for failing to bring medical help to the boy.

The physical labor of sawing, exacerbated by the effort of doing it all with one hand, had Rex played out. He retired to one of the lawn chairs by the fire and thumbed through Hank's book. Rex preferred Louis L'Amour western stories to the more literary matter Hank read, but regardless of Hank's personal tastes, all paperback books made acceptable toilet paper. He looked through the book for a dog-eared page and, before removing a few of the pages before that spot, hollered over at Hank who was intent on stirring dumplings. "Hank, ole buddy, we're fresh outa toilet paper, can I take a few pages from your book to read out in the woods?"

"Sure thing. Just take the first chapter or two. I'm beyond that."

Rex closed the book and, without putting on his coat, darted from the camp into the blistering cold to where the men had previously dug a deep hole beneath a low-hanging horizontal branch and where the pages of Hank's book would prove useful.

The men continued to work with determination around their camp throughout the day, trying their best to keep warm and preserve their supplies. Each man thought of the boy still lying unconscious on the table and worried about the young man's survival. Each waited for some change in the boy's condition, wondering whether Question Mark would ever awaken from his current day-and-a-half slumber.

CHAPTER 6

Lying semiconscious within the rough-hewn camp, beneath five snow-capped towering spruce spires, Chris struggled to open his eyes or move his limbs. His torpid thoughts floated about, bumping into each other like helium balloons at a New Year's Eve party. Try as he might, he could not achieve a level of consciousness sufficient to understand his current mental or physical condition. He'd once read about veterinarians who tranquilized animals with muscle relaxants that left them hazily aware of their surroundings but temporarily paralyzed. He felt similarly drugged.

He wondered whether he might be dreaming one of those crazy dreams where you thought you had awakened, to find yourself still asleep and dreaming of being awake. Something was not right, but he couldn't figure out what it was. There was also that very peculiar sensation of hot, damp air spreading across his face at even intervals. His face felt misted every time he exhaled, and he puzzled over why his every steamy breath returned to its origin. And his chest ached, especially when he drew in a breath. He envisioned a Saint Bernard sitting on him panting over his face, with every clammy breath taunting him because he couldn't dislodge the beast keeping him prone.

In the deep recesses of his consciousness, Chris questioned whether he might have died. But he couldn't ignore the ache in his chest when he inhaled or disregard the spinning sensation of having just stepped off a dizzying ride on a Tilt-A-Whirl. Such undeniable pain, head-to-toe, queasiness, and fogged disorientation made it clear he had not achieved permanent slumber — he was alive, and to some extent, awake.

Unsure of his surroundings, Chris stumbled upon a trace of contemporary awareness. He began to perceive olfactory clues that suggested he was in the woods. In response to an incongruent combination of odors — a musty blanket, damp cardboard, smoky wood fire, body odor and sweat, pinesap, dried blood — his stomach twirled like a Maytag on spin cycle. In the distance, he heard the wind howling, branches rattling, and men's voices reverberating against a hollow background, as if their words were being spoken through an oscillating fan.

Sweat beaded on his upper lip, and he held his breath to secure a thought that might otherwise evaporate if he so much as exhaled — *If I'm not dead or asleep, why can't I move?* The accumulation of disconcerting realizations edged his growing anxiety closer to panic. He exhaled slowly. *Oh, Lord, please don't let me be paralyzed!*

Chris strained to rein in his galloping heart, control his rapid respiration, and scatter the fluffy down fouling his thinking. He tried to lift his head, but it remained planted on the rigid surface where he lay. He urged one then another hand to scratch his nose or wipe the sweat from his upper lip. Nothing. Just to open his eyes to see where he was would be a relief. From beneath what he feared would be permanently closed eyelids, tears streaked his bruised cheeks and uncontrolled terror reigned within his otherwise nonresponsive body. He cried for help, but only he heard his unspoken summons; his vocal chords refused to oblige him a sound and his lips remained sealed tight. He was a prisoner within his own body, unable to communicate with others outside his skin. He wanted to scream to gain someone's attention.

The horror he faced might have driven him crazy, had it not

been for the blessings of his injury-induced bewilderment and the daydreaming distraction that kept him from focusing for long on his internal captivity. Like a fishing reel with a backlash, the young man's truant mind could not play out a single straight line of thought for more than a few seconds before the notion came to a jerking tangled halt.

A Herculean effort was required for him to maintain anything near focus, and consequently the overwhelming dread of paralysis subsided as Chris's thoughts regressed from his present surreal situation to his most recent, albeit transient memories. In a halting movie-like rewind and fast-forward review, ephemeral images began to replay in his mind's eye. He was at home, having breakfast.

Maggie and I have just finished our oatmeal and toast at the breakfast table. Mom is baking Christmas cookies, and I've worked on a few math problems to complete my homework before finishing breakfast. Shortly after eating, we go out the door, heading off to school. Maggie and I laugh and joke along the way. At school, I take Maggie to her homeroom and then I go to mine, but the morning seems to sour as soon as I enter my own class.

The day is long and tedious, and near the end of the last period, the second hand on the dingy classroom clock barely creeps around its ugly, yellowed face. Worse yet, its hands seem to stop and defiantly stand still whenever I take my eyes off them. I lay my head on my arm and bury my face sideways into the crook of my elbow, staring alternately at the clock and the second-floor window of the red brick house across the street, wondering who lives there.

For some reason, I'm thinking of Christmases past, all the while ignoring Sister Rose as she prattles on about the Saturday evening Christmas pageant. She's wearing a ridiculous electric, pulsing Christmas tree pennant on her habit and sits there, on the corner of her desk, beaming stupidly, swinging her rosary beads. What a joke! The old wannabe hipster is just killing time, trying to keep a lid on the classroom chaos that is about to erupt. The bell rings, and my classmates jump from their seats and begin darting about, cackling like a startled flock of barnyard chickens. 'Babel-

like happy sounds,' Father Byrne calls it; I surely can't make any sense of it.

Bill Johnston stops by my desk on his way out of the building to invite me sledding with him and the others, but I beg off. He frowns but moves on. I'm anxious to get out of this tired school with its tiled halls and hideous Navy gray wall lockers. I just want fresh air and solitude.

Chris's consciousness was aroused by a new scent, overpowering the collage of odors that had turned his stomach previously, but he couldn't quite put his finger on what it was. His mind mulled the aroma and his senses reacted sharply to its sharp bite. *Coffee!* That was it. Great, he must be home, in bed, and asleep. *I need to get up and get going.* But he wasn't asleep or at home, he soon realized, and he fretted again about his sense of oblivion. Once more, he heard men talking—something about decorations being gaudy, followed by laughter . . . a reference to ransom . . . a hushed conversation about being charged with murder. Chris's mental processing foundered, his thoughts jumbled like gathered wool, and his attention drifted.

Upon leaving the nearly empty building, I'm not ready to go home. I need to get away from my family and the other kids for a while. Suddenly, I feel an urge to walk up the tracks to the Cresson Trestle, where it will be quiet and peaceful. I shouldn't attempt the walk without changing into something warmer, but if I go home first, Mom will just make me stay. So, I headed out the school door with the bridge as my destination.

While leaving Immaculate Conception, I slip on the icy landing just outside the front doors, throw my hands in the air, and almost tumble down the stairs with a comedian-like pratfall. I make it past the flagpole okay and then onto the snow-crusted public sidewalk, the hard-packed snow crunching under my slick leather soles.

Heading toward Montgomery Street, I pass the cemetery's black metal gate, where my classmates are gathering to sled. They call and wave me over, but I just wave and keep walking toward downtown. My eyes remain focused on the slippery sidewalk until I get to the stretch of Hollidaysburg

73

with all of the decorated homes. I can't help but admire the view.

Scenes were flashing through Chris's mind like rapid-fire snap-shots: elaborate wreaths adorning massive recessed front doors set into even deeper entryways within expansive front porches; mansions; a mélange of Georgian, Victorian, Tudor, and Federal architecture with ornate porches, cupolas, columns, towers, doorways, brickwork, and stonewalls and walkways.

I keep going, past these huge homes, down Montgomery Street, past Spruce, then Walnut, and into the business district. Once in the town center, it will be a matter of only minutes before I reach the Pennsylvania Railroad tracks across State Highway 22.

At Allegheny Street, I go into the town square, where I see the Village's thirty-foot Christmas tree. It blazes manically, with thousands of flickering white bulbs blinking on and off like paparazzi taking photographs outside the Emmy Awards. Such a waste – another year, another dead tree.

The sparkling lights, dim due to the snow covering them, reflect like kaleidoscopes in the windows of the bank building. I stop for a moment and lean against the town's cast-iron, four-faced clock, resting my forehead against the frigid metal. Overhead, beyond my reach, the old timepiece is draped in pine bough, red ribbons, and a bow. The clock reminds me it's probably time to go home, but I can't. Instead, I cross Allegheny Street and gaze eastward, toward the municipal building and the County jail on Mulberry, which looks like a medieval fortress. Midway down the street, I see Dad's insurance agency, all decorated for Christmas – so fake.

One of the tiny trees that line Allegheny Street is aglow outside Dad's office. Like the Christmas tree in the town square, this tree's mini lights mesmerize me. I close my eyes for a minute to put the image out of mind and then start across the street.

As I cross, I look to my right. The same decadent line of sparkling trees runs downhill toward the red Insul-Brick tavern sitting dark and dejected on the corner. Like the town clock, all of the gas lampposts lining both sides of the street are covered with greenery, holiday banners, and crimson

74

ribbons. A Dickens scene straight from the Christmas Carol, but I leave it all behind, encouraged onward by a ghost from Christmas past.

In his dreamy semi-consciousness, Chris reflected on the origin of his hometown's name. Was Hollidaysburg named because of its festive holiday-like nature or did people decorate exorbitantly for holidays because of the town's moniker? It was the old chicken and egg conundrum. Whichever the case, it was definitely a holiday-oriented burg, especially around the Fourth of July, Thanksgiving, and Christmas, when the mayor would run around town cajoling business owners to pitch in and portray the Village as especially wholesome, quaint, and festive.

There's Gearhart's department store. I glance into the large glass windows at the Christmas displays. Visitors from as far south as Roaring Spring and Bedford and as far north as Tyrone and State College line the sidewalks from Thanksgiving to New Year to view Mr. Gearhart's antique train set rumbling among crowds of mechanized carolers, festive families, and children ice skating on a frozen pond.

There's no one here right now but me. Holidays past, Grandpa and Maggie were here with me . . . I stop briefly and stand looking . . . I'm not alone after all . . . Grandpa and Maggie are with me . . . I can hear Grandpa and Maggie discuss each window scene, just like we used to.

After seeing the holiday displays, Grandpa always led Maggie and me across Allegheny Street, where we'd stare in awe at the town's gigantic Christmas tree. He'd escort us to the hotel restaurant and order French fries and steaming mugs of hot chocolate topped with marshmallows. We'd dip our fries in mayonnaise while Grandpa periodically glanced at his pocket watch. At just the right moment, he would stand up, straighten his suit, slip his fingers into his vest pocket, and magically produce three theater tickets. Then he'd say, as though he'd just thought of the idea, "What do you two think about seeing whatever that magnanimous Mr. Wasserman might be showing for Christmas this year?"

Grandpa always made it a point to tell us that the theater owner obtained at his own expense each year's blockbuster Christmas film to show throughout the holiday season. Rumors had it that Mr. Wasserman projected pirated versions of the films, but Grandpa said the movies were obtained honestly and shown as a generous gift to the community. Grandpa said we should pay no never-mind to rumors.

Each year, Mr. Wasserman also dressed as Santa Claus and gave gifts and candy to patients in the Hollidaysburg Hospital. Grandpa always called Mr. Wasserman a mensch, whatever that means. I will ask him. But as I turn toward Grandpa, I see he's no longer with me. Neither is Maggie....

I've delayed long enough and feel a guiding hand on my shoulder urging me forward. After walking past the old historic Sheridan Hotel, opposite the Pennsylvania Railroad switching yard at the edge of town, I cross Highway 22 and step over the guardrail onto the limestone siding of the train track. The rank rail yard smell, diesel fuel and exhaust fumes, is nostalgic and somehow comforting. I tuck my face out of the chill and into my jacket collar, step from tie to tie toward the Cresson Trestle, and leave the village behind. As the incline grows steeper, I begin to perspire and unzip my jacket. I take off my tie and stuff it into the backpack and keep trudging upward. It feels as if someone is walking with me, so I look over my shoulder, but no one's there.

The higher I climb, the colder the air feels. At least the breeze that gusts up the mountain from the valley evaporates the sweat from my face. About three miles out of town, the towering graffiti-covered cliff alongside the track comes into view and I'm soon dwarfed by it. While passing the sheer-faced stone, I read a few of the names scrawled on the wall, many I recognize as my parents' friends: Kaminski, Salvatore, Hopkins, Bender, Fiore, Ancel.... The trestle is only about a quarter-mile farther up the mountain. My heart is pounding and my palms are now moist with sweat. Why? What am I afraid of?

Chris lay on the wood door choked with the dread of an impending disaster, incapable of getting out of its way and unable to call for help. Panic flooded over him. *Why can't I move? Why can't I yell?* Unable to stem the flow of fearful thoughts and recent memories, he continued to bob along the churning current that had swept him away from his home and deposited him where he now lay.

I look beyond the curving track to the trestle, waiting for me like an old friend. Far below, the winter waters gush down the mountain stream, splashing over rocks and boulders. I pause for a minute or so before stepping onto the bridge, just long enough to toss my backpack to the apron of the track. I'm shaking.

Chris's respiration labored as his racked body remained imprisoned on the tabletop. His nose itched torturously from the dew now covering his skin from forehead to chin, yet he could not wipe away the mist.

Maybe it's the height of the trestle and the stark landscape that has me so riled. The last summer when Grandpa and I were here, it didn't seem as high as it does now. It felt safe then. The leaves were soft, shortening the distance to the horizon and the stream below. I wasn't afraid then.

I sit on the cold iron rail, mid-trestle, watching the sunset. The frigid metal bites through my corduroys and stings my bottom. My shaking stops as I remember sitting here with Grandpa summers before. Calm once more, I pull my knees against my chest and rest my feet on the snowcapped railroad tie before me. Muted rays of sunlight merge with the distant mountains to form a massive steel-gray wall. The wind is picking up, and gusts of sharp, cutting snow scratch my cheeks and forehead. Is that a squall I feel approaching? Should I be worried?

The air has gotten much colder. I zip my jacket to the top and put my hands in its fleece-lined pockets. I am shaking harder now. Is it just from the cold? Is there something else, something ominous? What is it?

The warmth and crackle of the men's campfire worked its way into Chris's consciousness, and he began pondering the tremors he'd experienced while on the trestle. Still, he couldn't understand why he shook so. He recalled that while daydreaming on the bridge, the sun had sneaked behind thick, threatening clouds. Aware that he sat alone mid-trestle with scant light to guide him from his precarious position, he had stood and begun stepping toward his backpack. The temperature had plummeted, with gale force winds blowing icy snow in staggering gusts. All alone, he'd known he needed to get himself off the trestle in the dark and under risky weather conditions.

Under the blanket and plastic film, Chris strained to lift his head to view the danger he felt pressing upon him, but he remained in place, unable to defend himself from whatever it was that pursued him. Panting now, he struggled to open his eyes just wide enough to glimpse the looming peril, the demon he felt was in his presence. As in a horror film, the lurking fiend broke into his recollection with a gut-punch startle. It burst onto the scene through an opaque curtain of swirling snow, its presence announced by three eardrum-shattering blasts of an air horn.

His pursuer's bright searchlight arced through the woods, searching for him as it rounded the tracks. Chris recalled ducking low to avoid being seen, but the blinding lamplight shone its menacing ray full on him. His rattled mind knew he must escape the stalking predator, still unsure of what it was that sought him. Chris's throat tightened, as he belatedly paired the rumble of the approaching monster with its headlamp. The frightening fiend that had caught him off-guard was a train rounding the curve, preparing to rumble onto the trestle.

About thirty yards away from his backpack, Chris had first tried to scamper toward the false safety of his belongings, but soon realized the distance was too great to cross before the locomotive would block his retreat. Rather than challenge the massive engine head on, he balanced as best he could in the gusting winds and stepped away, placing one foot in front of the other, along the endless line of slippery, snow-frosted beams. His own grotesque shadow, cast down the track in front of him, dissipated along with his confidence every second the engine edged closer.

On the tabletop, Chris quivered fitfully. Mentally struggling to stay afoot and escape the massive locomotive, he saw himself throwing his arms in front of him as he was tossed onto the old wooden bridge by a temblor from the rumbling train. *Doesn't the engineer see me? Why isn't he trying to stop?*

With his floodgates of memory now breached, the remainder of the horrific event cascaded like a waterfall before Chris's eyes. The train, a long collection of boxcars, coal cars, tank cars, and flatcars, was impossible to stop short of a mile, even if the engineer had seen Chris. Proceeding at a glacial pace ahead of the train, Chris lowered his head out of the gale to keep from being blown from the trestle like litter. Guided only by the boundaries of the two iron rails and the approaching headlight, he shuffled like a crab from crosstie to crosstie. His reddened, tender hands, stiff from the cold and chaffed from clutching the rugged creosote beams, bled.

It was apparent that crawling was not going to save him, so Chris got onto his feet once more and tried to step off the distance at a measured pace, but faster than his previous creeping crawl. As the train undulated side to side and the grumbling diesel engines sent shuddering pulses throughout the trestle, Chris once more lost traction. His leather-soled shoes slipped on the slick, creosoted tie and he was heaved forward. His chin struck a splintered beam, his chest deflated like a burst balloon, and his nose cracked when it slammed against the rough wood.

Dazed and tottering above the rocky ravine on the fulcrum of a single tie, balancing on his bruised belly with his legs dangling into the abyss, Chris felt certain he would fall to his death. He kicked desperately, trying to raise himself onto the trestle. As he rocked his aching body rhythmically in his struggle to get atop the tie, his legs shot between two beams and his right shoe flung loose and disappeared into the gurgling rivulet below. At last, the toe of his left shoe snagged the very edge of a beam and held. Chris dragged himself to his feet once more, uncertain where he was but hearing a voice urging him to stay afoot. However, before he could regain either his full balance or his senses, he was sucker-punched by the wobbling trestle. This time, he knew he was out of the fight for good, but he pulled himself up once more in a defeated stance on a single tie. He stood, defenseless, his arms hanging at his side, and awaited the knockout punch he knew would soon be delivered.

Although his face was bloodied and his mind reeled, somewhere deep inside he heard then, as he heard now, a voice demanding he lift his head with dignity. His body resisted the simple command, but in one last frustrated attempt at deliverance, Chris raised his head and through swollen, half-closed eyes, glowered at the headlamp of the locomotive, now just thirty feet away and gaining fast. He edged toward the very end of the rugged crossbeam, as if the train might pass by, leaving him unscathed, and faced the dark valley below. He inhaled deeply with the engine nearly upon him, and as pungent diesel fumes filled his lungs, he sprung off the track, legs splayed behind, like a frog leaping from a lily pad ahead of an approaching snake.

Lying on the tabletop, Chris saw himself sailing downward, away from the trestle, through the snow-swirled chasm, anticipating the inevitable impact. During that brief but interminable moment, he thought he would at last be with his beloved grandfather, but his heart sank at the cost—the crushing blow to his family. He would never again see his mother, his father, his sister, or Grace on earth. He regretted his stubbornness and for not allowing his mother and father into his heart after his grandfather's death.

The first of two consecutive Pennsylvania Railroad locomotives—straining with scores of freight cars trailing behind— creaked, groaned, and clattered onto the trestle egress, its engineer unaware of Chris's presence. At the same moment, Chris, too, ceased to be aware.

In the spruce camp, the men were alerted to their patient's recalled struggle by his seizure-like thrashing, helpless as they watched the boy flailing on the tabletop. To them, it appeared as if Chris had been electrocuted, convulsing as though ten thousand volts coursed through his body. His eyes fluttered open and closed, his arms shook, and his legs jerked, kicking aside the blanket and thick plastic sheet covering him.

Out of necessary and benign abandonment, Leo held Rex and

Hank back, refusing their efforts to intervene. He knew nothing could be done for their patient during such a violent seizure except preventing him from falling off the table. After what seemed like several minutes of frantic battle with some unseen foe, Chris's body lay spent. His eyes, bulging and hemorrhaging from strain, stared heavenward unfocused. With his last short exhalation, he moaned a final utterance.

The men's hearts sank. They had done what they could to care for the boy after Rex and Leo had risked their lives to rescue him from the pond. In the boy's final moments, they stood by doing nothing as they watched him die from a massive seizure.

CHAPTER 7

The sun rose bright on that bitterly cold Saturday morning in Hollidaysburg. Pleasant Valley and its surrounding mountain backdrop, veiled by a deep cover of snow seldom seen in the vicinity, looked the picture of a Chamber of Commerce commercial for a ski resort. But Valley temperatures had dropped to below zero, making the wind chill inhospitable; temperatures in the mountains were about ten degrees colder and proportionately more perilous. The sky was clear except for the crystalline cirrus clouds that wisped above at high altitudes. Cirrus formations generally foretell fair weather, but the high-flying icy feathers fanning across the sky were dishonest harbingers of what was to be.

Throughout the valley, radio and television stations advised people to stay indoors and cautioned them to gather supplies for an emergency survival kit should conditions worsen. In Hollidaysburg, diligent, loving husbands fretted because they had postponed their Christmas shopping until too late. Stores would not open this morning due to the snowstorm and ungodly temperatures; the menfolk anticipated their wives' deep-freeze response to a giftless Christmas morning. Local media were broadcasting long lists of cancellations for events throughout the region.

Residents phoned the State Police barracks to inquire whether the mountain roads were passable, only to learn another storm was imminent and all roads would remain impassable for the foreseeable future.

Saturday had arrived in the Ballentine home without word from or about Chris. After a sleepless night, morning had brought Mary and Joe alternating feelings of hope and despair compounded with worry and fear. By midmorning, their thin veneer of confidence had cracked, and their anxiety was palpable. Pushed beyond her limits, Mary accused Joe of driving Chris away with his impatience; Joe snapped back a criticism that Mary hovered and didn't allow Chris to work things out for himself. Both were terrified and seeking explanations for why their son was still missing.

The parents found themselves asking questions of God and the municipal authorities about their son's whereabouts but were getting answers from neither source. They shrunk from and cursed the ever-ringing telephone, yet they prayed each time the phone rang the caller would be their son. In their minds, they seemed to be alone in feeling the urgency that Chris might be injured and in harsh weather conditions. Although the situation was a gut-wrenching emotional crisis for the Ballentines, it was just another local news story for the media, with routine questions to ask, and for the police, standard procedures to implement.

Mary and Joe sat at the kitchen table throughout the night, drinking coffee and listening to the wind, each gust sounding deceptively like Chris's voice or Chris entering the house. By sunrise, after a long night of auditory hallucinations and accompanying adrenalin rushes, the two worn parents were in no condition to interact with others. Joe was worn out. His back hurt from the snowball fight he'd engaged in yesterday, and he chided himself for playing like a kid thirty years his junior.

Maggie and Grace had both slept through the night, but now that Maggie was awake, her youthfulness contributed to random episodes of weeping. The family, with their lives now turned upside down, found everything that occurred on a typical Saturday morning annoying because nothing in their lives was normal any-more. Their son had disappeared, and although they prayed for the best, they feared the worst. In contradiction to their personal night-mares and imagined catastrophic scenarios, Mary and Joe felt as-sured Maggie that Chris was okay and that there must be some reasonable explanation for his absence. They felt dishonest and on the verge of decomposing, which they avoided only for Maggie's sake.

Mary's conversation with the police Friday evening was any-thing but helpful. Officer Bartkowski, pulling phone duty while the Chief collaborated with the hospital and emergency medical tech-nicians to coordinate storm-related emergency services, had been dismissive of Mary's concerns, leaving her on the other end of the phone in tears. He'd conjectured thoughtlessly that Chris had prob-ably spent the night with a friend. The inexperienced police officer told Mary, "You watch! Tomorrow morning he'll come home sheepishly because he didn't ask permission to spend the night with some classmate, figuring you would have said no if he'd asked. It happens all the time. There's nothing to worry about. If your son doesn't come home tonight, he'll be there first thing in the morning. Mark my words."

The patrolman had been unwilling to come to the mourning parents' home last evening to discuss the matter further, saying "I'd come by and chat, but we'd just end up having a cup of coffee to-gether and that would be that. I'm sure your boy's all right. Trust me. Now, call Saturday afternoon and let me know where he spent the night. All right? G'night now."

After pressing the cordless phone's talk button to discontinue the call, Mary had furiously pressed the talk button again and punched in the rectory phone number to call Father Byrne. Father shared Mary's frustration over the young police officer's thought-lessness. He helped her cope with her resentment by focusing her attention on locating Chris instead of on the bungling officer. He promised Mary he'd ask Sister Mary Agnes to use the school's phone tree to telephone every Immaculate Conception family to alert them that Chris was missing. If Chris, as the young police officer believed, was spending the night with a friend, the phone tree would locate him within an hour or less.

Each of the five nuns who taught at Immaculate Conception agreed to set aside their preparations for the Saturday night school pageant. Each nun would call three families on the tree. Within about twenty minutes, the phone tree would get in touch with all 264 families with students at Immaculate Conception School. Word would spread throughout the community that Immaculate Conception's eighth-grade student Chris Ballentine was missing.

The Ballentines had been awake for hours, since well before sunup, when Father, accompanied by Sisters Mary Agnes and Bernadette, rang the Ballentines' doorbell. They had coffee and donuts in hand from the Donut Hole. The trio had been surprised to see the Donut Hole open, but when they trudged through the deep snow in route to the Ballentines', they noticed a few haggard souls huddled at the counter inside. The shop's owner had asked the nightshift to work through the snowstorm, rather than closing up and going home. The weary crew was bone tired and had stayed awake only because of sugar and caffeine they'd consumed throughout the night.

Father Byrne counseled Joe and Mary, sharing his experience that missing adolescents typically return safely to their homes; however, he admitted every situation was unique, and it was not in anyone's interest to count on favorable probabilities. Discouraging Mary and Joe from following through on their plan to go out in search of their son, he said, "The conditions are far too dangerous for anyone to be outside for more than fifteen minutes or so. Besides, you need to be right here in case someone calls with important information."

Reluctantly, Mary and Joe agreed to stay home and give the media and police a chance to find their son. After twenty minutes or so of consolation, Father went to work placing calls to prod the media into action. Because the priest was only intermittently placing calls, he took all incoming from family friends and parishioners following up on the phone tree calls of last evening.

Because the church enjoyed far more influence in this Irish, Polish, and Italian Catholic community than did the two worried parents, the media had responded more positively to this missing person report than they otherwise might have. With Father Byrne's connections, the missing Immaculate Conception student had now become a touching human-interest story picked up by local radio and television stations. Breaking news about the missing eighth grader complemented each station's hyped report on the early winter snowstorms. Both news media had created broadcast teasers using the missing student's name to their advantage. Hollidaysburg's sole FM radio station, WHOL, asked the community to "Help put Chris back in Christmas," and Channel 6, the Johnstown television station covering Hollidaysburg and the region, was similarly ingenious, teasing viewers by saying, "Stay tuned for an important Chris Missing story."

After Sister Bernadette heard Mary describe Officer Bartkowski's insensitivity the previous night, she excused herself from the living room. From the kitchen phone Sister called the young rookie at his home. When Mrs. Bartkowski answered, Sister Bernadette asked his recent bride to put her husband on the phone. Father Byrne picked up the cordless telephone in the living room to place another call just as the sleepy off duty police officer answered. After the man mumbled a barely audible "Hello," the priest heard Sister say, "Jimmy, this is Sister Bernadette. I'm calling to tell you hell has frozen over and I'm not at all happy about it!" Thinking it best not to listen in on the rest of the conversation, Father turned off the phone and sipped at his coffee a few puzzled minutes before placing his next call.

Newly minted police officer James Bartkowski replied, "Um, Sister? Sister Bernadette?"

"I told Father I thought hell would freeze over before Chief Jamison would hire you as his new patrolman. Damned if he didn't do it! Well, I put up with your bad attitude and indifference when you were in eighth grade, and I can see you haven't changed your ways one bit in the seven years since. Well, mister, I've had enough of your nonsense. Get your lazy bottom out of that warm bed you're snuggled in and get over to the Ballentines' house to help us locate this missing young man. Do you hear me?"

"Yes, Sister, I hear you. I'll get dressed and come over right after breakfast."

"I mean now, son! No one in this house has had much of an appetite this morning. You could afford to pass up a meal or two, you good for nothing lard butt! I want you at the Ballentines' house within fifteen minutes or my next phone call will be to the mayor."

The young cop stammered, "Y-yes, Sister," and then he heard the call terminated at the other end.

Mrs. Bartkowski watched as her husband stared at the handset, ran his hands over his sleepy face, and then gently placed the phone in its cradle. "What was that about, sweetie? Is everything okay?"

The flustered cop lied as he crawled out from beneath the warm and inviting bed covers. "Uh, Sister Bernadette at Immaculate Conception had asked for my assistance in a missing person case and I promised to help her this morning. I just overslept a little. She called to remind me. I gotta get going, hon."

The man's thoughtful new wife asked, "Can I make you a toasted ham and egg sandwich and pour some coffee in a traveling mug for you?"

"Um, naw, but thanks anyway. I'd better get going. They'll have some coffee and donuts, I'm sure."

Mrs. Bartkowski lifted her chin for a kiss from her brave husband and said, "I'm so very proud of you!"

The police officer doubted his wife would be very proud if she knew the truth. He also doubted he'd get anything to eat once he left the house but deferred to Sister Bernadette and her unveiled threats. He would rather leave the house with his stomach growling than arrive at the Ballentines' house with Sister growling.

The pudgy officer dressed without showering or shaving his peach fuzz and strode out the door, forcing his handgun into its stiff new holster. Without activating the siren, he flipped on the police vehicle's lights and drove faster than was prudent, given the inclement weather and hazardous road conditions. With his All-Weather tires spinning through slick intersections, he zigzagged across the small town in the direction of the Ballentines' home. As it turned out, neither the emergency lights nor the siren was necessary. There were no pedestrians on the streets this cold, blustery morning, and his was one of the few vehicles that was not snowbound along the quiet village streets.

After hanging up at the conclusion of her call to the young cop, Sister Bernadette reverently rejoined Mr. and Mrs. Ballentine in the living room, where, under the scrutiny of Father Byrne, she picked up a framed photograph of Chris from the mantel above the fireplace. "Mary, may I borrow this picture? Officer Bartkowski has offered to help locate Chris this morning and said he would be stopping by as soon as he could get here to pick up a picture of Chris to copy and distribute."

When Bartkowski arrived at the Ballentines' house, he left his winter coat in the midnight-blue Chevy Suburban and marched past the sole television reporter and cameraman huddled together on the Ballentines' un-shoveled driveway. He gave an imperious "no comment" to the reporter's questions about the missing teen and tramped forward, with his head held high, to the concrete and fieldstone porch outside the Ballentines' home. He rang the doorbell, and as he stood shivering on the snow-covered porch, he studied the replica Colonial Williamsburg wreath on the Ballentines' maroon front door, wondering whether the apples, oranges, and miniature pineapples were real. They sure looked edible. He was about to dig his fingernail into the skin of one of the yellow delicious apples to test its authenticity when Sister Bernadette opened the door and stepped out onto the porch, her habit rustling in the gusts.

The startled patrolman wondered why Sister had come outside to talk when he thought his services would be needed inside. Before

the officer could ask about her intentions, the shorter Sister Bernadette reached up and twisted his nearly frozen left ear with the
stealth of a ninja. She pulled his head downward to her face, looked
into the young man's watering eyes, and said between tightly
drawn lips, "Now, listen up, mister. You put on your best humble
pie face and get into that house and apologize to those good people
of your parish for how you talked to them last night. I want you to
promise you will not quit searching for their son until he is found.
Here is a photograph of the boy. When they've finished with you, I
want you to get your tail to the Copy Cat and make a couple hundred copies of that picture and post them everywhere possible between here and Altoona. And don't even think about stopping by
the Donut Hole. Lord knows, you'd never leave that warm little
slice of heaven if you ever got your chubby cheeks inside!"

The police officer snatched the photo from Sister and considered the curly-haired young man's face smiling back. The way Sister had talked down to him as though he were a grade-school
student left him feeling no older than the missing youngster. As the
officer stomped the snow off his shoes and stepped forward to enter the house ahead of her, he queried, "And who's going to pay for
all the copies, Sister?"

Sister, mouth agape, was nudged aside by the police officer as
he stepped over the doorway threshold. At about one-half his
height but three-fourths his weight, Sister grabbed hold of the sassy
cop's web belt and jerked backward with enough force to stop the
lawman dead in his tracks. Before he could respond, she reached
her hand into his back pants pocket, pulled out the man's wallet,
and withdrew two twenty-dollar bills. As he turned back toward
her, Sister handed the cash and wallet back to him and said, with-
holding none of her wrath, "This ought to cover it, don't you think?
Thank you for your contribution to the church and your service to
the community, Officer Bartkowski!" With that, Sister pushed the
man nearly off the porch and entered the house, leaving him stam-
mering on the porch stoop.

A humiliated Patrolman Bartkowski fumbled his wallet back

into his pants and, after several failed attempts with stiff, cold-clumsy hands, unbuttoned the pocket of his tailored uniform shirt and shoved the two crumpled bills inside. The police officer dropped all pretense of self-importance and approached the Ballentines with his hat in his hands and head hung in shame. He made a whispered confession of his failings to Mary and Joe. The rookie's voice cracked as he looked first at Mary and then Joe and said, "Mister and Missus Ballentine, I am so sorry to have added to your grief and worry over your son. I should have come over last night to pick up this picture and to get enough information to involve the media. I promise I will do everything I can to make up lost time. I also pray you will forgive me."

Mary hugged the humbled man and thanked him for his promise of help. Father looked upon the poor soul with compassion, envious of the power of conversion the Sisters could bring about. When the opportunity for salvation presented itself, the Sisters were always quick to seize it. As an offer of friendship and respect for the young officer's contrition, Joe asked, "Jim, can I get you a cup of coffee? It's mighty cold out there."

Officer Bartkowski shook his head, "Thank you, sir, but I better get going."

The patrolman hoped to leave the Ballentines as soon as he could get out the door to avoid Sister Bernadette grabbing his other ear as a passing final admonition. He put his hat on and trod to the front door with purpose in his step, glancing over his shoulder to see whether Sister followed. Outside and on his way to the SUV, the officer stopped to talk with the reporter and cameraman, telling them there was nothing new to report to the media. He thanked them for their interest in the Ballentines and asked for their assistance in making Chris's disappearance known.

With the Ballentines' forgiveness and blessings, and Joe's staple gun and staples, Officer Bartkowski planned to go to the Copy Cat. If the Copy Cat wasn't open, he would return to the Police Department and use the department copy machine to duplicate Chris's photograph. It was against regulations to do so, but the Chief was out of the office, coordinating emergency services today and he'd be none the wiser.

Bartkowski turned the engine over in the high-horsepower police vehicle and began backing out of the driveway. He thought he now understood why sometimes he slept fitfully. For years, he had a recurring dream in which he was summoned to the school office, where a taller Sister Bernadette towered over him. In his dream, Sister was two-faced. One face was a specter threatening to haunt him the rest of his life, admonishing him for his shortcomings. The other face was that of an angelic soul radiating love and encouragement. It was an unsettling dream that had caused Jimmy Bartkowski many sleepless nights and incredible anxiety since middle school. That deep-seated angst caused the inexperienced officer to accelerate too quickly and fishtail the SUV several times, before gaining control and steadying the vehicle. It would take the remainder of the day for him to steady his nerves similarly.

By late afternoon, Father and the two nuns had done as much as they could for the Ballentines. An aggressive community search was in motion, the media were onboard and participating, the Police Department was involved and distributing fliers with Chris's picture and contact information, and neighbors had delivered more foodstuffs than the family could consume in a week. Their house was orderly, thanks to the Sisters' efforts, and nothing required anyone's immediate attention, at least until Grace needed to be fed again or let outside.

Maggie, Joe, and Mary showed Father and the Sisters to the door, thanking them profusely for their support. Before leaving, Father knelt and hugged Maggie, saying, "I know you are worried about your brother. We will do everything we can to find Chris and bring him home. In the meantime, I hope you and your mother and father will celebrate Christmas Eve Mass with us."

Joe, standing behind Maggie with his hands on her shoulders, said, "I don't know, Father. I doubt we'll be up to getting out this Christmas Eve without Chris at home."

Father nodded but added, "I plan to ask the congregation for its help in locating Chris, and it would be good if at least one of you could answer questions."

Joe patted father's shoulder and conceded, "Don't worry, Father, we'll be there. We appreciate all you're doing for us, and we know Chris needs our prayers and the prayers of everyone at Mass. We also need the comfort and support of our friends who'll be there. No matter what happens, some or all of us will celebrate Mass tomorrow night with you. If Chris comes home, we'll all attend Mass together!"

The Ballentines saw Father Byrne and the Sisters out the door and watched them hike in the direction of the church. Father had promised Joe, as soon as they returned to the rectory, they'd employ the phone tree once more to reiterate Chris's absence and to cancel tonight's pageant in deference to the impending snowstorm. As the front door closed, the house drew quiet. Mary, Joe, and Maggie wandered in separate directions to deal with their grief as best they could. For now, there was nothing more they could do to bring Chris home.

CHAPTER 8

The first and last sound uttered by the mysterious youth was a barely audible "Abba." Then he stopped breathing. The young man had been lying comatose for a day and a half, and now, after undergoing a massive convulsive seizure, he lay tranquil, blue from oxygen deprivation. In his last frantic moments of activity, the young man's thrashing arms and legs had kicked off the plastic sheet covering him, and the blankets the men had wrapped him in lay loose and out of kilter across his body. The boy's transformation from slumber to seizure had been so sudden his caregivers had sprung away from him as though he meant to attack them, but as he regained absolute stillness in apparent death, they overcame their initial surprise and approached the lifeless body once more.

Leo was the first of the three to stand at the boy's side, preparing to revive the young man if he could. Hank and Rex stood behind and on either side of the ex-corpsman, like attendants assisting a doctor during hospital rounds. Leo reached for the boy's neck seeking a pulse from the carotid artery. Before he touched the boy's neck, the young man's body arced once more off the tabletop. He gasped first a long, desperate breath, and then he struggled for repeated breaths, until his color changed from ashen blue-gray to rosy-red. His bloodshot eyes blinked open and closed several times, then relaxed into a questioning, uncertain gaze. He was alive after all, and semiconscious.

While the men looked on, the boy's breathing settled into a regular, steady rhythm. Leo took the young man's pulse; his racing heart had slowed to a more normal pace of about sixty-eight beats per minute. Leo whispered calm assurances to the boy, whose eyes strained to focus on the man's face, but Leo got no immediate response. He feared significant brain damage, but hoped the young man was just groggy from his concussive injuries. Within a few minutes, the boy seemed conscious enough for Leo to pose routine mental status questions. He was anxious to assess the boy's alertness and clarity, hoping to rule out serious brain injury.

Chris stared at the smiling black face hovering over him like an eclipsed full moon. *Is that smile friendly or mean?* Before he could figure out the man's demeanor, the Black man spoke in a melodious tone.

"Hey there, young man. We were beginnin' to wonder whether you were gonna sleep straight through the New Year. How you feelin'?"

After a considerable pause, Chris replied, "Awful."

"I'm not surprised. Where do you hurt the most?"

Again, a significant delay in his response, and then, "Everywhere. I hurt all over. My head hurts the most . . . umm, yeah, my head is pounding."

Leo smiled and with empathy said, "You took quite a beatin'. I'm sure you're hurtin' bad."

Though he wanted to sit up, Chris wasn't sure he could lift his head if he tried. Instead, he lay as still as possible to avoid the pain that accompanied every heartbeat, every quiver of even the smallest of muscles. He shifted his head to the left, then to the right, trying to avoid abrupt movements that sent pain hammering through his brain. When he shifted his gaze right he startled at seeing two rough-looking men staring at him. He looked beyond the men and saw pine branches decorated with a weird collection of fruit, pictures, canned goods, and an odd assortment of junk. Everything was surreal.

Chris had a tough time distinguishing between memories of recent events and false memories brought on by injuries or medications. He figured for the time being he must be careful and not reveal too much information about himself to these men. He didn't know what their intent toward him was.

Cautiously, Chris lifted his hand and touched his mouth. After detecting stitches inside his lip with his tongue, he felt his swollen lip with his fingertips to assess the extent and nature of his injury. He swept his hand over his face, flinching as his fingers brushed his broken nose and then grimacing when he scraped the row of stitches over his right eye.

Leo probed, "What month is this?"

"Ah . . . December . . . I think. Depends on how long I've been out."

Leo nodded, "Yes, it's December. Okay, can you count backwards from a hundred by seven?"

Chris looked at Leo with alarm. "What? Who are you? What happened to me?"

Rex stepped forward. "You were up on the train trestle yesterday when a locomotive was a-comin'. You couldn't get out of its way, so's you bound off that bridge like a skittish jackrabbit. You was darn lucky to survive. You missed the rocks down below by just the fuzz on your cottontail before you splashed into the pond. Son, I gotta ask...what was you doin' up there on the bridge sittin' in the dark, anyway?"

Chris wrinkled his nose a bit, thinking of Rex's jackrabbit comparison, blinked his eyes, and answered honestly, "I don't know. I don't remember much about yesterday."

"Do you remember your name?" asked Leo.

This time Chris lied. "No. I don't know who I am. I hoped you could tell me. What am I doing in the woods? Where are my clothes?" Chris feared his "hosts" had taken his school uniform to keep him from running away. After all, he seemed to recall hearing them talking about ransom and what might befall them if he died.

Hank spoke up, "You are in our camp near the Cresson Trestle. When you leapt from the bridge yesterday, Rex there almost broke his neck running down the ravine to find you. Leo here risked his life to pull you out of the water. The two of them carried you up the ravine to our camp. We took off your wet clothes to dry them and so Leo could check you over for injuries. He's given you all the medical care you've needed so far. I washed out your clothes and hung them out to dry." Hank pointed to the clothes, now hanging stiff and dry on the clothesline.

Chris pressed, "Can I have them back?"

"Of course you can. They wouldn't fit any of us!" Leo chuckled, thumping his chest to emphasize his beefy size.

"Now?" Chris asked in a serious tone.

Hank observed the boy's trepidation and said, "You can have your clothes as soon as you're fit to dress. Right now, you're in no shape to struggle into them."

Hank paused a bit and then asked, "By the way, do you go to a Catholic school?"

"Why would you ask that?" Chris asked, somewhat alarmed.

The three glanced at each other imperceptibly. Hank responded, "Well, it looked like you were wearing some kind of school uniform—blue cords and a white dress shirt."

"We figured you went to a Catholic school," Rex followed up.

The teen stammered a bit, feeling trapped and uncertain about how to talk himself free. These vagrants were keeping his clothes from him and pressing him with nosey questions. Hadn't he heard them say something about being charged with murder? He was certain they'd keep after him until they got the information they wanted. He'd have to lie about who he was, at least until he knew what they were up to.

"That's right! I remember now. I was visiting my grandparents in Hollidaysburg after school on Friday. I decided to walk the tracks up to the trestle. My parents thought I had gone to a movie. And, yes, I do go to a parochial school, Bishop Guilfoyle, in

Altoona."

"Hmm, so what's your name? Do you remember now?" Hank asked, trying to conceal his skepticism.

"Yes, my name is . . . uh, Bill Johnston."

"Well, Bill, I am Hank Canaday, and these two fellas are Leo Regis and Rex Sawyer."

CHAPTER 9

Down the snow-covered railroad tracks leading to the festively decorated town of Hollidaysburg, the Christmas holiday was off to a slow, and possibly terminal, start. By midday Saturday, shop-owners lamented significant lost sales. They had figured that frantic, last-minute Christmas shoppers, including the harried husbands who had not yet bought gifts for their wives, would boost the bottom line of their year-end balance sheets. This year, however, holiday sales would be curtailed due to the triple-whammy snowstorms: the first storm that hit Friday, December 21, followed by the substantial snow that would fall Saturday night, and the even bigger storm with gale-force winds that was expected to barrel through during the early morning hours on Christmas Eve. The retail season appeared to be all but over.

Officer Bartkowski had posted pictures of Chris in the few shops and stores open for business throughout the late morning of December 22, but there were no helpful leads as of yet on Chris's whereabouts. The local television station, now determined to do its part in the rescue effort, made Chris an instant holiday celebrity as its announcers alternately interrupted regular broadcasting to mention his name and desperate situation and decry the lost revenue for local retailers. It was the same every Christmas, the human-interest and spiritually rejuvenating story of the birth of a special child contrasted with the chronicle of retail sales. This year the story had an added human twist.

In contrast to the glacial pace in town, up the mountain, across Cresson Trestle, the three rail-riders were in a frenzy readying their encampment for the imminent storm, which they could see gathering in the south like an invading horde before battle. Throughout Saturday, the caregivers tended the young man who sporadically dozed on their tabletop and withheld information from them while awake.

Chris slept little. His body, wracked with pain, throbbed from his bruised and battered head to his scraped right foot. Leo still did not know what internal injuries the boy might have sustained during his near-fatal fall or, more precisely, from the sudden impact bringing his fall from the trestle to an abrupt conclusion. Although Chris did not feel lucky, Rex assured him only a miracle would allow the boy to survive a fall of five stories, while avoiding the boulders surrounding the pond.

During his brief moments of wakefulness, Chris remained in a dreamlike haze, feeling as though he were in the center of a Christmas snow globe with scattered flakes of confusion swirling about him. He struggled without success to keep his thoughts focused for more than a few minutes at a time—he wanted someone to stop shaking his world so everything would settle down and lie still. He worried he'd live the rest of his life in this swirling snow globe. Leo explained that he experienced symptoms of Traumatic Brain Injury and, hopefully, the condition was mild, and his headache, confusion, and related cognitive symptoms would clear after a few days, or within a few weeks. "You got your bell rung hard, boy. Give it a little time," Leo explained in his best nonmedical language.

After sleeping a few hours, Chris awoke late Saturday afternoon to the smell of chicken broth warmed over a wood fire. He lifted himself onto an elbow, but he lay back down when his head began pounding to the beat of an overly enthusiastic marching band. He closed his eyes as his vision blurred, and his stomach somersaulted.

Chris knew he couldn't escape this secluded camp on his own, at least not right away. He was too weak and too nauseated to stand, let alone dress, and hiking down the mountain was out of the question. He also realized he was dependent on his captors to care for him, at least for now. He would cooperate with them until he was mentally capable of developing an escape plan and physically able to implement it. Maybe early the next morning he'd feel better and make his break while the hobos slept.

Leo was the first to notice that the boy had woken up. He shambled to Chris's side and asked, "Do you feel like you could eat some chicken soup, Bill?"

Chris stared back at the smiling face with confusion, "What?" Then he recalled the fake name he had given the bums. "Um, uh, yeah. I'd like that, but I'm not sure I can sit without throwing up. My head feels horrible and I'm real dizzy. In fact, I think I'm gonna be sick right now."

From his sleeping compartment, Leo retrieved a plastic grocery bag, which he laid next to the teen. "Okay, don't worry about gettin' sick." He also brought out a heavy wool sweater, which he rolled into a pillow. Leo lifted the boy and placed the sweater beneath his head and neck. "Here, try this. Let's see if we can't get you up a lil' bit at a time."

While Leo helped situate Chris, Rex filled a green bowl with thick chicken broth and hearty noodles. With the hand of his good arm, Rex cut the noodles and chicken into bite-sized pieces, removing bones as he discovered them. Taking the soup, Leo blew on a spoonful and put it to Chris's lips. Little by little, Chris ate. With each bite, he grew hungrier and felt better.

When Chris finished eating, Hank offered him coffee, to which Chris replied, "I don't drink coffee at home, but I smelled it when I was sleeping, and it smelled really good. I'd like to try a cup. Do you have sugar and cream?"

Hank laughed, "No, son. We don't stock a full refrigerator or pantry up here. I'm afraid you'll have to drink it black if you want some."

Rex rejoined the group with coffee pot in hand and poured a round for everyone. Despite their genuine care, the boy was wary, and his eyes darted about the camp, exploring its structure, contents, and possible escape routes. Hank suggested that the men not press the boy for information, wanting to first develop a sense of trust with him. Leo understood the need for trust, but he was even more concerned about getting the boy to the small Hollidaysburg Regional Hospital.

In an effort to gain the kid's confidence, Hank said, "Well, Mister Bill, after you've finished eating, how about we get you back into your britches if you feel up to it? You must be chilly lying there as bare as Leo's scalp! How about it?"

Hank's suggestion had some of the effect he'd hoped. Chris reasoned that, although he was a prisoner of weather and impaired health, he might not be a captive of these men after all; however, he still wasn't certain and thought he'd risk addressing the issue directly.

"I'd like that. I think I could get dressed, with some help. That would make me feel a lot better. But there's a question I have to ask."

"Shoot," said Hank.

Chris hesitated and then spit it out, "When I was asleep, I heard you guys talking about ransom. Are you gonna try to get a ransom from my parents? Because my mom and dad aren't wealthy at all . . . they sometimes have difficulty paying all their bills. They won't have any money to pay a ransom for me." Chris turned his head a bit and then admitted to the men as well as to himself, "And my dad would probably pay you to keep me anyway."

The three adults looked at each other incredulously, trying to understand why the young man thought he heard them talking about a ransom. Then in a rare moment of enlightenment, Rex bellowed a knowing hoot. When his laugh wound down to just a coyote-eating-chicken smile, he said, "Y'all, I think Bill heard us talkin' 'bout our travels, and he might'a overheard me tellin' you 'bout my stay-over in Branson. That would be Branson, Missouri, young man."

Hank added, "Son, we aren't interested in ransom. You don't have any reason to fear us. All we want is to get you to the hospital as soon as it's safe."

Although he was relieved to hear what sounded like a sincere and believable response, Chris retorted, "But I heard you talking about what would happen to you if I died. You were afraid you'd get arrested for murder. It doesn't make any sense."

Hank reasoned, "Well, Bill, we aren't known in these parts, and we're concerned someone would think we hurt you or we didn't do our best to save your life. We have done everything we could for you, but we might not be believed."

"I can see that. You're just three bums living way out here in the woods. I probably wouldn't believe you either. Who are you hiding from, anyway? And why wouldn't you be interested in collecting a ransom or at least a reward for saving me?"

Rex hooted again at Chris's suspicious questions, "Young man, we ain't bums and we ain't hidin' from nobody—not even ex-wives! You've been listenin' to too much country music."

"I don't get it." Chris replied.

"You know, 'All my ex's live in Texas. That's why I hang my hat in Tennessee'. We didn't run off to Pennsylvania to hang our hats so ex-wives couldn't find us."

Chris crinkled his face in response to Rex's explanation.

"Never mind." He threw his head back with the cocky superiority of a barnyard king rooster, "We're kings, young man. Kings of the road. You know, like that ole Roger Miller song?"

It was obvious Chris had never heard of Roger Miller or of his song about kings of the road. Almost in unison, Rex and Leo broke into song, "Trailer for sale or rent, rooms to let fifty cents . . ." Hank was familiar with the tune but hadn't learned the words. "King of the Road" wasn't a huge hit among the surfers, fishermen, beach crowd, or wine vintners in Monterey, or among the urban folk from Los Angeles for that matter.

Chris's face continued to show confusion.

Rex pointed at the boy, "Son, I was wrong. You gotta *start* listenin' to some good ole country tunes. It's obvious you ain't been very far out'a Pleasant Valley!"

These self-proclaimed kings were doing their god-awful best to entertain Chris and help him relax a bit, and despite Rex's woeful singing the boy worried about having accused them of being bums. He tried to deflect the accusation, "If you three are kings, why aren't you home in your kingdoms or castles? Why are you living out here in these woods?"

"Cain't beat the rent!" Rex chortled and slapped Hank on the back and then mouthed a piece of pine straw.

Hank scratched his bare cheek, "We don't really know why we're up here living in the woods. It's just kind of where we ended up. We've talked about it a lot over the past few months, and we still don't have a clue. But we're happy we were here to help you out, anyway."

"Yep," Rex chimed in, "Bill, my man, you've given us a little extra reason for the season while we try to figure out why we came here."

Chris looked quizzical. He liked Rex, but he didn't understand his humor. He seemed goofy, in a kindhearted way.

Chris didn't understand what Hank and Rex were talking about and was about to follow up with additional questions, but Leo held his hand up and said, "We gonna have plenty of time to be talkin' this evening while we ride out a doozie of a storm that's a-blowin' an' a-comin'. Now, let's get you dressed so you can sit in a chair for a while an' maybe get some more grub in ya. If the weather gets bad tonight, you might be needin' to bunk in one'a them refrigerator boxes. If ya do, you gonna wanna be dressed warm an' have a full belly to get ya through the night."

Hank and Leo raised the teen to a sitting position on the tabletop with his legs dangling over the edge. "Damn it, Rex. Look here! Mouse droppings on the table, right next to where the boy's been lying." Like muttered thunder, he added, "I told you those mice were nasty! We have to get rid of them and you've got to stop feeding the little buggers. You hear me?"

Rex stopped sucking on the pine straw and studied the tabletop, "Aw'right, aw'right. You're right, L.A. I'll stop feeding my cute lil' friends, but I ain't seen as many lately anyway. Maybe they're leavin' on their own accord. I think they might be scared a somethin'. I found the entrails from one yesterday and thought you musta stomped it. I didn't say nothing, knowin' how you feel about 'em."

"I don't like them a bit—they give me the willies—but I wouldn't hurt any of them. I just think it would be best if they lived somewhere else."

"Aw'right. Agreed. Let's get the kid dressed, and I'll clean up them mouse turds."

Shaking his head in disgust, Hank began to dress the young man, who flinched and groaned in response to every part of his body being touched or moved. With the boy half-dressed, Leo suggested taking a break. Chris's breathing was quick and labored, which Leo noted as he took his pulse. "'Bout what I expected, considerin' the beatin' you took. Y'all, we gotta slow down a bit gettin' this boy up and about. He ain't quite up to it."

Anxious to get his clothes back on, Chris assured them, "I'm okay. I'll let you know if it's too much. I really want to get dressed."

"Aw'right, then," Rex consented, "but let's be gentle with the boy. No sense in losin' ground with his recovery."

After a brief respite, Hank and Leo helped Chris with his shirt. Requiring more concentration than usual, Chris zipped and snapped his pants and buckled his belt. Kneeling, Leo and Hank put a sock on each of the boy's feet, while Rex adorned his head with a stocking cap that sat on his pate like a crown. They slid his arms into his jacket sleeves, and Leo helped him stand on shaky legs. Chris was weak, hurting all over, and unable to stand alone, but he felt better now, dressed, sitting up, and off the hard door.

As Chris stood before the tabletop, hunched forward like an old man, an intense pang of panic jolted him upright. He realized the men had not given him his shoes. He could not escape through deep snow without shoes, and they knew it. Trying not to show his alarm, Chris wiped perspiration from his upper lip and whispered, "Umm, the pine needles are sticking to my socks. Can I have my shoes?"

The smiling Black man reached down near one of the 55-gallon drums and hoisted one sodden, black shoe and frowned, "This is all you got left, son. You either hiked up that mountain with one shoe on and one shoe off, or you lost a shoe when you scooted off that bridge." He added with a genial smile, "I suspect the latter bein' you seem bright enough to put both shoes on in the mornin'."

Chris recalled his legs dangling between crossbeams on the bridge and then standing, feeling the rough railroad tie through the sock on his right foot. He knew Leo had told him the truth about his shoes, but, even more assuring, Rex held high a pair of what looked to be rattlesnake-skin cowboy boots, and said, "These are gonna be a bit big for ya, *amigo*, but they'll keep your feet warm an' dry, an' class up your school uniform some. If'n you'd go to school wearin' jazzy boots like these after the holidays, you'd be the envy of all your classmates, for sure!"

Again, Hank and Leo shook their heads as they knelt before Chris and pulled the incongruous boots onto the boy's feet. Rex draped a sleeping bag around Chris's shoulders like a cape. With considerable but manageable discomfort, Chris sat in one of the aluminum chairs hugging the crackling fire, his mind still swimming, but otherwise warm and sated from the meal he had eaten. The three kings went about their normal non-majestic evening routine of preparing dinner, brewing the final remains of their coffee grounds, stowing tools, fastening the tarps securely, and doing what they could to batten down the camp before the arrival of the impending storm.

Rex cleaned up the mouse droppings and poked around through the pine straw looking for signs of the mice. "Y'all, somethin's been diggin' around here. I'm a-thinkin' somethin's been a-thinnin' mah herd, right here in front of us. Have either a'you seen anythin' around camp rustlin' strays?" Neither man had seen anything unusual and said so; both were relieved the mouse "herd" was getting smaller, no matter who or what was responsible.

As Chris considered his situation and these men who appeared dedicated to his well-being, he recalled feeling horrible about his family as he flung himself off the trestle, and his stomach turned at the thought of what his parents and Maggie must be going through, worrying about him. He missed his family, who he knew cared about him no matter how strained his relationship with his father had been, and he wanted to get home and make up for the pain he had caused them. "What's today's date?" Chris asked with another round of panic.

"It's Saturday, December 22nd. Just a couple of days before Christmas." Discerning the reason for the boy's unspoken concern, Hank added, "If things aren't too bad after this next batch of snow arrives, we hope to get you to the hospital or home to your family, possibly as soon as tomorrow. But don't get your hopes too high, I suspect we're going to be snowed in for a couple of more days. And we can't transport you until Leo says you can be moved, and we still need to figure out how best to do that. I want to be honest with you, Bill. You need to be prepared to stay up here a couple more days. I just don't think you're going to get home until after Christmas."

CHAPTER 10

Mary looked out the window at the forlorn, undecorated tree on the patio, but she couldn't bring herself to think about decorating it. But then, her thoughts turned to Maggie, and with a nagging sense of responsibility to her daughter, she retrieved the tattered boxes of ornaments.

"Why don't we set up the video recorder and tape the tree decorating. That way, we can tell Chris how much we miss him," Mary suggested.

"That's a great idea," Joe said with feigned enthusiasm. He wandered away to rummage through the storage closet under the first-floor stairway to locate the recorder, tripod, and necessary power cords. He returned to the family room with an armful of equipment and a tangle of wires and cables dragging behind him. He began assembling the video camera, cattie-corner from where the tree stood, at an angle where the event could best be viewed and taped.

As tradition would dictate, Mary blended instant chocolate powder with hot milk in the saucepan on the stove and poured four mugs of hot chocolate, one for each of them, including Chris. After dropping a couple of marshmallows into each mug, she carried the hot drinks into the family room on a tray, along with red and green

Christmas napkins.

Joe hauled a small bundle of logs into the room from the rack on the back patio, and with ample kindling and outdated newspapers, he opened the flue and held a flaming match to the newspaper crumpled beneath the kindling. After the initial smoky fire began to take hold and he'd added additional kindling, Joe hung Maggie and Chris's stockings on opposite ends of the mantel away from the growing heat. Grace found a spot to lie opposite the video recorder, close to the hearth. She basked in the growing warmth of the fire and soon fell into a deep slumber.

After chipping the bucket-shaped ice block off the white pine's trunk, Joe placed the tree in his father-in-law's green tree stand in front of the double door leading to the patio. Joe adjusted the tree, so it stood as straight as a Nutcracker Soldier and clipped off a few wayward branches. After putting the brush saw and clippers away in the garage, he re-entered the house with an eight-foot stepladder over his shoulder and proceeded with flair to wind one string of lights after another around the tree. He planned to double the number of lights on the tree this year, wanting it to be brighter and more colorful than ever before. Mary began unpacking boxes of ornaments, ensuring each decoration had a hook attached.

With Christmas tunes like *Up on the Rooftop* and *Frosty the Snowman* playing in the background and the tree sitting firmly in its stand, the setting was as cheerful as it had been any previous year, even if the participants weren't. Each of the Ballentines had successfully faked appearing upbeat and optimistic to each other, while feeling empty inside. Unable to maintain her façade any longer, Mary collapsed on the floor crying. Joe knelt beside her. She held a frayed yarn ornament Chris had made in the third grade. Joe wiped tears from Mary's eyes and hugged her against his chest. Together they hung Chris's childhood masterpiece in the center of the tree, without Maggie noticing their memorial gesture or her mother's brief cry.

As a family, they talked about Chris, summer vacations, family outings, and all sorts of other fond memories. They sang along with the music playing in the background, and they did all of this with considerable enthusiasm, trying very hard to keep the evening merry. After all, Joe thought, Christmas is the season of hope, is it not?

Grace jerked her chin off the floor and scrambled to her feet. She dashed about the family room, searching for something, anything, to pick up as a gift for whomever she alone heard approaching the front door. She found and mouthed a stuffed cloth Santa Claus, which muffled her flurry of happy woofs and growls. Within these few seconds Joe, Mary, and Maggie each paused and held their collective breath, recognizing Grace had heard someone on the front porch.

A moment later, the doorbell chimed its Westminster Abbey tones, and all four Ballentines raced to the foyer, with Grace beating the other three by far more than a wet nose. Her tail wagged wildly and she growled a long deep-throated welcome to whoever stood outside. Joe held his breath and then jerked open the inner door. Although he maintained a welcoming smile, his heart sank as he discerned the police uniform through the frosted glass. Unable to make out the patrolman's facial expression, Joe's insides wrenched at the sight of the police officer. He stood momentarily massaging his shoulder and then opened the storm door. Officer Bartkowski stepped forward carrying a large, heavy cardboard box, and entered the house like an old friend.

Jim set the container beside the coffee table in the middle of the Ballentines' living room floor. "It seems everywhere I went today hanging pictures of Chris, someone had something they wanted to share with you. Everyone in Hollidaysburg seems to have the Christmas spirit, and they all want you to know they are thinking about you and Chris."

Joe closed the door behind the patrolman, and the three Ballentines regrouped physically and emotionally in the living room with Jim Bartkowski. Maggie popped the lid off the box and peeked inside, eyeing a cornucopia of candies, fruit, canned meat, sardines, crackers, smoked salmon, green and black olives, anchovies, tea, a

109

bottle of cabernet sauvignon, bread sticks, apple cider, and many other delights hidden beneath the visible top layer. Grace abandoned her slobbery cloth Santa to join Maggie in the more exciting activity of digging through the box of treats.

Officer Bartkowski continued, "Everyone I talked with today wished you a Merry Christmas, and they want you to know Chris is in their prayers. It seems no one in Hollidaysburg is prepared to have Christmas without Chris. They also told me they will not rest until we have found your son and brought him home."

Within a few minutes of thanking Jimmy for his message of hope and for the box of treats, and after seeing him out the door, they heard the doorbell chime once more. Again, the hopeful Ballentines, including Grace, this time tenderly mouthing a tangerine from the box of offerings, raced to the door. Roberta and her parents had stopped to express their concerns and offer their sympathies. The family stayed only a short while and had no sooner left when the doorbell rang again, as it did all evening.

After the rush of visitors from the neighborhood had long departed, another neighbor and member of Catholic Mothers, Janie Schultz, and her three-year-old son came to the door. Janie's son, Andy, fell to playing on the floor with a small red pickup truck he received in the wood-framed Advent calendar his grandfather had built. After listening awhile to the adults' conversation, Andy said to his mother, "Mary Chris Miss."

Janie muttered, "Yes, honey, Merry Christmas."

"No," Andy retorted, "Mary Chris Miss."

"Uh-huh," Janie muttered as she followed Mary's gloomy gaze out the bay window toward the dark street.

"Momma! Mary Chris Miss!" Andy said with hands on his hips.

Before Janie could respond, Mary turned toward Andy, reached down and ran her fingers through his brown, satiny tufts, and said, with moist eyes, "Yes, Andy. Mary misses Chris, very much."

She smiled misty-eyed, met Janie's eyes, and shook her head, "From the mouths of babes…"

"I thought…" Janie stammered in disbelief.

110

"He's such a dear…no, Andy, not a reindeer…you're a sweetheart."

Finally understood and with his truck in hand, Andy crawled toward Grace, who slept beside Mary's chair, and drove his red pickup over her mountainous blonde belly. Grace, comfortably serving as a playground for Andy, didn't open an eye.

After Andy and Janie left for home, two more couples stopped by the Ballentines' house, offering support. It was just before Saturday night turned to Sunday morning when Joe and Mary shepherded the last well-wishers out the door, having shared all the goodies Officer Bartkowski had brought earlier in the evening. The Ballentines were grateful for their many spontaneous guests and the thoughtfulness of their friends, neighbors, fellow parishioners, and even strangers who'd walked through the worst of the weather to offer help and encouragement. They were worn from the continual adrenalin rush as the doorbell rang and the disappointing realization each time that Chris was not the one outside.

After closing the door for the last time, Maggie joined Grace in the family room where they both fell asleep on the carpeted floor before the fireplace. Joe picked up his sleeping daughter and carried her to bed, leaving Grace asleep in the warmth of the fire. He lay on the bed covers next to Maggie for a while and soon dozed. Mary sat exhausted, looking out the front bay window at an empty street. It had been a long evening, and the visitors had helped the night pass, but sleep would not come easily to Mary on this second night of Chris being out *there* somewhere. Mary straightened the pillows on the couch while she fretted about where her son would sleep tonight. She retraced her husband's steps and found him asleep next to Maggie. She whispered in his ear, "Come on, honey. Let's go to bed."

Leaving Maggie snuggled in her bed, Joe shuffled behind his wife while trying to rub away the persistent pain in his arm. They needed to get some sleep. There would be plenty to do tomorrow to prepare for the next storm and continue their vigil.

As with the Ballentines, Chris and his attendants in the mountainous woods had also called it a night. It had been an arduous day for everyone. Chris stretched out on the hard door covered with blankets and the plastic sheet thinking of his mother, father, and Maggie. He also missed the unconditional love of his dog, and as he lay there, he prayed he would soon see his family and Grace.

CHAPTER 11

As families across western Pennsylvania awoke on Sunday morning, December 23rd, threw open blinds and curtains, and looked out onto the world, they were greeted with more snow than anyone had seen in decades. Communities and households, already stretched thin in terms of available power, supplies, and patience, struggled to cope with the compounding winter emergency or, as the television meteorologists liked to say, "major snow event." The inclement weather intensified Mary and Joe's agony over Chris's absence. They worried too that the good-hearted citizens of Hollidaysburg had far too much to deal with in their own lives to be concerned about their missing son. Joe and Mary weren't being cynical, just realistic.

This snow event had reached historic proportions, and yet another tempest, already considered the big brother of the previous storm, drove hard and fast across the midwestern United States, and was predicted to cross the Pennsylvania mountains sometime early Christmas Eve. Residents of western Pennsylvania, wont to describe any distant location or event as occurring "just over the mountain," referred to the approaching blizzard as such, and forecasters were predicting it would bury Altoona, Hollidaysburg, and Pleasant Valley like an avalanche when it crossed the distant range.

Joe hauled firewood from the iron rack on the patio through the back garage door and stacked a substantial supply of wood in the garage, where it would be easier to get to than on the snowy, wind-swept patio. He prepared for whatever the next squall might dump on the valley, his home, and his family. Although he still felt a bit peaked, he was determined to leave nothing about safety to chance.

Mary prepared too. She ran through a personal emergency checklist: candles, batteries, manual can opener, blankets…. She was thankful once again she'd been adamant about installing both a natural gas stove and hot water heater when they built their house years ago. No matter what this next storm might bring, they would have hot meals and baths, and the fireplace would provide at least a modicum of heat in the house should there be an electrical out-age — that is, everyone except Chris would be guaranteed hot show-ers and meals. Mary would not fully enjoy any of these amenities, however, until her entire family was together under one roof.

Maggie and Grace were oblivious to the impending dangers. Maggie had put *Prancer,* her favorite Christmas DVD, in the player and watched the movie on her bedroom television as she made her bed and straightened her room. Grace, asleep at the foot of Mag-gie's bed, made it impossible for Maggie to pull the sheets tight. Grace did not budge as Maggie smoothed the covers as best as she could around the snoozing sixty-pound creature. The dog stirred only when the celebrity reindeer in the film snorted while standing injured on the snowy road before the headlights of an approaching truck. At the sound of the deer's mournful bleat, Grace lifted her head, looking as if she expected to see the injured animal in Mag-gie's bedroom. The dog scanned the room and, once assured she was not sharing space with a reindeer, snuggled down against Maggie's comforter and resumed her nap.

On the mountain crest, the men rose and dressed before sunrise, and like the concerned folks in Hollidaysburg they tended to chores and prepared for the coming blizzard, which they could see inten-sifying on the western horizon. Fortified as it was by the encirclement of spruce trees, the camp was still dry and warm inside, but the men realized this snowstorm was likely to dump enough snow to penetrate the natural barrier.

Hank had begun preparing breakfast, combining dried prunes and apricots with fresh orange segments and a pint of blackberries in a deep pot, which he positioned on a side grill near the fire. The fruit simmered in its natural juices, which Hank diluted with a splash of water.

In the soot-covered skillet, Hank separated slices of bacon from a one-pound slab, the last of their meat. Afterward, he whipped the remaining half-dozen eggs into a froth. As the bacon finished frying, he poured off most of the grease and fried the eggs with chunks of the remaining cheddar cheese. Despite the formidable breakfast, Hank brooded. Rex approached the younger man, having inferred his thoughts from his behavior.

Throwing his good arm around Hank's shoulder, Rex asked, "No coffee this morning, huh, *gringo*?"

With a dejected look, Hank shook his head, "I'm afraid not, Rex. We used the last of the beans last night and it looks like it's going to be a long haul before we taste real coffee again. It's darn cold this morning and an espresso sure would hit the spot, wouldn't it?"

"Yep, pardner, it sure would. You know it's against my nature to do such, but I think our *numero uno* camp cookie deserves his Christmas gift a little early."

Rex trotted across the camp and retrieved a package about the size of a large bag of flour from his bunkhouse. He held the sack behind his back as he strutted back to the campfire and offered the gift to his gloomy friend with a cheerful, "*Feliz Navidad!*"

As soon as Hank accepted the burlap bag, he recognized and appreciated what Rex had given him. He ripped open the five-pound sack and ran his hands through the precious green beans as if they were cut diamonds. Shaking his head, Hank asked, "Guatemalan? I didn't think you knew Guatemalan was one of my favorites!"

"Hey, *compadre*, how could I not know your favorite beans the way you rave about coffee? I couldn't get Kona or Blue Mountain, which you crow about even more, so I figured Guatemalan was the perfect solution. I told the man at Brewmeister's that not just any bean would do for *mi amigo*—and then I had to wrestle the durn raw beans away from him. He insisted on roasting the suckers and didn't want to take 'no' for an answer, saying you can't brew raw beans!" Rex gave his friend a hasty Dutch rub and said, "Now, git roastin', man! Toast them beans up and brew us some good, strong Joe to wash down the stewed fruit you've got simmerin' over there."

Hank's mood soared as he contemplated the gift Rex had just given him. He thumped Rex on his good shoulder with his fist and said "Rex, my man, you just made my day . . . my whole week! This is the best Christmas gift I've received in years. I'll perk us some praiseworthy coffee, you wait and see! And I guarantee once that stewed fruit works its magic on you, you'll be praising my cooking too!"

Rex guffawed, "You know I always compliment your cooking and love your liberal use of Tabasco. I'll thank you later for the stewed fruit and my regularity! Can we just get started with the coffee for now? I'll eat some of your blockbuster fruit later."

Leo and Chris sat warming by the crackling fire, Leo talking about the deer, bears, and mountain lions that lived in the mountains. Smoke from the campfire drifted into Leo's eyes and then the boy's, and they alternately wiped their irritated eyes and fanned the smoke toward the other person. Leo scrolled rings of thin bark off the small straight shaft of a trimmed five-foot sapling with Hank's red-handled Swiss Army knife, making a crudely decorated spear.

"When I finish sharpenin' this tip, we'll lay the spearhead over the fire, so it'll dry out and harden. Then we can whittle the point a little bit more and you'll have a weapon that could kill a rabbit at twenty feet, if you could get that close and throw straight. With a few tools like this, a man wouldn't ever starve in the woods."

Chris was uncertain why he'd need a spear to kill rabbits for food. He wanted to go home before hunting for their meals was necessary, but fear raised its ugly head once more and he worried that the men had other ideas.

Hank reached deep into his jacket pocket and approached the pair. As he pulled his hand from his jeans, he said, "Leo, see if Bill feels good enough to whittle a little with my knife. You should be using your own knife. Merry Christmas!" Hank smiled and handed Leo his very own Swiss Army knife, still in its original box. Chris turned his head right then left to see if there was another person who had joined the troupe, someone named Bill. Then he remembered Bill was his alias. He realized he wasn't a skilled liar, especially in his current confused state.

Leo handed Chris Hank's knife and opened the box containing the new one. Chris planned to hold onto the knife Leo handed him, if he could, to use as a more effective weapon than the spear should he need to escape.

With the new case in the palm of his hand, Leo rubbed his thumb along the tooled chocolate-brown leather. The beautiful, embossed case was snapped closed, stowing the knife securely within. Leo saw where he could slide a belt through the insert at the back of the knife holder if he were wearing jeans instead of bib overalls. After unsnapping the flap and removing the knife, he examined each of its ingenious features, including the various cutting blades, scissors, screwdrivers, and corkscrew. Leo slid the plastic, ivory-colored toothpick from the end of the knife handle and picked his teeth and then tucked the pick back into its sleeve.

To Rex, Hank bellowed, "Heads up, buddy! I got something else for you later, but I thought you'd like this now." Hank tossed him an eight-ounce bottle of Tabasco in its traditional Christmas-looking red and green box.

Rex stepped back to catch the box, and as he did, he heard the squeak of a mouse under foot. Hopping aside to avoid harming the mouse, he missed his catch and the hot sauce fell to the ground. To Rex's relief, the straw-covered camp floor cushioned the box and kept the bottle from breaking. But as Rex turned to pursue the hot sauce, he saw the mouse was not squeaking because he had frightened it. The terrified mouse ran for its life from a large skunk that had sauntered into camp.

Rex stopped in his tracks and froze as the skunk moseyed forward, nose to the ground, unconcerned about the lanky man standing nearby.

"Hey, boys! Lookie here," Rex called out, with his hand cupped over the right side of his mouth. "We got us a visitor."

Hank and Leo spied their latest guest, picked up Chris's chair while he still sat in it, and cautiously back-pedaled away from the unwelcome intruder. Rex joined them at the far edge of the camp opposite the skunk, quipping, "Man this camp is beginnin' to get crowded!"

Being the city boy that he was, Hank asked, "So, what are we going to do? We can't share our campsite with a skunk, and it's too cold for us to be leaving the camp to him."

Leo put a hand on Hank's shoulder and said, "Don't panic, man. That's the last thing we be needin' with that skittish critter in our midst. Let's jus' see what the ole boy does."

The black and yellow-white fur ball nonchalantly stalked the mouse through the camp, digging its front paws into the pine straw near one of the barrels and sniffing along the pallets upon which the men's sleeping compartments lay. While the humans skirted the interior edge of the camp to remain opposite the varmint, the skunk made no threatening movements toward them. After eating the few breadcrumbs it found scattered near their table, the unexpected nocturnal guest tucked its head low and squeezed through the pine boughs, leaving the campsite, and entered the dark morning as unassumingly as it had arrived.

With tentative steps, Leo peeked around the bunks, barrels, and low-hanging boughs, making sure the skunk was gone. Hank said, "Man! That was close. Rex, now you know where your furry little buddies have gone. As much as I detest mice, I think I like the prey a bit more than I like the predator."

Rex concurred. "I'm with you there, good buddy!"

With everyone breathing a little easier, Leo recalled earlier days in Georgia. "You know, I had me a coon dog that tangled with a skunk down on my farm . . . stunk so bad it made my head hurt. Vet said to bathe him in tomata juice. I used a quart'a shampoo, a case'a tomata juice, one whole bar of Lava soap, and all the dish detergent I had on that hound, and he still stunk for weeks. Poor thing was a housedog too, and he jus' couldn't understand why I wouldn't let him inside . . . he stood at the back screen door an' cried all night! Pitiful thing. I could still smell him through that door, but I din't have the heart to run 'im off any farther. Unh!"

"I think it's safe for us to cozy back up to the fire," Rex said. "I'm freezin'."

"Me too," Hank agreed, "Come on, Leo, help me carry the boy back to where we can all get warm again, and I'll serve up our breakfast." The two men transported the boy and his chair back to the campfire, and the four campers sat around the flames eating, positioned so they could watch all four directions for a possible encore appearance of their unwelcome guest.

Chris discerned uneasiness among the three men whom he still feared might be holding him captive. He couldn't help but wonder whether they were concerned about the impending storm or worried about him escaping as his health improved. The approaching storm would make it all the more difficult for him to sneak away and descend the mountain. If he were going to break free, he'd need to slip away tonight after the men fell asleep and the blazing fire turned to flickering shadows, but before the storm raged.

CHAPTER 12

I t was a blustery evening that December 23ʳᵈ. The three caregivers hovered around their young patient as if they were
three hens caring for one lone peeper, uncertain which was its
true mother. Peeping was still about all the young man had done to
this point, especially since Hank took back his jackknife before carrying the boy away from the skunk.

Chris had been fretting as the weather worsened during the
day. He was determined not to stay another day in this makeshift
hobo camp, but he was afraid he'd be unable to steal away unnoticed, and if he did manage to flee, would he be strong enough to
make it home? He also considered how far he'd get before the men
realized he was gone and set out to track him down. He'd bide his
time, rest, and wait for his opportunity to break out.

Earlier in the morning, Hank had dug a hole about two feet
deep in the unfrozen, sandy soil within the camp interior. He pulled
several medium-sized rocks from the fire and laid a foundation in
the newly dug pit. After filling the Dutch oven with two large cans
of baked beans, he layered two pounds of hotdogs in a crisscross
pattern. He stirred a little pond water into ready-mix cornbread ingredients and poured the batter over the hotdogs. After slathering
the batter over the dogs,

Hank crowned the oven with its heavy rimmed lid. On his knees, he reached into the pit and placed the Dutch oven onto the heated rock foundation. He then surrounded the pot with fist-sized stones as he pulled them one by one from the fire pit. He capped the pot with two large flat rocks to hold the lid in place and to keep dirt and debris out of their meal. Hank then scooped dirt back into the hole with his bare hands, burying the charred rocks, the Dutch oven, and their dinner.

Around dinnertime, Hank acted the part of a befuddled archeologist searching for buried treasure. After racing around the camp like Charlie Chaplin, his hands behind his back, he stopped abruptly. Standing over the buried bounty and scratching his chin like Stan Laurel of Laurel and Hardy fame, he shuffled his feet across the dirt like an uncertain Gomer Pyle. His foot-shuffling antics turned up the loose soil and a subsequent "Ah ha!" Borrowing the spear from their young guest, Hank shoved the lance deep into the soft ground, striking the rocks that covered the pot. With mock surprise, he opened his mouth and eyes wide at the realization of his discovery.

"What have we here?" Hank asked no one in particular as he rubbed his hands together.

He dropped to his knees and began burrowing in the loose dirt like a groundhog, with dirt flying between his legs. When he reached the stone encasement surrounding the treasure he delicately removed and set aside the stone cover, whereupon he tapped the iron lid with a small stone. When the metallic chink was heard by his amused audience, Hank scraped away the remaining dirt and removed the stones encasing the Dutch oven. With gloved hands, he lifted the oven out of the hole and held high the ancient pot, bellowing to the treetops, "I am rich! I'll be famous. Everybody will want what's inside this pot. But you, you alone will be allowed to see it tonight."

Turning to the others, Hank said, "Would you like to be the very first people on earth to see the jewels and bullion that's filling this pot?" Leo and Rex nodded their heads enthusiastically, like hayseeds listening to the spiel of a sideshow carnie. Chris managed to smile at the sight of three adults acting silly in the face of a dangerous storm and diminishing supplies.

Fitting the significance of his discovery, Hank set the pot on the table reverently and stepped back to admire it. He examined the pot from several angles, and as he did so, Leo and Rex approached the table with anticipation, to witness the dramatic unveiling. Both men stood aside so their patient could also watch from his chair near the fire. Hank feigned a moment of solemnity and lifted the lid so only he could peek inside. He gasped and then set the lid back in place. Leo put his hands over his mouth in mock excitement, while Rex clambered, "Let me see! Let me see!" With a magician's bow and a dramatic sweep of his hand, Hank removed the lid, exposing the entire meal to the anxious audience. Leo bounced up and down like an excited toddler, exclaiming, "It's beee-uuuu-tee-fuuull." Chris stifled a laugh.

Rex, just as enthusiastically, called out, "Hot damn, *frijoles!*"

Even after six hours below ground, the buried pot was too hot to touch with bare hands, and the aroma of a steaming pot of "beanie weenies" and cornbread permeated the camp, making everyone's mouths water with anticipation. With the dramatic pre-dinner entertainment complete, Hank dug into the mélange with a long-handled aluminum spoon, scooping beans, hotdogs, and cornbread onto each waiting plate. He served Chris and handed him a cup of coffee. Everyone ate his fill of dinner; aware how little food was left in camp and that this might be their last full meal.

A couple of platefuls of cornbread, beans, and franks remained in the Dutch oven after everyone had had his fill. Hank approached Rex and Leo stirring the quarter-filled pot. Rex just shook his head. A step toward Leo brought two upward hands and a "No way, man." Turning toward Chris, Hank stopped in his tracks as the boy grimaced while rubbing his distended belly.

"All right, then. There's plenty more food in here if anyone gets hungry later." The others looked at each other doubtful whether they'd be able to eat beans anytime soon. Rex swallowed a burp,

"Let's give'r 'til tomorrow, Hank. I might be able to eat a little more for breakfast, with some Tabasco on it."

Shaking his head, Hank replied, "Eat it however you wish, but let's not waste it." Then as Hank set the beans on the tabletop, he recalled, "Oh yeah, what about dessert? I almost forgot!"

Rex lifted his eyebrows as Hank poured the camp's last can of peaches into a small tin pot. He then added a couple jiggers of brandy from the nearly empty pint bottle he pulled from the back pocket of his jeans, thinning the compote some. He stirred the sliced peaches and spiked compote with flair, adding a little cornstarch as he did so, repeatedly digging deep and bringing the spoon's sticky contents to the surface. He set the pot onto the grill until the mixture bubbled. After most of the alcohol had evaporated, Hank served the thickened brandied peaches over sliced pound cake he'd retrieved from his apartment. He had bought the Christmas treat at the Hollidaysburg day-old bread store while Leo and Rex were digging through the A&P dumpster. It wasn't Christmas, but he thought this might be their last opportunity for a holiday celebration.

Later, after pouring off soapy dishwater and rinsing and drying the dishpan, Hank left the dinner plates, cups, and eating utensils on the tabletop to air dry. He pulled up an oak high-back chair with a tattered cane seat, another prize salvaged from a Hollidaysburg curb, and joined in the discussion Leo and Rex were having about the approaching weather front.

As if the conversation had brought on the storm, the furious winds started to blow. Chris looked apprehensively at the heavy snowflakes dropping like parachutes through the pine boughs, forcing their way into the normally dry, protected encampment and landing on everything within. Escaping would be all the harder in this weather.

Rex misinterpreted Chris's uneasiness and tried to reassure the boy, "Don't you be worrying, son, I ain't gonna let us freeze tonight." Rex hefted onto the fire a couple of large hunks of hot-burning coal harvested from along the railroad tracks. Wiping his oily hands on his jeans, he added, "Thank God for coal cars!" He stirred the coals and repositioned several logs to keep the fire close and personal for each camper. Pulling his flannel shirt collar up around his neck, he challenged the bombastic sky, "Bring it on, Momma! We're ready for ya."

Chris sat huddled in his chair beside Hank's, withdrawn and not contributing to the men's conversation. Listening to their light-hearted banter, he began to accept the three meant him no harm. Somewhat emboldened, Chris asked the lanky Texan, "Rex, where are you from? You sound like you're from Alabama or Mississippi. And what are you doing in Pennsylvania, anyway?"

The unexpected intrusion brought the men's repartee to a sudden halt. For a moment, only the crackling fire, the howling wind, and the tree branches raking against each other could be heard within the camp. But Rex always perked up when he heard any invitation to talk about his home state, and before the silence had a chance to germinate and grow, he laughed aloud and chortled, "Alabama? Mississippi? You must have batting in your ears, boy! What you're hearin' is pure-as-cotton Texas drawl." He smiled to himself and pondered the boy's second question a bit more seriously. Where he was from was not difficult to answer, but he had never been certain what he was doing in these Pennsylvania mountains. How could he explain his presence to the kid? In the ensuing silence, Chris wondered whether the tough-talking cowboy might be on the lam.

Rex cleared his throat, "I'm originally from Corpus Christi. Like in the great state of Texas, not Alabama or Mississippi! When I was a youngster, my parents let me work on my uncle's shrimp boat in the Gulf of Mexico. I always wanted to buy his boat when he retired, but I was too young, still in school, and couldn't afford to buy a shrimp boat when

he called it quits. So, after high school I went to work in the East Texas oil fields. But I wan't gettin' steady work and wan't gettin' rich like I thought I would. Damn Texas crude was too expensive to pump out of the ground with oil prices bein' so low. Then I

124

worked a while as a cowboy, drivin' cattle 'cross the state. Yee ha! Now that's one job I loved. Me an' the open range, it don't get much better'n that. I learned one thing doin' the cowboy thing though: cowboys don't make much money gittin' all them saddle sores on their behinds. A little later, I had an opportunity to go to Saudi Arabia to work in the oil fields and make tons a'money, but by then I realized despite being a natural wanderer, I really didn't want to leave Texas for any length of time. I decided being rich wan't the most important thing in life. I knew my family an' friends were far more important to me than money, an' I chose to be king of my own little place out in the Texas countryside. I do a lil' mechanical work, repairin' just about anythin' broken, includin' machines on the big rigs way out in the Gulf.

"Man, do I miss Texas, though!" Rex added with more than a hint of melancholy.

Rex's response did not clarify why he came to western Pennsylvania, so Chris pressed a bit more, "If you miss Texas so much, why did you leave your home and come to Hollidaysburg?"

"Well, we tol' you yesterday we ain't bums. We ain't fugitives on the run, neither. An' we ain't hidin' from no wives or girlfriends! I have my little ranch in South Texas, down in the valley near the border . . . really, nothin' much at all, but it's where I call home. I love the land, the people, fishin' in the Gulf, Tex-Mex food, an' just about everythin' about the place. Ever' once in a while my brother and I go over to South Padre Island an' do some fishin' at the beach...." He rambled on for quite a while, embellishing in true Texas style the virtues of living in the Lone Star state. He eventually returned to the boy's question. "Work was slow during the late fall, an' one night I sat outside my backdoor contemplatin' the heavens above when a train passed on the tracks behind my property."

Rex turned up the affectation on his Texas drawl, "I saw that durn diesel a-comin' an' I was drawn to look straight into its head-lamp. The light was not only some-kinda bright, but it called me. I had to pay attention to it—it had a holta me an' I couldn't look away. The train was creepin' 'cross the highway into McAllen, the town near my ranch. I watched the train pass from left to right until it was clear out of sight. You know, I didn't think much more about it. That is, until the train came through the next night, an' the next, an' the one after that. Each time it squeaked and squealed past, its bright beam seemed to be callin' out to me above all the noise the engines made. I was mesmerized, transfixed, discombobulated!

"Feeling the draw of the train's headlight, I packed up some of my campin' gear an' cowboy boots into an old rucksack an' I hurdled my wandering butt into an open boxcar the next time that train rolled through. I rode the train for miles until I saw another one headin' north with a headlamp brighter'n an' somehow more compellin' than mine.

"I hopped off the first train an', without even thinkin' 'bout it, crossed the tracks an' climbed right onto the next one. I rode train after train through Texas, into Arkansas, and on to Missouri. I laid over in Branson a few days and took in some country shows. After a while, though, another train came by a-callin' me. I left Branson an' rode freight trains onward through Illinois, Indiana, Ohio, down a bit into West Virginia, an' back north into Pennsylvania, followin' one bright headlight after another.

"I jus' hopped on trains whose beams beckoned me forward, not knowin' where they was gonna take me. As strange as it sounds, I left my family an' followed the lights an' a narrow path of cross beams until I ended up here, all alone . . . without a clue why. Now, I've got me a little money in the bank an' no debt to speak of, so I am okay just withdrawin' a little cash whenever I need to buy somethin'. But frankly, I ain't needed much since I've been followin' those rails an' that guidin' light.

"I was in Hollidaysburg jus' a couple days when I ran into Leo. He had this look about him an' I knew he was okay. He an' I started talkin' at the lunch counter an' we was like old friends catchin' up.

"He asked me if I'd ever been to the Horseshoe Curve, an' I told him, 'Heck, never even heard of it.' That day was warm an' real pleasant. The leaves up in the mountains was bright with color. We just decided to snag us a train passin' through Altoona an' we rode

126

it clear up to the Curve. What a sight! It was so beautiful with them colorful leaves a-fallin' an' the blue water in the reservoir down below, you know what I mean?"

Chris nodded. He had been to the Curve in the fall many times and the sight was beholding.

After Chris leaned forward to indicate he was paying attention, Rex went on, "We rolled off the train at the top of the curve an' went straight down the stairway to the gift shop where I bought myself a book on the history of the 'World Famous Horseshoe Curve.' We caught us a short southbound train a little later, an' I read the whole book on the ride back down to Hollidaysburg, cover to cover. Jus' a tiny lil' thing.

"When we got back to Hollidaysburg, that's when we ran into Hank at the local donut shop…you know, the Donut Hole. Leo an' me are just ole country boys an' we was dunkin' our donuts in our coffee like bumpkins, yakkin' up a storm. Hank, a refined, gentleman rail rider—you know, the kind that don't like mouse turds on his tabletop—was havin' his fancy apple pie à la mode, and don'tcha know he was savorin' that donut shop's fine coffee!"

Chris laughed at Rex's description of Hank. He'd seen firsthand how Hank felt about mice.

Rex continued, "Hank's a city slicker, a little better educated and a bit more courtly than the two of us more common kings of the road, an' we was a tad dubious of him at first. He had some 'airs about him' as my momma used to say. But after jus' a few minutes hearin' him talk about his travels and his home, we knew he was okay too. We knowed Hank was a good guy, a fellow traveler. He told us about this place up in the woods where he had started a camp near the trestle an' he invited us up to join him an' share his place. We took him up on his offer, an' that's how the three of us got together. It was a good decision, and it sure didn't take us very long to learn the ole boy can cook!"

Leo elbowed Hank when Rex described his "courtly ways," to which Hank rolled his eyes, patted Chris on the shoulder as if he'd heard enough and rose to begin putting away the cooking gear. Rex got up and gathered an armful of branches and logs and fed the dry wood into the fire until flames kicked high into the evening sky. Leo leaned forward, rubbed his hands together, and prepared to pick up where Rex left off.

Leo sidled into the conversation. "Son, my story is like Rex's in some ways but different too. I got me a lil' farm down in Bethlehem, Georgia. Me and my Sis was raised in Athens, not far from where my farm is now. I always wanted to be a football player for the University of Georgia. I was big enough and was pretty decent at high school ball, but I jus' wasn't quite good enough to run with the Dawgs. So, I joined the Army jus' to leave home, and I ended up in the Special Forces. They trained me to be a medic, an' I spent several years providin' medical treatment to the troops in my company an' anybody else that needed a band-aid."

Hank's head snapped toward the humble man when he heard his last comment. He and Rex both hooted at Leo's modest self-appraisal.

Ignoring his buddies' ribbing, Leo continued. "After re-enlistin', I hurt my back in a night jump an' couldn't stay in the Special Forces any longer. My back got worse an' I ended up gettin' out of the Army on disability. I took my bad back an' disability home an' found that farmin' was good for me an' for my back. I used my medical trainin' to work off an' on as a part-time veterinarian's assistant, an' I bought me a farm. I raise some poultry — chickens mostly — but I also got some geese an' ducks, an' a few pigs, a couple cows, an' one beautiful, strong, jet-black horse I named Sugar Cube. Everybody thought I was bein' funny with the horse's name 'cause he was all black an' with a sugar cube bein' so white. Truth be told, I didn't even think 'bout his color, he just loved them sugar cubes I gave him every mornin'. The name just fit.

"I got me a plain an' happy life. I'm a deacon at the Bethlehem AME church an' I sing in the choir. One day last winter, my sister, her husband, an' their three little ones got burned out'a their place in Atlanta. The space heater they had runnin' one February night shorted an' their apartment caught fire. Thank God, they all got out safe, but Brenda lost everythin' 'cept her three kids an' Melvin.

"I invited the whole clan to move in with me in my old farm-house until they could get back on their feet. What else could I do? Durin' the spring an' summer months it was cramped in the house, but it was okay. We spent a lot of time outside workin' the farm. Melvin took to farmin' like he been doin' it all his life. When the temperatures began to fall, we were spendin' more time together inside, an' I could see it was gonna get real crowded. I talked with my sister, Brenda, an' later I talked with her husband, an' they agreed to manage my farm while I traveled north for a spell.

"I bought me a train ticket to Washington, D.C., an' went to see the White House an' all them memorials. I 'specially wanted to see the Lincoln Memorial. One day, on the corner outside Union Sta-tion, I met a real interestin' fella who'd been ridin' the rails. He seemed unusually peaceful, kinda like a laid-back flower child on tranquilizers." Chris's face screwed up when he heard Leo's de-scription of the man. "You know, he kinda beamed an' glowed all over in a gentle kinda way. He tol' me he'd show me how to ride freight trains an' I could ride wherever I wanted to go. Livin' the life of a rail-bum sounded excitin', so I decided to give it a try. I rode the rails with the man from D.C. to Maine, but one day near Bangor, he up an' disappeared. I looked for him a long while, thinkin' he'd be back, an' then I continued ridin' the rails. I never did run into the man again.

"One warm fall day, with my legs danglin' outside a boxcar door, the train I was ridin' came upon the Horseshoe Curve. I didn't know nothin' about the Curve, so I wasn't knowin' that at some point on this long freight train the engineer an' brakeman would be 'cross from me as the train rounded the curve. I could see the ole engineer scannin' the track ahead of him an' the brakeman was watchin' the rest of the train takin' the curve. As his eyes went from car to car, his gaze stopped on my car. He saw me for certain! He pointed in my direction an' began speakin' into a hand-held radio as the engineer too looked my way.

"I was discovered. What could I do? Well, I waved, all friendly-like at the engineer an' the brakeman, but they didn't wave back. I figured before we reached the rail yard I'd better slide off the slow-rolling train an' hoof the rest of my way into Altoona. Now, there ain't all that many Black people in Altoona, so I knowed I was gonna stand out like the proverbial black sheep in a flock of white lambs. I guessed I'd get arrested for hitchin' rides on freight trains or somethin' like that. I was scared and knew somebody would come lookin' for ole *mister you-know-who,* but no police came pokin' around an' nobody else seemed to give a hoot about me. Only God knows why I didn't stand out as different to anyone who saw me. I was surprised, but nobody commented about my southern accent, about me being black, an' no one asked me what I was doin' in Altoona. Not one person I met acted as if I was different in any way from the mostly white Appalachian folk livin' up here. It was kinda like someone'd made me transparent...no, not invisible, 'cause people talked with me just fine everywhere I went. More like, what people saw standing before them was not a Southern Black man, but an Appalachian white man. Man, oh man, that was weird. I'm a-tellin' ya!

"All in all, if it wasn't for that strange man in D.C., I most likely woulda gone home...but for some reason that man picked me out of more than a million folk in that capital city to talk me into riding the rails. I still don't understand why he singled me out for his attention. Do I gotta sign on my forehead or somethin'?"

Chris bent forward to get a close glimpse of Leo's forehead. He put his palm to his chin, studied the Black man's brow, and then started laughing. He shook his head, and said, "I don't see anything there...not even any hair."

"Unh, thank ya for noticin' that minor detail, young man! An' thank ya for confirmin' my suspicion that I ain't got a sign sayin' 'Pick me'! . . . Okay, where was I? Oh yeah, when Rex and I met up at the Donut Hole, I knew right off I'd found an old friend. Then when we ran into Hank, it was like we was three lost folk meant to be together again. We soon became best friends an' knew there was some reason we were meant to be together in these mountains. We been tryin' to figure out what we're doin' here, but we ain't solved that problem yet. An' here we sit."

Hank came back to the fire, poured another round of coffee, and set the pot back on the grill. He ran his hand over his stubbly chin, and said, "Well, I guess it's my turn, huh?"

Momentary grief enveloped Hank as he considered his life story. He had a hard time getting started, but he rubbed his face and eyes with his hands, let out a sad sigh, and recomposed himself. He drew his shoulders up around his neck and leaned forward with his metal cup in both hands, elbows resting on his knees. He nodded, squinting at Leo and Rex, and began his tale. "These two men are like lifelong brothers. We just didn't happen to know we were related before we met in Hollidaysburg. I don't have any family I trust or love more than these guys. They are honorable and righteous men, and they'd risk their lives for anyone. What am I saying? That's exactly what they did when they found you. That's just the kind of men they are."

As if on cue, Rex and Leo leaned back in their chairs and began to sip their coffee. Chris craned forward with growing interest. He blew on his coffee, no longer cognizant of his own bruises and injuries, as he waited to hear the story about to be told.

Hank continued, "I was born and raised in Los Angeles—that's why ole Rex sometimes calls me L.A. After high school, I went to UC Berkeley and got a degree in small business administration. I worked for a couple of restaurants in management training over the next few years and cooked in others, until I met my wife on a weekend getaway.

"She was at the beach in Monterey, near Carmel, and I saw her lying on a blanket from my hotel balcony. I grabbed a towel from my room and went trotting down to the beach before she had a chance to get away. I laid my towel right next to hers, and when she opened her eyes, she saw me staring at her beautiful face. She was startled and a little scared of me—she was a smart girl! I didn't know what I would say or do, but I smiled and told her I had seen her from my balcony and very much wanted to meet her. We talked that afternoon on the beach and we had dinner together that evening. Sunday morning I joined her for Mass at the old Carmel Mission. Afterward we walked the Carmel-by-the-Sea beach hand in hand. It was the best day of my life, at least until we married.

"I fell hard and fast. Becky and I married four months later at that same historic Spanish mission where we'd attended Mass together. I moved up from L.A. and she moved down from where she'd been living north of San Francisco. We opened a small restaurant along Highway One in Monterey with a friend of mine, and we worked and lived among the kind of characters that John Steinbeck wrote about and made famous."

Hank looked down into the fire for a long moment, took a deep breath, and then continued. "We were married just two years and three months when Becky died of complications from a virus. When she first became ill neither of us was concerned. Why should we be, it was just the flu. She picked up a respiratory bug going around. I did too. I got over my virus in a couple of days, but Becky didn't get better. She got weaker, tired easily, and began to breathe with a rattle.

"One night she had night sweats as she lay next to me. When she awoke and complained of pain in her chest, I got us dressed and took her to the hospital. I thought she might have pneumonia, but they thought she'd had a heart attack. She had a virus, and it had infected the sac surrounding my girl's sweet heart. Because her illness was a virus and not bacterial, there was nothing the doctors could do to treat her infection except keep her comfortable and hope for the best.

"But . . ." Hank's voice faltered. "She got weaker and weaker by the day until her heart gave out. My Becky died after being sick for just three weeks from myocarditis caused by a simple flu many people got that year and got over, like me, within a few days, without complications."

As Hank told his story, he wiped tears from the corner of his eyes.

"Without any life insurance money, I got a second mortgage on our house in Monterey to pay for her funeral and eventually left the struggling restaurant with my buddy who's trying to run it by himself. Like Rex, I was drawn toward a train's headlamp and sat, depressed, at a railroad crossing with a trunk-load of produce for the restaurant, waiting for an oncoming train to pass. I was missing my Becky and thought if I just pulled my car ahead another ten feet or so the train would take me to her. I couldn't do it though. I knew Becky didn't want me to come to her that way. It might sound crazy, but it was almost as if Becky was the light on the front of that train and she drew me toward a promise of new hope and purpose.

"After the train passed, I crossed the tracks and drove down the gravel road running alongside the train tracks. I passed the train and then watched the headlight in my rearview mirror. I stayed well ahead of the slow-moving train until I reached the next town. I parked my car in a grocery store parking lot, got out, and waited. Within minutes, the train pulled into the small town and slowed even more to pass through the crossroads community. I ran alongside the train, grabbed onto the ladder of a railcar, and stood on the bottom rung for a while, wondering what I was doing. Who knows why, but I climbed up the ladder and crawled into a car filled with pea gravel, planning to ride a while with my girl.

"I stretched out atop the small grains of smooth stone and just stared heavenward for miles; finally fell asleep as evening approached. All the while, the train just kept rolling east. Somewhere around midnight, after awakening from my deep sleep, cold hungry and thirsty, I sat up and looked over the top of the car into wide-open desert. We were out in the middle of nowhere. Sometime later in the morning before the sun rose, we were in western Arizona, approaching the lights of a city named Casa Grande. That's Spanish for big house. It was in Casa Grande where Becky spoke to me. She was saying, 'Don't go home, Hank. Keep going.'

"I could have gone home from there easily enough. My car sat idle in a parking lot near the tracks, where it still may sit today with rotting produce in the trunk. I had enough money left over from shopping to catch a bus or a passenger train back to Monterey.

There was nothing to stop me from turning back, except the message from Becky in Casa Grande encouraging me to 'Keep going.' So, I bought some sturdy clothes, traveling rations and bottled water, a shaving kit, and a few things I thought I might need on a trip that could take me anywhere...threw it all in a grip and kept going.

"I called my business partner and told him I wouldn't be coming home for a while and caught the very next train passing through Casa Grande and rolled on toward Texas. From Texas, I followed a route similar to the one Rex described, with some minor variation. My train didn't go through Branson like Rex's did, and my travels up north detoured into Michigan. I left the train for a layover in Flint and spent a day throwing stones at passing freight trains and feeling sorry for myself. The next morning a long line of Chesapeake and Ohio railcars filled with Buicks from the local assembly plant was leaving town, and I decided it was time to move along. I dodged a yard clerk and climbed up into one of the cars hauling luxury Buicks and jimmied my way into one of those rolling living rooms and rode in splendor eastward for a long while.

"I arrived in Hollidaysburg just about two weeks ahead of Rex and Leo and, for reasons I can't explain, I jumped off the train at the trestle, followed an animal trail leading down the hill, and started a camp within these pines. In town, I picked up more camping equipment, pots and pans, and some groceries, and began dragging discarded materials to the site. I threw the empty oil drums off the train on one of my trips up from town. Another day that door lay at the curb of someone's house and I managed to throw it onto the train as it was passing by and then tossed it off and followed along behind it up here on the mountain. Little by little I began setting up housekeeping, believing there was some reason Becky wanted me to do so."

Hank's voice had lowered to a whisper, and above, the pine trees pitched to and fro in the gusting winds. The storm was getting worse—dead branches large and small broke free from swaying trees and crashed to the ground with resounding thuds and earth-shuddering quakes. The four campers huddled around the fire, their eyes darting in the direction of each cracking and falling branch, or sometimes entire trees, growing increasingly anxious about the severity of the storm and the possibility of a tree falling within the camp.

Hank spoke louder so his voice could be heard above the whistling, whipping winds that were sending sparks swirling from the campfire and blowing Leo's cutout pictures off the interior tree branches. "We each have just enough money to get by. We've got friends and families that love us. They don't understand what we're doing up here any more than we do. Off and on they're okay with us livin' up here in the woods, but they worry about us, and wonder if we've cracked, living like bums when we have happy homes waiting for us."

Rex added, "We've been thinkin' it might be about time for us to drift on home, but we've been waitin' for somethin' to tell us it was time. We knew we were here for some reason, and we couldn't leave until that reason no longer had a hold on us. We kinda thought, kinda hoped we'd be travelin' on before Christmas, but it don't seem like we'll be off quite that soon. Maybe we'll be home with our families before the New Year, who knows?"

Leo rubbed the chill from his arms, and asked, "What about you young man, what's your story?"

Moved by the honesty of each man's history and what each had given up to come to this camp, Chris prepared to share his tale. He took a drink of coffee and groaned like an old man when he set his cup on the ground, and then he sat upright, as best as his aching body would permit. Before speaking, Chris met Leo's gaze and then looked above Leo's bald head, distracted by the wind swirling snow within the camp through the well-insulated pine branches and boughs. He began to speak but hesitated again, once more looking over Leo's head. The pine boughs shook and then pushed open, as if the storm had blown its way into the camp, but it wasn't the wind blowing through the pines. What forced its way through the boughs and into the camp was far more threatening.

Unaware that the winds were gusting just as forcefully down in

Pleasant Valley, the group could not see the distant skies lighting up with blue-yellow explosions, or the trees uprooting throughout the valley and falling across electrical wires. From one end of the valley to the other came the characteristic flashes of transformers blowing. In quick succession, power stations shut down, neighborhoods and towns went dark, and soon the entire regional power grid was offline. West central Pennsylvania was powerless.

CHAPTER 13

For a moment, Chris stared wide-eyed in disbelief. As in a scary dream, he sat speechless, unable to move or yell a warning to the others. He sat with his mouth agape. Just as the men followed his shocked gaze over Leo's shoulder, Chris managed to yell, "B-B-Bear!" He pushed himself out of his chair, trying to stand and scramble from the approaching danger, but his legs failed him. He fell back into his chair, clawing at the armrests in an effort to stand again.

Leo put his hand on Chris's shoulder, pressing him into his chair, and stood protectively by his side. Rex positioned himself between the bear and Chris, while Hank took the lead position. Confronting a very hungry, determined bear with a frying pan, Hank yelled, "Get! Get! Get out of here!"

Drawn to the camp by the smell of barbecued beans, hotdogs, and cornbread, the hungry omnivore had left her seasonal hibernation for a snack. She sniffed the air, seeming to consider Hank standing before her as either a minor nuisance or a possible feast. Snarling, the bear reared up with her front paws a foot or so off the ground and leaned back on her haunches, threatening to pounce. Leo and Rex picked up Chris's chair, with him in it, and sidled away, as they had done when the skunk visited the camp earlier.

Shock preceded consternation as Hank mused, "First mice, then skunks, and now bears—what's next?" Despite a pounding heart and sweaty hands, he stood his ground against the massive beast holding nothing more than an 18-inch iron fry pan. He raised and lowered the skillet menacingly, ready to strike the bear in its most sensitive body part, her nose, if she attacked. As the beast stalked her prey, Hank again yelled with a trembling voice, "Get out of here—Go!"

Hank saw the bear was not intimidated by his menacing stance. She strode forward with her broad shoulders and large head swinging side to side. With the bear too close for comfort or safety, Hank yielded ground and stepped back. He startled as he edged into the tabletop, wedged between the hungry animal and the unyielding table.

As the bear drew one more challenging step closer, Leo warned, "Get back, Hank! Get out'a there. There ain't nothin' she wants we cain't do without. Let momma bear have her way. She prob'ly jus' wants them beans an' dogs. An' you're standing between her an' dinner. Let her have it. 'Sides with all the gas those beans been givin' me, she can have my share for sure! Y'all can fight 'er for your shares if ya want, but I say let *her* stink up the woods for a change."

Inside the bear's snout was a dreadful display of teeth, including four canines and twelve incisors, bared for Hank to examine. Throwing her head back, she growled one last warning at the one person standing between her and the food that would satisfy her needs. Hank read her determination correctly and decided he'd concede the dinner and anything else she wanted.

Fearful of turning his back on the mammoth beast, he edged sideways until he reached the end of the table, where he then backed away. Fortunately, neither Hank nor momma bear were determined to fight, at least for now. Pressed against the pine boughs as they were, the four campers considered the pros and cons of dashing out of the camp underdressed for the life-threatening temperatures, with everyone fending for himself, or remaining together where they stood, hoping the bear wouldn't attack.

Rex summed up their situation. "I'm feelin' a bit like chopped steak, knowing I'm gonna be tossed either into the deep freeze or onto the grill. An' I ain't carin' much for either option. I vote for four-on-one. I think we've got a better chance ganging up on ole missy if we have to." Leo opened his Swiss army knife, and Rex unsheathed his Bowie knife. Hank still wielded the large iron skillet, preparing to strike the bear's sensitive nose with all his might. Chris sat holding the spear Leo'd made for him, hoping the sharpened point had hardened enough to penetrate the raging monster's furry hide.

The four watched anxiously, handling their meager weapons, as a massive paw swiped leftovers onto the ground. Lapping beans and franks like a dog eating from its bowl, the bear licked the pot clean. When the Dutch oven was empty, she shoved it aside and considered the huddled campers, as if sizing up each of them as a possible entrée. She snorted, her attention appeared to be focused on Chris, the smallest, weakest member of the group. Each of the campers read her intent, and the three men stepped in front of the boy. She growled a clear warning, reminding them who was the biggest, baddest, and meanest creature in the woods.

Saving her entrée for later, the bear continued picking off easier foods. She sniffed out the remaining cornbread and pound cake and scraped it off the tabletop onto the ground. With baseball glove sized paws, she scooped the snack into a pile and licked it up with a single swipe of her thick tongue. Apparently still hungry, the bear tipped over the camp table, continuing to graze on whatever she could find. The near-starved animal rolled each of the 55-gallon drums around, rocking one then the other back and forth, listening with interest as objects clanked within the interior. She reached deep inside the first barrel and retrieved a potato, two onions, and an orange.

As she chomped the vegetables and fruit, Hank commented, "There go your Vidalias, Leo."

"Unh. She sure knows how to hurt a guy!"

After the bear ate the pantry remnants, she stuck her head

inside the barrel.

Rex edged forward saying, "This would be the time to jump her. We could whoop her good with the fry pan and scare her off. What'a all say?"

"Whoa, man!" Leo grabbed his friend's arm. "Let's not be doin' anythin' stupid. Leave her be unless she comes after us. Then we'll take'r on if we gotta."

"I like that plan," Chris added.

"Me too," Hank concurred.

With nothing more edible in the barrel, the bear stuck her long forearm deep into the second drum, where she pulled out a partial loaf of bread. Her sharp claws tore through the plastic bread bag, and she stuck her snout in and emptied the contents. She reached deeper into the barrel and found a box of Brillo pads. With the ease of a seasoned pot-scrubber, she tore through the cardboard, sniffed, and then licked one of the bluish pads. Snorting with distaste for the soapy biscuits, she abandoned the rest.

Sitting on her haunch, licking her snout, and surveying the camp for something else to fill her winter-empty stomach, she ambled toward Leo's doublewide sleeping berth. Looking fiendish in her ice-matted and molting winter coat, she reared her hefty frame up on her hind legs and bound to the top of the cardboard box. She belted a loud snort when the box beneath her crushed like a peanut shell. She growled ferociously and backed away, regarding the box as if it were a potential aggressor.

"Whoa, missy! That's my rack you be tossin' about. Get!"

The bear responded with an angry, threatening snarl and ripped Leo's sleeping compartment apart, rummaging fiercely through his clothes and personal effects. With his belongings strewn across much of the camp, Leo sighed. Alarmed as he was, Leo yelled, "Get outa here or you're gonna to be in big trouble."

After swinging her powerful right paw toward Leo, she left Leo's rack and sauntered toward Rex's sleeping compartment.

It was Rex's turn to step forward and heave idle threats at the famished brute. "Wait, you hussy! You've done enough damage to

140

our place; now get away from my bunkhouse. And I mean now!" Surprisingly, the bear did as Rex directed. She backed away from Rex's compartment.

Believing his yelling had the desired effect, he added, "Aw'right, now you just keep goin'! You know I mean business. I think you know I'm the nastiest hombre in these mountains. Now, get along back to where you came from!"

The bear, however, was not attending to Rex. Instead, her eyes hadn't moved from his sleeping compartment. She reared back ready to pounce on the cardboard box, but as she prepared to leap, something black and white stepped out of the bunkhouse.

Rex jumped back, falling over Chris's legs and onto the ground. "If she gets squirted by that skunk, she's gonna have a fit, an' she'll likely wanta take it out on us."

Leo and Rex picked up Chris's chair and moved him into the overlapping spruce branches, concealing him from the bear. Leo said, "If she charges, I'll throw the boy over my shoulder and make a run for it. Rex and Hank, you two run in other directions. That way, at least some of us will get away."

But Hank was determined to stay put and protect Chris and his buddies. "You guys sneak out now. I'll stay here and divert her attention. Go now." He stepped forward and waved the skillet threateningly while he paced side to side. To the bear he yelled, "Get going. Go on!"

The bear ignored Hank, intent on the skunk. The skunk wasn't fazed by her interest and threatening stance. As the bear cautiously stepped forward, the skunk turned around as if to walk away, but its tail was lifted in one final warning, as it stood its ground. The bear hesitated for a moment and then inched forward. With the beast within four feet of the small creature, the skunk let loose a well-aimed stream of pungent spray, without so much as a snip, yip, or whisper.

The stomach-churning spew sent the bear somersaulting backwards, howling. Snorting in agony, she rampaged throughout the camp, rubbing her massive head on pine straw, cardboard, clothing, anything she could find to get the horrible stink off her muzzle and broad forehead.

In an act of desperation, she plowed headlong toward Hank. He leapt aside, but her muscular front left shoulder struck his leg, tossing him high into the air. He bounced off her fleeing rump as she bolted through the pine boughs toward Leo, Rex, and Chris. She lowered her head as she prepared to burst through the greenery and howled when her massive forehead struck a thick, low hanging branch. The limb cracked and flew forward, striking Chris across the chest and knocking Leo and Rex to the ground. The beast did not stop but instead ran into the woods.

Hank opened his eyes, thankful to have survived the attack. He lay face-to-face with the offending skunk; fearful he'd be sprayed next. But the varmint was finished with its dirty work. It tucked its tail and sallied nonchalantly through the pine boughs, leaving behind four distraught campers and a stinking, disheveled camp. The bear's agonizing howls resounded through the woods as she fled, crashing through brush and brambles.

Getting to his feet and brushing himself off, Hank lamented. "Oh, man! I'd rather wrestle the damn bear than smell that stench."

Rex chided Hank from deep in the spruce as he pulled himself to his feet, "Be careful what you wish for, Hank. We might get both if that angry, hungry hussy decides to come back lookin' for food and revenge."

Rubbing his bruised leg while taking stock of the others, Hank asked, "Are you guys all right?"

Rex replied, "I am, but I think the kid got the worst of it."

Leo lifted the dazed young man in his arms and carried him into the camp, laying him in clean pine straw, distant from the reeking wreckage. Rex brought in the broken and bent chair and tossed it atop Leo's destroyed sleeping compartment.

Leo began examining Chris. His injuries, mostly scrapes on both biceps and chest, were not serious. The broken branch had knocked the wind from Chris's lungs, but the boy was resilient and had mostly recovered on his own by the time Leo took his pulse and asked, "How you doin'?"

Chris did not want to be pampered any longer. He said, "I'm fine, thank you very much. How are you?"

Leo laughed, "Well, I was about scared to death, but I am doin' better now we all okay!"

Chris surveyed the demolished camp, while Leo began barking orders. "Burn everything that smells. Burn it all! Burn my coveralls, the cardboard, pine straw, anythin' and everythin' that stinks like skunk. You know that stuff's gonna linger anyway, but not so bad if we can burn the most of it. I'm 'fraid we're in for a rough night, for sure!"

They burned Rex's sleeping compartment and sleeping bag, and the bear had destroyed Leo's. They burned much of their clothing and all of the soiled insulating pine straw they could scrape into the fire, without actually touching it. They continued to add logs to the roaring fire, which offset the miserable cold that lay beyond the pines. In their efforts to burn everything that stunk, they also consumed much of their firewood reserve. Comforted a little by the flames kicking high into the sky, the men grew hungry as they worked, but there was now very little edible within the camp. What little food remained would have to be tomorrow's breakfast, lunch, and possibly dinner. Given their limited provisions and nonexistent shelter, the men became stoically quiet.

Rex summed up their dire situation succinctly, if not eloquently, "Boys, we're in some real deep dung!

CHAPTER 14

With evening settling down, the camp regained a semblance of order and the foursome gathered again around the roaring fire. Instead of sitting on the stinky caned chair that was now well on its way to becoming charred embers, Rex perched atop one of the barrels still lying on its side. He looked like a cowboy mounting a bronco, Leo joked, "Now, don'tcha be fallin' off yo' horsie, cowpoke."

Rex responded to the taunt by grabbing hold of the barrel rim with his good hand and throwing his injured hand high in the air. He rolled the barrel side-to-side, forward and backward, looking like a rodeo star on a Brahma bull. After ten seconds or so of frenzied riding, the cowboy made the "awnnnnnh" sound of a rodeo horn, indicating the end of his successful ride. He stood with the barrel still between his legs, flashed a toothy smile, and waved to imagined fans sitting on the pine branches surrounding him.

"Thank you. Thank you. That's the way rodeo's done in Texas!"

Rex hadn't noticed that Hank was behind him. As Rex bent his knees to sit, Hank booted the empty barrel forward with a solid kick, shooting it out from under the cowboy, leaving Rex falling back. Hank caught him around the chest and pulled him upright, saying, "And that's how California rodeo clowns save bragging

144

Texans' butts."

After letting Rex go, Hank smelled his hands suspiciously, "Man! You stink like a Texas polecat."

Rex was offended at the insinuation of him alone smelling badly. "We all do . . . don'tcha think?"

The campers sniffed themselves warily, Chris included, but no one had skunk spray on him, except Rex. "You must have gotten some of the spray on your boots or pants, Rex. I hate to be the one to tell you, but you stink ole buddy! Why don't you drag your buckin' barrel downwind from us?"

Rex puffed up. "The hell I will! Y'all ain't too good to smell a little skunk."

The banter helped settle the group, and the camp took on a more relaxed atmosphere. Despite the trauma they'd experienced and the massive storm that lay ahead, the group hunkered down with coffee, which they still had plenty of, and picked up the conversation where it had trailed off. Hank turned to Chris and said, "Son, I think you were about to share with us your life story before all of that excitement. You feel up to telling us a bit about yourself?"

Chris nodded and launched into his story. These men had many of the characteristics of his grandfather: they were smart, thoughtful, and protective. He now felt safe with them. He opened up to them and found himself explaining every aspect of his life, beginning with his real name.

"I have to tell you something first. My name isn't Bill Johnston, it's Chris Ballentine. I lied to you because I didn't trust you and I was trying to protect my family. My mother and father have been worried about me for a long time because I've been sad and difficult to live with. . . .. I've missed my grandfather so much since his death that I just haven't felt like doing anything. I know I've hurt my mom and dad, especially my dad, acting the way I have, but I just couldn't stop myself." Chris hung his head in shame, expecting a rebuke or a cavalier response from one of the men. But the three men only listened.

Chris continued, sharing a lot of information about his

grandfather. He also told the men about how close he, Maggie, and his grandfather had been. He explained how his grandfather had made him laugh, like Rex did. How he'd been strong, thoughtful and reflective, like Leo. And, like Hank, his grandfather had liked to cook, often fixing meals for Maggie and Chris. "Grandpa used to make the best cucumber and ham salad in the summer, with mayonnaise in it."

Hank reflected, "Chris, you know you could make that salad too and think of your grandfather when you and your family enjoy eating it. But I'd be willing to bet your grandfather used sour cream, not mayonnaise."

"Sour cream, you think?"

Hank nodded.

Leo added, "Oh man, I'm hungry. Mmm, now wouldn't it be good 'bout now with a little Vidalia onion minced in?"

Rex jumped in, "Now, you're gonna think I'm crazy, but I could see spicing it up with a lil' Tabasco."

Chris laughed and pointed at Rex, "That's what I mean. Hank had the recipe right. Leo had a good idea when he suggested adding onion. And Rex made us laugh by wanting to add Tabasco."

Rex crossed his arms over his chest and snorted with feigned indignation, "Well, I'm sure glad I make y'all laugh, but I bet it would taste dandy with some hot sauce, just the same."

Leo looked askance at the man while holding his nose and said, "Tex, your idea smells just about as funky as you do right now . . . pee-yew."

Bringing the conversation back around to the serious stuff he wanted to unload, Chris described how he'd been sitting on the trestle, considering jumping when the train came along. "I have been so sad after my grandfather died of a heart attack two years ago, just after New Year. I not only lost my grandpa, but I lost my best friend. My life hasn't been right since. Grandpa lived with us after my grandma died four years ago. He was always around and did things with Maggie and me. Dad tries to do things grandpa used to do, to help me feel less sad, but I just get mad at him for

146

trying to act like grandpa. He tries so hard to be close to me, but I can't seem to let him."

Hank sniffed the backside of his hand and rubbed it on the back of his pant leg. He refocused his attention and said, "You know, I lost my Becky about the same time you lost your grandfather. I understand the pain you've experienced. Becky was my life. But these guys," pointing to Rex and Leo, "have helped me see there are people who can pull you out of your gloom if you let them."

Chris looked down ashamed, "I know I have to try harder. My dad's done everything he can to help me, and I've mostly ignored him. It hurts him, I know, but somehow it makes me feel better."

Hank nodded his head. "You kind of want someone to share the pain you feel, don't you?"

"Yeah . . . I guess that's it. I don't really want my dad to be sad. I don't know what I would do without him. But I want him to talk to me about me being sad, rather than trying to cheer me up all the time."

"Have you talked with your school counselor or priest?"

Raising his voice and shaking his head, Chris blurted out with considerable emotion, "Religion is bogus! If there was a God, He wouldn't have taken my grandpa."

After Chris's sudden outburst, Leo jumped in. "Hey, Bill, er Chris, you know your grandfather's heart just gave out, it wasn't God that stopped his heart from beatin'. Your grandfather must'a had diseased arteries. You know, rather than blamin' God for those diseased arteries, maybe you might consider thankin' Him for lettin' your grandfather live long enough to be as big a part your life as he was. What a shame it woulda been if he died when you was too young to get to know him."

Chris replied, "Yeah, I guess. Maybe God didn't kill grandpa, but I miss him just the same." After a long pause, he added, "I know I'm too old now, but I miss how, when we were little, I sat on one knee and Maggie sat on his other knee, and the three of us sang *Little Green Frog*."

"Oh, yeah, I remember that one," Leo said, beginning to hum

the tune, and when Chris nodded, Leo sang in a deep, soothing voice, "Little green frog, swimmin' in the water. Little green frog, doin' what he oughta . . . Those are the only words I remember."

Chris nodded. He smiled into the fire for a long minute and then went on, "My grandfather said the water snake at the end of the song was symbolic. You know, the mean snake that ruined everything for the white duck and the green frog and that ate the black bug, leaving none of them sitting happy in the water anymore. He said many old books, even the Bible, used snakes as a symbol of evil and we shouldn't be like the snake and ruin things for others. After singing the song a bunch of times with us, Grandpa would always get serious and say, 'Chris, Maggie, now be sure to always do what you oughta, you hear?'

Hank added, "Chris, your grandfather sounds like a wonderful man. You know, you're not too old for the message of that song; I think your grandpa would have told you the same thing today. You have to do what you oughta. I think you know you have to let your dad get close to you again. He's not your grandfather, and he'll never replace the special love you had for your grandpa, but he didn't cause your grandfather to die either. He loves you and is just trying to help you."

Chris considered what Hank had said, tears welling in his eyes as he thought of the pain he had caused his father these past two years.

Leo added, "Chris, we are all kinda like bulbs on a string a' lights. Some of us be shinin' bright and some not so bright. Jus' like all them little lights on that big ole Christmas tree down in Hollidaysburg, when one of them lights go out on the tree, the whole string a' lights don't go out. Even after a bulb burns out the tree shines just as bright, minus the one ole burned-out bulb. Your life is more'n just you an' your grandfather — you don't have just two light bulbs on that string a'yours. You got lotsa folk in yo' life. You just gotta let their lights shine on you. If ya do that, your light gonna shine brighter too. Ya know what I'm talkin' about?"

Before Chris could answer, Rex chimed in, "We're probably just *loco hombres*, but we came to Hollidaysburg following some ole train headlights. We ain't sure where those lights came from that brought us here, but I got a feelin' your grandpa, Becky, and others felt your pain an' wanted you to keep on shinin' bright, an' not be a dimwit any longer."

Chris wiped his eyes on his sleeve and laughed at Rex's play on words, but he understood what the man was getting at.

Rex continued, "We didn't know what we were s'posed to do once we got to Hollidaysburg, but I think we was s'posed to help you see the light that guided us here. We know now we needed to be here because you needed us. We came to celebrate the joy o' Christmas with you an' hopefully bring some light back into your life."

Hank added, "You know, I think Rex is right. You are the reason for us being here, or as he once said, 'the reason for the season.' We each had something in our lives pushing us away from where we were and something pulling us here; you were what drew us to Hollidaysburg. It might be time for us to deal with what pushed us out of our comfortable nests."

Leo wiped his broad forehead and said, "I think the boys are right, but y'all remember, we ain't done yet. We gotta get this young man home to his family. Then we'll know for sure if that's why we're here."

Leo reached deep into the watch pocket of his overalls and considered what he had in his hand. He leaned forward and held out his big paw. Chris put his hand under Leo's and Leo released a 1904 Double Eagle twenty-dollar gold piece. He said, "Chris, I'm a thinkin' we ain't gonna have a lot of time for goodbyes tomorrow, but I got somethin' I want you to have. My granddaddy gave me that coin 'fore he died and tol' me not to spend it, but to hol' on to it, 'cause as long as I had gold in ma pockets, I was a rich man. *He said, 'Lee, you keep dat coin handy, som'aday you gonna meet someone dat might need luck mo' den you. Gib it to 'em when you fine' em.'* He tol' me I'd know who was deservin' of a gift of gold an' who was down on his luck when I met 'im, an' I know you that person. Chris,

149

friends are worth more than all the gold in the world. My grand-daddy wants you to have his coin. Merry Christmas, my friend."

Chris held the small but heavy coin in his hand, disbelieving Leo had traveled all the way from Georgia to save him from drowning, bring light back into his life, and come bearing this gift of gold. Chris studied the gold piece and said, "Thank you, Leo. I'll treasure you and your grandfather's coin forever." He shook Leo's hand and added, "Merry Christmas, Leo."

Rex pulled the ruby ring from his long narrow finger and polished the stone on his ragged jeans. He then took Chris's hand in his own. He slid the ring on Chris's right ring finger and said, "Chris, ole buddy, the ruby in this ring came from India. My own grandpap bought the stone from an Indian farmer during World War II. He learned the Sanskrit word for ruby means 'king of gemstones.' When he came home from the war, grandpap had the stone polished and placed in this gold setting. He wore the ring for years. When he died, he left the ring to me. Chris, my man, this ruby is better suited to you than it is to the likes of an old cowpoke like me."

Chris was overwhelmed with the generosity of the man who had given him his grandfather's prized ring. With choked voice and tears again building in his eyes, Chris said, "Rex, I'll do the best I can to live up to you and your grandfather's expectations. Thank you."

Hank walked to his sleeping compartment and retrieved a small velvet pouch. He slid what was in the pouch into his hand and studied it. He palmed the object and approached Chris. "Chris, this silver pocket watch was *my* grandfather's. He received it from the Ambassador of Spain more than 60 years ago. Three thugs attacked the ambassador's daughter near Chinatown in San Francisco. My grandfather fought off the muggers as best he could until a beat cop heard the young woman's cries for help. Two of the thugs were arrested on the spot. One got away, but the police caught him later. My grandfather was in the hospital for a couple of days, but the ambassador's daughter was not hurt. The watch was a gift to the hero who'd saved the ambassador's daughter."

Hank opened the watch and under the picture of a smiling young dark-haired woman and her somber-looking mustachioed father, was an inscription that read, *forever indebted, forever a friend.*

"Chris, let this watch remind you that you have many friends. You're going to touch the lives of a lot of people during your lifetime, but you have to befriend them first. I'm pretty certain you were the reason we were drawn to Hollidaysburg. Our work here is almost done, but yours is just beginning. We'll soon be going home to our families, as you will to your family. We hope when you go home, you'll have a changed heart and recognize the importance of your family and friends in your life. My grandfather's watch is symbolic for now is the time for you to change your heart."

Chris didn't know what to think. He looked at the photograph and the inscription, and then at Hank. With choked emotion, he said, "Thank you, Hank. I know how proud you must have been of your grandfather. I will never forget you guys and I will be forever indebted to you too. The watch is even more meaningful than you may have thought. You used an expression my grandpa always used. He'd always say, 'now is the time'. I think you're right. Now is the time for me to change."

Chris sat close to the fire with a sleeping bag swaddled around his shoulders. He stared into the flames with a clear mind and a heart that ached to see his mother, father, and sister. For the first time in two years, he realized his grandfather was still with him. In fact, he was certain his grandfather had something to do with bringing these three men to Hollidaysburg.

CHAPTER 15

A t 5:00 a.m. the sky was dark, and it stayed gloomy all day. Christmas Eve arrived with a fury never before witnessed by the quaint Borough of Hollidaysburg. Snow continued to rage over the mountains and into the valley. The Governor of the Commonwealth of Pennsylvania declared a state of emergency for western Pennsylvania, but few people in Blair County were aware of his proclamation. Electricity was out throughout the region, as was access to television and radio, except for battery-powered devices. Even telephone service was nonexistent.

Families gathered inside frosty homes trying to stay warm, worried about how long they could survive in such primitive conditions. The lucky ones had fireplaces warming their homes to temperatures somewhere just above freezing. Some enjoyed hot meals and showers because they had natural gas-fueled stoves and hot water heaters, but many families sat in the cold without the radiant heat of a fireplace, unable to cook or bathe. Everywhere, the foreboding topic of conversation was how long before plumbing would freeze, and pipes would burst. Along the length of the valley, hot and cold-water spigots dribbled to forestall freezing.

With a battery-powered radio broadcasting in the kitchen, the Ballentines hovered nearby to glean emergency news and weather reports, eager to hear something about their son. Instead, they learned the local weather forecasters predicted blizzard-like conditions continuing late into Christmas Eve. Although Joe, Mary, and Maggie had become aware of how serious the situation was for them, they each worried the weather would not only hamper search efforts for Chris, but if he were exposed to these conditions, he likely would not survive.

To prepare for their own safety, the family searched cabinets and closets for extra batteries, candles, matches, anything that might be useful in the uncertain hours and days ahead. Maggie, too, realized how serious the weather conditions had become, and she set aside her childish interests to join in the family's survival mission.

Sitting at the kitchen table with lukewarm coffee in hand, Joe shook his head, "You know we promised Father we'd come to Mass, but I just don't see how we can do it in these conditions. I suspect Immaculate Conception will hold both masses this evening regardless of the weather, as Father promised, even if he expects that only a few parishioners will attend. The church will be candle lit, and people will sit close together, as near the altar as possible to stay warm and to hear the homily. They'll play the piano instead of the organ. You and I both know he wouldn't let anything stand in the way of holding Christmas Eve Mass. But I think—"

Mary interrupted Joe, "Honey, I agree, we can't go to Mass in this weather, especially without Chris home . . . I'm afraid this is one Christmas we won't be attending church."

Joe nodded, "I'm certain Father Byrne would understand, but how about I walk you two to Mass, and then I'll come home and wait with Grace for Chris to return? If the snow is passable, you two can walk home on your own."

Mary held her hands up and shook her head. "That's too much. You aren't even feeling well."

"Mary, we promised Father we would come to Mass this evening. He and the Sisters have been so supportive of us. We owe them this, and we need the community's continued prayers and help."

Mary considered Joe's argument. "Come on, Joe! It's a blizzard out there. We haven't got electricity. This makes no sense. Let's keep the family together and safe."

Joe shrugged. "Honey, I'll walk you there and come get you after Mass if the weather is too bad. One of us has to be there to answer any questions our friends might have about Chris, or to learn anything they might know. We must go to church tonight, for Chris, for us, and for Father."

Mary gazed at Maggie for a moment and threw her hands in the air, "Okay, you're right. There's no reason Maggie and I can't bundle up and walk to and from Mass – it's not that far. And you never can tell, by some miracle Chris might just show up at Mass."

After setting his cup on the table, Joe winced and tried once more to rub the pain from his arm, "Okay. It's settled then. You two will go to eight o'clock Mass and I'll keep the home fires burning. If Chris comes home, I'll be here; if he ends up at Mass, you'll be there."

For the rest of the day, Mary, Joe, Maggie, and Grace each in turn stole into the living room and looked out the bay window to judge how much snow had fallen or to see whether some distant shadow might be Chris pressing through the waist-deep snow. Hour after hour, the snow continued to accumulate, but none of the hopeful shadows miraculously converted into Chris.

Near Cresson Trestle the campers awoke to much more wet, thick snow than they'd anticipated. The snow worked its way into the camp, and everything was soaked. Hank's compartment sagging from the heavy snow settling on its unshielded roof and melting into the fire-warmed cardboard. Hank and Leo dozed in the two remaining lawn chairs, covered by a shared sleeping bag and nylon tarp. Chris slept inside the two 55-gallon drums joined open-end-to-open-end, set near the fire. When the "sardine can" was fully assembled, as Rex referred to it, Leo had helped the boy climb in. As a final act of hospitality, Leo handed him the electric blanket and a sweatshirt to use as a pillow, and asked, "Boy, are you feeling all right?"

Chris beamed, "Yes, sir. I'm just anxious to get home."

Impulsively, Rex had thought aloud, "Let's hope ole momma bear don't come back here and decide to play Kick-the-Can with our kid-in-the-can!"

Leo had tapped the sardine can and reassured the boy, "You sleep tight now, Chris. Rex and me are gonna be right outside here. That ole momma bear ain't gonna be comin' back tonight. She's had enough of us. 'Sides," he concluded, "I think we'd smell her nasty hide a mile away should she decide to stroll toward us."

As the early morning chill hastened the eventual call of nature among the campers, Leo put on his boots to walk through a snowy camp interior, before leaving the camp to relieve himself. Only beneath some of the low-hanging branches, nighttime nesting spots for at least one deer and several smaller animals, was there bare pine straw.

"Brrrr," Leo said, slapping his hands together. The air was crisp. The heavy snow continued to plummet like leaden flakes, and the blustery wind blew a biting, damp chill. Brushing snow off the woodpile, Leo chuckled, "Now ain't this beginning to look like Christmas!"

Rex, talking from beneath the warmth of his covers, answered, "I 'preciate your enthusiasm as well as the next man, old friend, but we got nothing to eat, little to burn, and no more shelter for protection. That don't remind of the Christmases of my childhood."

Leo stoked the coals of the previous night's fire and began ripping pieces of damp cardboard from the last surviving sleeping compartment. Now far more serious, Leo responded, "We'll make do, Rex. We just gotta keep our heads about us."

As soon as Hank climbed out of his bed, Leo tore into the cardboard. Hank blurted, "Whoa, dude! That's my apartment you're destroying there."

Ducking and weaving, trying to avoid the smoke and steam rising from the nascent fire, Leo reminded his companion, "Hank, you ain't gonna be needin' your bunk any longer, remember? We gotta burn as much of this stuff as we can before we break camp. But we'll save some'a yo' box to use as we planned."

"Yeah, yeah. I know, but I just hate to get rid of the only shelter we have left . . . you know, just in case."

Rex, still sitting in the lawn chair he'd slept in, piped up again from under his covers, "Hank, if my memory serves me right, you and the boy was the only two who slept in a shelter last night. We're gonna burn that *apartment* a'yours, regardless. If we have an emergency, Leo and I got a place for you right here between us by the fire."

"All right, point taken. Let's burn it up — all the more reason for us to get down the mountain today."

Hank joined Leo at the fire and passed him logs and pieces of coal to add to the previous night's embers and the blazing cardboard and boards from the shipping pallets. The roaring blaze finally caused Rex to lift his head out of the covers. Looking toward the barrels, Rex tapped on the top one and said, "Yo, sardine. You in there?"

"Yes, I'm in here. Can someone help me get out?"

Rex patted the drum and replied, "Sure 'nough, I'll pop the top on your can, kid."

As Rex slid the "bottom" barrel down and Chris emerged stiffly, then looked right, left, up, and down, and said, "Wow! Leo's right, it does look like Christmas."

"I 'ppreciate your enthusiasm too, young man, but snow don't make Christmas. I'll take a little warmth, family, and hot food — you can have all the snow you want."

Rex helped Chris to a lawn chair near the fire and then stood the barrels upright, wiped the snow off the tabletop, and reassembled the table. Hank pulled the sooty pots and pans out of the wooden crate the tabletop had sat on all night and considered what he could make for breakfast this morning. As the fire roared, Leo scraped aside a portion of the existing coals and began roasting beans under Hank's watchful eye. Soon a char rose from the beans, and Hank admonished "Remember, Leo, city roast, not Italian. And

156

don't be stingy with the beans. Let's roast enough coffee for several pots. I'm afraid we're not going to have much else to keep us going today."

While the first of a seemingly endless series of pots of coffee began to perk and the campsite filled with the visible aroma of steaming coffee, Hank rummaged through their remaining food. There was just one can of corned beef hash, tomato soup, and fruit cocktail. With corned beef hash sizzling in the fry pan, Hank diluted the tomato soup with half as much water as recommended on the can label. The smoky fire, coffee aroma, and food frying caused the hungry campers' gastric juices to flow and their mouths to water.

In happier days back in Monterey, Hank had enjoyed creating one-of-a-kind omelets on Saturday mornings for Becky; her favorite was a fragrant mixture of onion, broccoli, and ham sautéed in butter, seasoned with yellow curry, and topped with Provolone. She'd laugh at what Hank served today: tomato soup fortified with corned beef hash. He also opened the can of fruit cocktail, spiked it with the last of his brandy, and set the mix to a low bubble.

Chris, sitting in a lawn chair near the fire, was still too weak to help the men in any meaningful way. Once Leo and Rex reassembled the table, Hank served the brandied fruit, soup, and coffee. Chris stared into the fire while he ate, and the men dined standing at the table as they made final plans to get the boy home. They had a lot to do before they could leave.

No one would be moving around outside in either Hollidaysburg or the woods until midday Christmas Eve at the earliest. It was dangerous just to be outdoors in treacherous conditions. The unprecedented storm had brought chaos to the valley, and there were no ambulances, police cars, or fire trucks capable of responding to emergencies. The Phoenix Fire Company and its rescue squad were as snowed in as everyone else. In fact, there would be no one available even to receive a call for help because the telephone landlines and cell towers lay dead throughout the region. A minor fall, a careless cut, or a domestic fire could potentially have life-threatening consequences. Caution was the watchword in Hollidaysburg and on the mountain.

CHAPTER 16

Maggie and Mary dressed in layers for their walk to Christmas Eve Mass, and Joe got ready to escort them to church. He tried not to let on just how badly he felt, but his pale skin, glistening with perspiration, gave him away. He insisted he'd be okay just to walk to church and back, and Mary reluctantly took him at his word.

Up on the mountain, the campers made last-minute preparations for an arduous cross-country trek to town. With his good arm, Rex had felled two fifteen-foot poplars, stripped off their branches, and trimmed their tops. Leo and Hank lashed one of the 55-gallon drums to Rex's nine-foot poles to create an Indian-like travois. The men planned to haul Chris down the mountain in Rex's ingeniously constructed sled. The barrel's smooth exterior was set low on the poles at the base of the drum and pitched higher than the poles at the top, creating an angle that would allow the travois to sled through the deep snow. Rex lashed a branch across the bottom of the drum to hold the barrel in place and a second crossbar under the top lip of the drum.

Inside the barrel, Hank packed the crushed cardboard from his demolished apartment, upon which Chris would sit while riding down the mountain backward. Because Rex's shoulder was still out of commission, he planned to carry Hank's grip and Leo's medical bag; Hank and Leo would pull the sled.

After eating the remaining oranges from the tree branches and downing the last of their coffee, Leo doused the campfire, and Rex stored the remaining gear in the one remaining upturned barrel. Leaving the camp otherwise intact, the group set off, with Chris inside what Rex called "the world's first armored sled."

Hank and Leo lifted and pushed against the horizontal sapling lashed to the poles that served as a yoke, and the group was on its way. By the time they completed the short uphill trek from their camp to the tracks, snow was falling hard and heavy. With the sled now on the railroad tracks, positioned between the two iron rails, Rex said, "Okay, guys, its time to get this sleigh airborne. Christmas is closing in on us, and it's time for some real holiday magic!" Rex threw back his head, waved his good arm maniacally toward the sky, and yelled to the snowy clouds swirling above, "Now Dasher! Now Dancer! Now Prancer and Nixen! On Cupid an' Stupid, and all the rest of you guys. Come on, let's get over the porch an' over the wall! Let's dash away! Dash away! Dash away all!"

In response to Rex's mangled call for Christmas magic, Leo and Hank threw their weight into the yoke like reindeer pulling taut the leather lead of Santa's sleigh, and the sled began bouncing, *thump, thump, thump,* from snow-covered tie to tie. Rex's two "reindeer" found it easy to pull the sled straight, because the single iron rail on either side of the track served as solid guides.

The team kept up a brisk pace until they reached the entrance to the stark-looking trestle, with its rails and ties covered deep in snow. The men looked across the span; snow was falling so hard they could see only halfway across. None of them had vocalized their fears about crossing until this point, but all three recognized the challenge that lay ahead. It wasn't going to be possible for Leo and Hank to walk side-by-side on the outsides of the rails *and* pull the travois across the narrow snow-covered trestle. Leo also didn't like the idea of Chris being trapped in the sled on top of a windy bridge during their crossing. Under his breath, Leo expressed to Hank his fear of Chris cascading over the edge of the trestle inside the barrel and into the churning stream below.

Their trestle-crossing conundrum was compounded by Chris's physical and emotional condition; the boy wasn't fit to walk across the bridge on his own. After some discussion and debate, Leo's suggestion for getting the group across was accepted unanimously. Hank would pull the empty travois. Leo would carry Chris on his back. Rex would throw the grip and medical bag into the barrel and follow behind, providing whatever support might be required from the rear.

Traversing the snow-and-ice-covered trestle would be like walking a narrow, shaking ramp without guardrails over Niagara Falls. And every icy step forward would be like walking on a surface covered with marbles. In addition to this tightrope walk without a net, the unpredictable, shifting winds and blizzardlike, whiteout conditions made the feat all that much more terrifying. In gut wrenching contrast to the unsettling ice and snow on the ties and rails, the wide void between each beam revealed deep, terrifying shadows that highlighted the roiling and rocky stream, some forty-five feet below.

The group was silent as they contemplated the challenge before them. Hank and Rex helped Chris, in all of his bulky winter clothing, onto Leo's even bulkier back. There was nothing for Chris to hold on to, so he wrapped his arms around Leo's shoulders as best he could and dug his fingers into the fabric of the man's coat. Leo warned, "Chris, my man, hold tight. Don' shift your weight at all once we're on the trestle. And no matter what happens, don' let go of me. If we fall, we go together. Jus' hold tight. D'ya hear me?"

Chris stammered, "Are you sure you can do this, Leo?"

Leo chuckled with false confidence, "Chris, I've carried bigger and worse injured men than you, farther distances, an' over rougher terrain. The main difference this time is nobody is shootin' at us! I can do it, don' you worry."

With trepidation, tempered by trust in the three men, Chris

agreed to do as Leo asked. This ordeal would test everyone's strength, balance, and agility, and it would try Chris's newfound faith in the men.

Hank took the lead and advanced the troupe onto the trestle. He tested his footing by kicking loose snow off the beams. A dangerous layer of ice coated each tie. Hank inched forward, wishing he were on the beach in Southern California rather than taking the lead for this treacherous trek across a lonely gorge under such perilous conditions.

As Leo approached the trestle, he took a deep breath and blew a billowing cloud of frosty fog ahead of him. With his arms under Chris's knees, he clapped his hands together, mentally preparing himself for the gusting, snow-driven 180-foot crossing. Chris pressed his forehead against the back of Leo's neck, closed his eyes, and said a silent prayer. Leo was well ahead of him there: his prayers had been said as soon as he realized he'd be carrying Chris across the span on his back.

Leaning forward and maintaining as low a profile as possible, Leo cantered along behind Hank's cautious lead onto the trestle. He dug the rubber tread of his boots into the snow to test his footing. Like Hank, Leo didn't like what he felt underfoot and didn't want to proceed further. No matter, he knew he had no choice but to walk as sure-footed as possible and trust each step would hold while he tread from tie to tie.

Rex followed behind, cussing each uncertain step.

The first third of the trestle crossing was shaky. Randomly the men threw an arm out in one direction or another in an effort to regain their balance after slipping on a tie. There was a lot of cursing and complaining, but so far everyone remained on their respective feet.

Just as Leo's confidence began to rise, a front-bearing frigid wind beat against his forehead, creating painful "brain freeze." Holding Chris as he was, Leo couldn't pull his knit cap down any farther to protect his bald head. "Chris! See if you cain't pull my ski cap down a bit. This wind's freezing my head bad!"

162

Chris loosened his grip to reach upward for Leo's hat. The shift in balance caused Leo to readjust his footing. At that moment when the two were slightly off-balance, the hammering wind shifted from its previous steady northerly direction to an unexpected thrust from due west. With Leo in mid-step, Chris's weight shifted right, and the gale blew Leo to the right. His foot struck the inside edge of the metal rail, and as he suddenly pitched sideways, he found himself looking over the side of the track and into the deep ravine. Instinctively, Leo over-corrected. He dropped low and shifted his weight forward and to the left. But in doing so, Leo developed a forward momentum that had him beginning to dart ahead toward the center of the track.

Leo held tight to Chris's legs, and belted out, "Whoa, man! I'm a-fallin', Chris! Hold on, buddy! We're going down."

Leo's stumbling misstep, compounded by the weight of Chris riding high and off-center on his back, sent him running forward, trying to get his feet to catch up with his front-leaning torso. Sprawling ahead of his lumbering feet, he stretched his stride farther with each step. Soon, Leo was jumping across two ties at a time trying to stay afoot. Leo called a warning to Hank into the wind.

With each bounding step, Leo knew he risked not finding suitable footing on the slippery ties, but he had no choice but to keep running. After he'd vaulted over ten or so consecutive ties, all the while fearing Chris would release his grip and fall off the trestle, Leo was running too fast to stop. He was going to collide with Hank and the travois within seconds. As he closed in on Hank, who was creeping ahead unaware of Leo's predicament, Leo considered whether to leapfrog onto the travois or sprawl flat onto the track ahead of him. The travois offered something to hold onto, but he feared the jolt would hurtle Hank over the edge.

Leo attempted a controlled sprawl. First tripping and then falling to his knees, Leo arched his body forward and stretched for the sled, like a drowning man grasping for a single reed. His forehead struck the barrel side, erupting into a shower of bright lights and stars. Spinning as he fell, Leo missed the barrel rim with his left hand and slid shoulder first off, the icy beam into the abyss; three fingers of his right hand snagged the upper edge of the barrel and held, keeping him from falling further.

Leo's body was splayed in all possible directions; his knees were supported by a single tie, his chest was flattened against a second, distant crossbeam. His cold, stiff fingertips affirmed his desperate grip on the rim of the barrel, giving him a brief opportunity to stretch his left hand into place beside its mate. Leo held onto the barrel with all his might and pulled even harder to secure his position on the trestle. Chris stayed with the big man, holding as tight to Leo's back as a tick to a deer's behind.

Although Chris and Leo were still on the trestle, the rear-end collision had jerked Hank backward and off his feet, as Leo had feared might happen. Blindsided by Leo's contact with the travois, Hank let go of his grip on the yoke, and like loose change falling through a grate, Hank vanished into the gap between two ties.

Leo winced, knowing a fall from this height likely would be fatal. There was nothing Leo could do for Hank at his point; he had to save the boy. He pushed and pulled himself in all directions, trying to raise Chris and himself above the barrel's edge. When he managed to obtain a secure footing, Leo stood and stared into the ravine. He saw no sign of his friend; Hank's body must have been carried downstream.

As Leo regained his balance, centering Chis once more on his back, he realized they needed to somehow get around the travois that blocked the track ahead of him. When Leo leaned over the back of the sled to see if creeping past was a possibility, he saw Hank's hands straining to hold onto the tie ahead of him; his body kicking wildly five stories above the stream. With his right hand, Hank reached as high as he could and grabbed hold of one the stout poplar poles attached to the sled, but that move wasn't gaining him a safer position.

From his place behind the travois there was nothing Leo could do to help as his friend was losing his survival struggle. Leo hollered over the barrel, "Hold on man, I'm comin'." But Leo wasn't coming. He couldn't get past the sled. The rails were too narrow, and he didn't dare sit Chris down.

Holding futilely to one of the poplar poles, Hank pulled hard but didn't have the strength to lift himself high enough to get his knees onto an adjacent tie. Dangling between two ties, he kicked and twisted, straining with what felt like virtually every muscle in his body. However, no matter how much effort he exerted, he wasn't able to leverage himself onto the tie. Hank pushed his left hand downward on the tie and pulled upward with his right, but his efforts were in vain.

Understanding what Hank was trying to do, Leo wrenched his body and pushed down on the back end of the barrel. As he did the yoke lifted, but the effort was not enough to raise Hank out of the abyss. Leo slapped at the barrel and pushed even harder, but Hank still didn't rise far enough to get a footing. His hands were slipping on the yoke. If something wasn't done soon, Hank would fall to his death.

From behind Leo, Rex had watched the entire event unfold. Rex was shocked when Leo and Chris began sprinting across the trestle. He stood and watched the pair, disbelieving that Leo would do something so stupid. It wasn't like Leo to panic and run, but it appeared that Leo had done just that. At the moment of collision, Rex understood Leo's dilemma and now he saw Hank's desperate situation as well.

Although he got a delayed start, Rex matched Leo's reckless stride step for step until he was upon the pair. As he leapt forward, he stretched his gangly arms around Leo and Chris, and his rough hands met Leo's big paws on the rim of the barrel.

Hank suddenly found himself thrown high into the air, and as he was propelled upward, he swung his legs over a tie, where he sat gasping. Rex's weight on the bottom of the barrel, along with Leo's and Chris's, was just what was needed to lift Hank to safety. Hank struggled to stand, anxious to get away from the gap that nearly took his life. On shaking legs and with weak, trembling arms, he sought to regain his balance and composure.

With everybody now back on their feet, shaken but only scraped and bruised, Leo regrouped the four panicked souls. "Okay, y'all. Is everybody aw'right?"

Hank's shaky voice reported first. "I . . . I'm okay, Leo, but I thought for sure I was heading into the ravine. Thank you guys for saving my butt. I wasn't making it on my own, and my arms weren't going to hold on much longer. I was within seconds of falling."

Leo nodded. "No problem, man. It's the least I could do after knocking you off your feet in the first place. We couldna' done it without Rex."

Leo released the barrel with one hand and placed his hand over Chris's, asking over his shoulder, "How you doin', pal?"

The boy's big eyes told his story. "I'm okay, but that just about scared me to death."

Rex chimed in, "Me too! I thought y'all was goin' for a swim and I'd be up here by myself. Don't y'all worry about me. I'm okay back here, other than still recovering from a near-fatal heart attack."

As the wind continued to whip the men from all directions and the snow cut at their faces, Leo shielded his eyes and said, "Glad to hear ever'body's doin' okay. Ya know, you gotta pay good money at a theme park for a thrill ride like that! Aw'right now, let's settle ourselves down and catch our breaths. We best be taking stock of where we are and how far we still gotta go. Pull yo'selves together now. I want everybody's head in this game b'fore we start movin' again. Y'all ready?"

The three men and the boy atop the narrow trestle were anxious to get off the bridge. Though their spirits were willing, each was too afraid to move as much as a single muscle forward. Were it not for the ongoing winter gale that heightened their very realistic fear of being blown off the bridge, they might have stayed put until spring.

The group huddled low to the track to avoid the wind and steadied themselves as they anticipated what the next ninety feet might bring. Despite his misgivings, Hank stood upright and picked up the travois yoke with shaking hands and stepped forward. Leo released his grip on barrel rim and followed behind. Chris had his fingers dug into Leo's coat, and Rex continued to press against Chris's back while the troupe inched forward.

Leo barked orders to the slow-moving group, "Okay, men! Let's get our butts off this bridge on our own b'fore we get blown off the damn thing."

Trying to buck up his buddies' nerves, Rex called out from behind, "Don't y'all worry none. I'm ridin' drag on this herd! I've got y'all covered. But, man-oh-man, please . . . *please*, let's not be havin' any more stampedes! Y'all hear me?"

Though no one spoke, everyone agreed with Rex's sentiment. Each of the three men focused his attention on the distant end of the trestle, their destination. Rex added, "Aw'right then, let's get this wagon train a-rollin'."

The four resumed their deliberate procession across the windy trestle with pounding hearts and oft muttered expletives. Gliding lightly, as if on thin ice, the foursome made it to the trestle entrance without further incident. When they passed the egress, the three men hooted and hollered, and jumped up and down like children. They hugged and slapped each other on the back, relieved to be on solid, albeit icy and deep snow-packed, ground again.

As soon as Leo lowered Chris to the ground, the boy hobbled off the track to the rail siding, which sloped toward the woods. Chris fell to his knees and began digging wildly in the snow. Assuming Chris was going to be sick, Leo scooted to the boy's aid. Putting his hand on the boy's back, he knelt beside the boy asking, "Whatcha doin' there, Chris? Ya' aw'right?"

Chris continued digging in the snow like a dog searching for a buried bone, and then beamed, "Here it is! Here it is, Leo." He pulled hard and then held his snow-covered prize high above his black and blue face. "I found my book bag!"

Anxious to get off the mountain, Rex shook his head in disbelief and hiked his thumb toward the sled. "Throw it in the barrel, son. An' climb in after it. We gotta get off this durned mountain and fast wouldn't be none too quick for me."

With the travois lowered onto the ground, Chris crawled into the barrel with his book bag resting on the bottom. Leo and Hank lifted the travois poles, and the group resumed its trek down the mountain. After following the track about three miles toward town, the group arrived at an eerily abandoned rail yard. The snowstorm had ceased all train activity; the town looked deserted. Despite how cheerless the village appeared, the men were off the mountain in one piece, more or less, and their spirits soared.

Rather than lifting the travois over the guardrail separating the rail yard from Highway 22 and pulling it through town center, the men agreed it would be easier to continue following the tracks until they reached Canal Basin Park. With their load and moods lighter, Rex had advised the group, "Let's take the easier, more scenic route through the park. I've had enough excitement for one day!" And off they set, each man walking with confidence.

The group passed the Canal Basin Park signage commemorating the now-defunct Pennsylvania Mainline Canal, Lock #38; the lock that once controlled a manmade stream upon which thousands of cargo-laden barges floated long before the railroad heydays. This snowy Christmas Eve, however, the park revealed nothing of its former life except for the antiquated lock.

Leo studied the luminous hands on his wristwatch: 7:10 p.m. If all went well, Chris would be home with his family within the hour, still four hours before Christmas. As the men pulled the travois over the covered bridge and through the park, Leo began singing "Silent Night." The four entered the west end of town as a solemn group, each deep in thought as they walked through the borough's deserted streets. After Leo finished singing, Rex led off with "Jingle Bells," after which the four sang any Christmas song that came to someone's mind. The quartet sang with gusto, and Chris glowed with battered happiness at being safe, in familiar terrain, and so very close to home.

The men were no longer on a downhill slope, or even level ground. Hollidaysburg is a hilly town, and Hank and Leo were beginning to strain under the weight of the travois they hauled over a seemingly never-ending succession of valleys and crests. Their strength had been sapped by the long trek down the mountain, and the life-preserving adrenaline surge that earlier pulsed through their veins was now beginning to dissipate. Yet, despite their fatigue, the men were elated; they knew they'd make it. And like a typical west Pennsylvanian, Chris encouraged his newfound friends on the crown of each rise by promising that his neighborhood was "just over the next hill."

As Chris looked past the shuttered tavern at the western end of Allegheny Street, the dark village had the feel of a wind-blown ghost town. Rex shared the perception, "Man, it looks like Dodge City, don' it? All that blowing snow reminds me a' tumbleweed."

The group stopped singing to observe the village's dramatic appearance, a change that caused Leo to reflect, "Chris, you were injured pretty bad just a couple days back. Your face is all black and blue, an' I had to close up cuts with stitches in two places. Your nose was broken, givin' you those two raccoon-lookin' black eyes. An' yo' lips are pretty swollen. Don't be surprised if your parents don' recognize you right away. In fact, you might scare the daylights outa 'em. I'm certain you don' look like the same kid that left for school last Friday mornin'."

Chris's glance went to the ground. "I'm not the same boy that left for school last Friday, but I am okay just the same — I'll be fine once I'm home. Besides, you don't know my parents. They'd know me anytime, anywhere. You wait and see how happy they'll be when they see me . . . and I can't wait for them to meet you guys!"

"Yeah, you're probably right," Rex replied, unconvinced about both claims.

As they pushed onward, bounding through the snow, Chris launched the group into an animated rendition of "Frosty the Snowman." The men sang with the joyful celebration of drunken carolers as they pulled the travois through the empty streets of the village, just blocks from Chris's home. But as they neared Chris's Street, the boy became somber. The men's moods also changed, and

169

they pressed forward in silence.

At 7:30, outside the Ballentine house, Joe, Mary, Maggie, and Grace were testing the depth of the snow in the driveway. Joe had opened the doublewide, wooden garage door manually, and Grace sprang out of the garage onto the snow-covered drive, where just two days earlier she had chased the girls. With Grace biting the snow as she bound through its depths, the Ballentines headed off into the darkness toward church, through the still falling flurry.

From the onset Joe's tee shirt was soaked in sweat. Once they arrived at the church, Mary and Maggie walked up the candle-lit aisle, entered the front pew, and knelt to pray. Joe sat in an empty back pew with Grace for a few minutes to catch his breath. Well before the Christmas Mass began, as soon as he felt up to the return trip, Joe stood and waved goodbye to Mary, who had looked back at him with unspoken concern. At the church exit, Joe dipped his fingers into the holy water, crossed himself, and walked out into the cold night air.

CHAPTER 17

C hris could hardly contain his jubilation when he saw and smelled the smoke rising from the chimney of his family's house. He called out from the street but got no response. Hank and Leo pulled the travois through the yard to the front of the garage, where Joe had left the door partially open. Footprints and trampled snow in front of the garage suggested the Ballentine family had been outside recently. In the dark of night, with no stars, moon, or streetlights to provide illumination, it wasn't possible for the men to tell whether the footprints led away from or toward the house.

Rex leaned down and lifted the heavy garage door with his good arm, throwing open the last obstacle keeping Chris from rejoining his family. He said with satisfaction in his voice, "Well, y'all, we made it! Let's get this boy inside with his family. They must be just about crazy with worry over him."

Hank and Leo lowered the travois poles to the ground and helped Chris climb out of the barrel. Hank pulled the empty travois around the side of the garage to get it off the driveway and out of the way, and Leo led the way through the garage. With beefy Leo propping up Chris, they stumbled between the Jeep and the interior wall of the garage leading to the utility room door, which Chris promised was just ahead in the cavern-black garage. After stomping their feet and brushing as much snow as they could off themselves, they entered the dark house.

Leo left Chris leaning against the island in the kitchen, saying, "You stay right here, son. We don't want you falling and getting hurt in the dark. We'll find your folks and bring them to you. Hold on now."

As the men ventured into the house calling, Chris was joyful about being home. Chris felt along the countertop for matches or a lighter and would have lit the candle on the island had he found either. Even in the darkness, Chris was overwhelmed with relief to be among familiar surroundings. He was home at last.

As he worked his way beyond the kitchen, Hank hollered, "Hello? Mister and Missus Ballentine? Your son is home. Chris is here."

Rex and Leo joined in calling for Chris's parents, and when they got no response, they began to investigate each room of the house, calling ahead as they went.

Leo hollered to the others, "Hey, there is a cracklin' fire a-burnin' in the fireplace. They musta been here not too long ago."

Rex climbed the stairs to investigate the second-floor bedrooms. Hank went down the hallway in the direction of the master bedroom, and Leo looked around the family room for any clues to everyone's whereabouts. Seeing none, Leo stepped out of the family room door and onto the back patio. A trail of footprints formed a path between the snowy patio and the back door of the garage, where firewood had been carried inside and stored, but nothing explained where the Ballentines had gone on such a stormy night.

While the men were searching the house, Joe approached from the street. As he plodded up the driveway, he found the doublewide garage door wide open.

"Huh? Didn't I close that door?" he asked himself. "I guess I'm more confused than I supposed."

In the darkness outside the garage, Joe was oblivious to the extra footprints in the yard, but as he entered the garage, he noted the snow-tracked floor. Chris must be home! With a much lighter step than he had had for several days, he felt his way toward the utility room, but stopped short when he heard a distant, unfamiliar drawl, "Looks like there ain't nobody here."

Joe backed away from the door, with his hand trailing the garage wall for guidance. His hand brushed against the aluminum baseball bat propped up near the garage door, and he stopped. He shooed Grace out of the garage and into the yard and told her to stay. He picked up the weapon and took off his cotton gloves so he could get a good solid hold on the metal grip. With his heart pounding, he sneaked through the utility room and into the kitchen. There at the kitchen island stood a man with a red parka pulled over his head. Over the hooded sweatshirt, the man wore an oversized, military-style fatigue jacket. The intruder was bent over, leaning lazily across the island countertop. Hoisting the bat and drawing it back, Joe yelled with a trembling voice, "What's going on here?"

Chris recognized his father's voice and turned toward him with arms outstretched. Leo, Hank, and Rex also heard Joe's voice, and they came thundering through the house toward the kitchen.

CHAPTER 18

J oe held the bat back, ready to strike as the shorter man turned and faced him. In the semi-dark kitchen, Joe searched the man's face but didn't recognize the stranger standing before him. The man threw his arms outward and stepped forward, mumbling through thick lips. Joe stepped back with his right leg, positioning his left leg forward and turned inward, resembling a batter waiting for the next pitch. Disregarding the batter's stance, the intruder lumbered forward, with his hard-heeled cowboy boots scuffing the floor. Joe swung the bat, aiming for the left side of the stranger's head.

The swing missed its mark and struck Chris on the shoulder. Just as Chris was struck, he yelled, "Dad!" Immediately, Joe realized he'd clobbered his own son. Joe dropped the bat and reverberating metallic pings sounded each time the bat bounced on the tile floor. No sooner had the bat fallen from Joe's hands than the nagging pain in his left arm exploded like a blown fuse, coursing electricity upward and into his chest, neck, and jaw. Joe's face contorted as he grabbed at the crushing pressure within his chest. Without another word, Joe crumpled onto the tile floor.

Chris yelled out, "Dad, Dad. What's the matter?"

He knelt where his father lay, taking his head in his arms,

crying, "Don't die. Don't die. I love you, Dad. I don't want you to die, too. I'm so sorry."

Transformed again into the well-rehearsed emergency medical caregiver that he was, Leo cussed, blaming himself for not protecting Chris, and then dropped to the floor, kneeling beside the boy. With Chris still holding his father's head, Leo first checked Joe's pulse and then listened for his breath. Joe's heartbeat with an unpredictable arrhythmia, and, more critically, he had stopped breathing.

Leo called out, "Rex! Find a phone and call 911. We need an ambulance here now!"

"You bet!" Rex replied. In the darkened room, Rex found the kitchen wall phone. He lifted the handset and began pressing 911 on the keypad. "Hey, what's the address of the house?"

Through his choked, tearful voice, Chris recited the address, "4347 Grandview... no, wait, 4743... uh, I can't . . .."

Leo said, "Don't worry; they'll get it from the phone trace."

Leo was already administering mouth-to-mouth resuscitation to Joe and massaging his chest in a consistent rhythmic manner. Breathing in, pausing, pumping; breathing in, pausing, pumping; breathing in, pausing, pumping . . .Finally, Joe was breathing on his own again.

Rex was unable to get a response from the call, so he punched the number in again. It took him a moment or two before he realized there was no dial tone.

"This ain't good, *amigos*. The phone is deader than ole Davie Crockett."

Leo rallied the others, "Well boys, we know what we gotta do. Let's get these two to the hospital and do it quick. Before we move them, I want to get a couple of aspirin into this man to start dissolving the blood clot and prevent any more clots from forming. Chris, where could we find some aspirin?"

"Umm, in the downstairs bathroom. In the medicine cabinet."

"Rex, see if you can find that aspirin bottle and bring it here."

Hank assessed the situation and assured Chris, "You sit right here at the kitchen table and don't move, son. We'll get you when we're ready. You might say some prayers for your father." He then added for the benefit of the others, "I'll see if I can find the keys to the Jeep."

He felt along the kitchen countertops for the keys, as well as on the dresser top and in the dresser drawers in Chris's parents' bedroom, and then he checked the Jeep itself. Nothing. To Rex and Leo, he said, "I can't find the car keys anywhere. We're going to have to pull these guys to hospital, but the travois will carry just one of them. We can't put both of them in the can. I'll look in the garage to see what else we can use."

With his hands out in front of him to keep from running into anything that might cause him to go down, he found his way into the garage where he rummaged around. After a few minutes of searching in the dark, he realized he could turn on the car's headlights. The reflective light from the vehicle eased his search. He found what he needed.

Rex brought a bottle of aspirin and a glass of water to Leo, who was monitoring Joe's progress. When Joe lifted his head during a moment of semi-consciousness, Leo placed two aspirin on Joe's tongue and told him to chew them and sip some water. Joe did as Leo directed, and soon thereafter lapsed back into unconsciousness. Leo checked his vital signs, which continued to be weak but stable.

"Shoot!" Leo said, "This wadn't s'posed to happen! Chris, we gotta get you and your dad to the hospital. Are you ready?"

Chris replied affirmatively and asked, "Leo, is my father going to die?"

"I don't know, son, but he's stable enough to move, so let's get goin'. We gotta get him to the hospital! Stat!"

Leo shouted these last two sentences with the urgency of a medical man who knew time was of the essence.

Hank came back into the kitchen and said, "I've found a toboggan. It'll do the job for Chris's dad."

The men placed Joe on the toboggan and carried him out of the house. They laid him in the yard, where they left him sunken in the snow, awaiting the trip to the hospital. Rex fetched the travois and dragged it around the house to the front. Hank and Leo carried Chris out the door and slid him into the barrel. Leo tucked pillows on either side of Chris's hooded head to protect him during their cross-country race to the hospital. Hank and Leo stuffed the remaining pillows into the barrel to keep Chris's body from bouncing around inside the metal can.

Within twenty minutes both of the Ballentine males were secure enough for transport, and the troupe set off running as best they could through waist-deep snow toward the hospital, leaving the Jeep lights on and the garage and front interior house doors open.

Mary and Maggie came home after Mass with glad hearts. They were thankful they had attended the Christmas celebration. As they approached their home, a whining, distraught Grace met them on the road. With Grace ahead of them, Maggie and Mary picked up their pace, stepping as fast as they could with Grace bounding ahead, leading the way. The garage door was open, and the Jeep's headlights were illuminating the garage. The living room inner door was open too, and there was debris scattered over the porch and front yard.

Mary gasped. From where she and Maggie stood on the street, the dark house and lit garage looked as though the place had been ransacked.

Even in the darkness from the street, Mary could see sets of tracks crisscrossing the snowy front yard. Her gaze followed the scene to the drag marks in the snow, where it looked as if something had been stolen from the house and dragged to the street and beyond.

Mary grabbed Maggie by her shoulders, and said, "We have to get out of here!"

Maggie protested, "What about Dad?"

"Honey, we need to run to the police station to get help for Dad. I'm afraid if we go in the house and meet up with whoever broke in, we won't be helping Dad at all."

She shepherded Maggie away from their home, pushing her in the direction of the intersection they'd just come from. Calling Grace to follow, the three Ballentines ran as fast as they could through the deep snowy streets of Hollidaysburg toward the police station.

CHAPTER 19

T he travois and toboggan crested the last hill before the hospital, to reveal the hospital's lights burning; the hospital generator was working. Guided by the bright *Emergency* sign, Leo and Hank tugged their two injured patients to the entrance of the busy emergency room. Rex had run ahead of Leo and Hank to alert the medical staff of their approach, and when the two men arrived at the hospital door a shivering nurse waited, speaking into a handheld radio. Because both patients had suffered serious trauma, one with head injuries and the other a heart attack, Joe and Chris were triaged right away.

After taking initial vital signs and listening to Leo's summary of Joe's, then Chris's conditions, one of the two attending nurses placed a page for a cardiologist and another for a neurosurgeon, both of whom were in the building in anticipation of snow-related emergencies. Officer Bartkowski, also present, noticed Chris and Joe's arrival. Jimmy and a second officer had been dispatched to the hospital to deal with an alcohol-related domestic dispute. The familial fracas resulted in minor physical injuries to three feuding men, but it created a dangerous situation and potentially escalating chaos within the emergency waiting room.

After separating the family members, obtaining their promise of peaceful behavior, and threatening each of them with arrest for disorderly conduct should they renege on their respective promises, Officer Bartkowski moved to the edge of the conversation taking place between Leo, Rex, Hank, and the emergency room physician and nurse. Leo did most of the talking, with Rex and Hank adding points of clarification from time to time. The moment he heard how Joe had collapsed as he swung at Chris with a baseball bat, Jim stepped forward and introduced himself. After additional information was forthcoming, he walked away from the group and spoke in a quiet voice into his walkie-talkie. He concluded the conversation with his superior by saying, "Yes, sir. I understand."

Jim rejoined the doctor and nurse and the three men, and announced, "Gentlemen, please follow me."

Reluctant to leave Chris, Leo hesitated. Bartkowski shifted his hand to his pistol handle and said, "Please come with me. Chief Jamison would like to talk with you men." Before leading the men away, Patrolman Bartkowski huddled with the second police officer. Jim then led the tired, disheveled mendicants, reeking of skunk, toward a secure room in the hospital to await the Chief. The three walked without talking through the emergency room waiting area, with sick and injured patients looking upon them as likely criminals. After entering the hospital's small conference room, Bartkowski spoke up, "You men are not being charged with anything at the moment, but please take a seat. Chief Jamison wants to talk with you to get a complete report on what has happened to Mr. Ballentine and how you came upon Chris."

At the Hollidaysburg police station, Chief Jamison approached Mary, Maggie, and Grace. Grace leapt to her feet in excited anticipation, tail wagging. The Chief patted the dog's head and scratched behind her ears as he looked into Mary's eyes and paused.

"Mrs. Ballentine," he started. "I just talked with Patrolman Bartkowski at the hospital. He is holding three bums who brought Joe and Chris to the emergency room a little while ago. We're trying to sort out their stories. Chris has sustained multiple head injuries over a period of the last few days. We need to get you two to the hospital right away. They will need permission from you to do whatever they deem necessary."

"Yes, yes…" Mary said, her mind reeling. "Umm, what about Grace?"

The Chief looked down at the dog, and said, "I think Grace will be fine here."

Zipping his heavy waistcoat, Chief Jamison picked his gloves out of his coat pockets and added, "I'm sorry, Mary, but we'll have to walk to the hospital. The roads are still impassable, even for emergency vehicles. I'll lead the way. I want to talk with these fellas."

Mary entered the Emergency Room entrance and caught sight of Father Byrne standing in the entrance waiting for her. She threw her hand over her mouth and cried, "No, no… Oh, no!"

Father strode forward and took her in his embrace, and said, "Jim Bartkowski sent Officer Shreve to the rectory to get me when Joe and Chris were admitted. I got here as fast as I could."

Mary was still sobbing when a physician approached them. "Mrs. Ballentine?"

"Yes?"

Extending his hand, the doctor introduced himself. "I am Doctor Schmidt, the ER doctor this evening. I attended to both your husband and son when they arrived about twenty minutes ago. Both have serious medical conditions requiring immediate attention. Will you sign these forms permitting us to run some tests and conduct follow-up procedures, should they be needed?"

Mary reached for the doctor's clipboard, "What kinds of tests, what procedures?"

"It appears your husband has had a heart attack . . ."

Mary's hand covered her mouth, and the doctor continued, "We want to use a catheter to probe his arteries, and conduct an angioplasty, if appropriate, or bypass surgery, if needed.

"Your son has had considerable head trauma, and we want to

run scans of his brain to ensure there is no bleeding. We have to get started immediately. Do we have your permission to proceed?"

"Yes, by all means." Mary signed the forms and handed the clipboard back to the doctor. She then stood looking lost, not knowing what to do next.

The priest returned from talking with the doctor and took her elbow. "Come, we have little time to see Joe and Chris while they are being prepped for their procedures."

Christmas Eve turned to Christmas morning before much more was accomplished in the hospital. Mary and Maggie were too worried to sleep, but too weary to stay awake. They sat in the waiting room and talked with Father Byrne, Officer Bartkowski, and the three men. The group shared every conceivable detail about the events that had unfolded on the mountain until they could no one could stay awake any longer.

By one in the morning, Joe was in a surgical suite and Chris had had x-rays and scans of his skull. A little after three a dark-skinned physician of Eurasian background came into the waiting room and awoke the group. He was worn but smiling. With a slight British clip, the doctor began to speak to the entire group, "Merry Christmas, huh?" he said with an ironic smile and a shrug of his shoulders. Directing his attention to Mary, he said, "Mrs. Ballentine, I'm Dr. Khanna. I am a resident here at Hollidaysburg Regional Hospital. How are you holding up?"

Mary felt disheveled. Her hair was out of place, her face drawn, and her clothes wrinkled from the long evening and night on the waiting room chair. "I'm okay," she said. "How are Chris and Joe?"

"Your husband and son are sleeping right now, and we are expecting them both to be fine. That is, with a little rest and recuperation." The doctor looked at his clipboard and added, "We're going to keep Chris for a few days to investigate the extent to which the blows to his head may have affected him. You know, compare his pre-morbid status to his current condition."

Mary blanched at the word "morbid," to which the doctor

182

smiled, "Your son is young, healthy, and recovering splendidly. Don't worry. He's doing well. We just want to make sure there are no surprises." After glancing at his chart again, he continued, "We also want to keep your husband for a few days, so we can better understand the extent of the damage to his heart. It appears he had heart attack symptoms for two or three days, culminating in a major cardiac event on Christmas Eve. We are uncertain about the amount of muscle damage he may have experienced. We found one blocked artery, which we took care of with an angioplasty and stent, as you know, but we want to check out the rest of his arteries. He's doing very well, too, and you can visit both Joe and Chris tomorrow."

The physician recommended that everyone go home and get some sleep. After the doctor walked away, Jim Bartkowski stood and said, "Mrs. Ballentine, let's get you home. If you are up to the walk, I'll carry Maggie."

"What about Grace?"

The Police Chief reassured her, "Grace can stay at the department for the night. The men on duty have been enjoying her. We'll get her back together with you tomorrow."

Before leaving, Mary asked to see the three men who'd saved her son and husband. Upon entering the conference room, she turned to the men and hugged them one by one. She cried with relief as she said, "I cannot thank you three enough for what you have done for Chris and Joe. If it had not been for you, I'm afraid I would have been a widow grieving over her lost husband *and* son. Because of you men, I hope to have many more Christmases with my boys."

Leo spoke for the men. "You have a wonderful son, Mrs. Ballentine. We were blessed to spend a few days with him. I'm

a-thinkin' you're gonna see a different child than you're used to. His heart has softened, and he tol' us how much he loves you, your husband, and his sister. An' he loves that dog of yours too! We want to stick our heads in and say goodbye to him, and then we gotta be gettin' on to our own families. You know each of us was searchin' for some purpose in our lives, not knowing where we'd find it. We found it in Chris!"

Mary nodded in agreement but couldn't say anything more.

As Mary and Maggie left the hospital with Jimmy, the men said their goodbyes to Chris. Actually, they said very little. Rex tousled Chris's hair; Leo held his face between his hands; and with memories of his last moments with Becky, Hank caressed Chris's shoulder. One by one, they left Chris's room and met up in the hallway.

Once the men were reassembled in the ER waiting room, they looked at each other, not knowing where to go from there. The Chief had questioned them earlier about their involvement in Chris and Joe's rescue, yet, hesitated in releasing them. Leo asked, "Chief, are we free to go?"

The Police Chief rubbed his jaw, "Not just yet."

Hank considered the police officer suspiciously and asked, "Why not?"

It was clear to the men that the Chief of Police didn't want to answer Hank's question, but he took a deep breath and began, "Well, you guys have done a lot for this community by saving Chris and his father, but—"

Rex now spoke up, "But what?"

The Chief grimaced, "Let's just visit a little while longer, and when I know there are no warrants for your arrest anywhere, I'll be happy to let you be on your way."

The men returned to dozing until they heard the Chief's handheld mike squawk. He listened to the report, eyeing the men all the while. When he tucked the radio back into his pocket, he leaned forward, "You men are free to go. Thank you for your patience and for rescuing our folks. You saved a lot of Christmases here in Hollidaysburg."

After shaking each man's hand, the Chief of Police walked off, leaving the men wondering where to go. Father Byrne held out his arms toward the men and said, "You guys must be exhausted. Please come home with me and be my guests at the rectory . . . have something to eat, take a hot shower, and see if we can't get you some fresh clothes. Stay tonight, or as long as you need to. The parish will work with you anyway we can to help you get home to your families but come . . . let's talk later."

The four men walked through the crisp, early morning air, too tired to talk, but feeling relieved that doctors were caring for Chris and Joe, and knowing Mary and Maggie would be resting at ease in their own home. The priest's visitors were hungry, tired, and pondering their returns to their homes. Now that their reasons for being pulled to Hollidaysburg were resolved, each man faced the personal issue that had pushed him on his journey.

CHAPTER 20

"Three, two, one . . . Camera One."

A finger pointed at the morning news anchor while the initial camera view zoomed from the smiling, three-person news team to the anchor, Donna Spellman. After shuffling and organizing the notes and papers before her, Donna began.

"We at Channel 5 would like to wish a very good morning to Altoona, Hollidaysburg, Blair County, and the surrounding areas. Electricity and phone service have returned to approximately eighty percent of the area homes and businesses. The remaining twenty percent of affected homes and businesses will have power by midday New Year's Eve, according to the power company. The State Police barracks report that most thoroughfares throughout the region are now passable, secondary roads are still problematic, and neighborhood streets won't be cleared for several days. Interstate 99 is open, the trains are running, and we seem to be returning to normal. We have much to be thankful for this December 28th.

"Channel 5 would like to spend a few minutes this morning sharing an event that was literally buried under our three historic snowstorms. On December 23rd, we reported on a missing Hollidaysburg youth, Chris Ballentine. We introduced the news event as a 'Chris Missing story.' We are pleased to tell you that Chris

186

Ballentine, our missing eighth-grade Immaculate Conception student, is safe and currently a patient in Hollidaysburg Community Hospital. He has experienced quite an ordeal, which we want to share with you. We will introduce many of the individuals who were involved in this Hollidaysburg Christmas miracle. Unfortunately, there are other casualties associated with this incident. Chris's father, for one . . . more on this after this commercial break."

After what seemed an interminable wait, the camera again focused on the news anchor.

"At Hollidaysburg Community Hospital, crowded into Chris's room is our own Susan McDougal. Susan, who is in the room with you and Chris?"

"Donna, I am here with Chris's mother, Mary Ballentine, his sister Maggie, and several students and faculty from Immaculate Conception School. As our viewers will recall, on the last day of school before Christmas break, Chris, a middle-school student, did not return home. Authorities report Chris spent several days with some hobos in the mountains near Cresson Trestle. Reportedly, the three tramps were living in a secluded camp within a circle of pines.

"We are not allowed to speak to Chris because he is recovering from injuries sustained during his ordeal. The doctors, however, expect his full recovery, and from the look of the large, excited group of friends who are here with him offering prayers and encouragement, Chris does indeed appear to be doing well—all things considered." The camera panned to Chris, whose swelling and bruising had just about peaked. He looked terrible, bandaged as he was, but his eyes were smiling.

Susan walked toward the crowd of supporters standing near Chris. "Donna, I am going to talk with some of the people in the room, including his mother, Mary Ballentine."

Susan held the microphone midway between herself and Mary, with both women facing the camera. "Mary, Chris was missing for several days. Weren't you worried your son might not return?"

"Yes, of course, we were worried about that possibility, but we prayed he would be safe. God answered our prayers long before

Chris came home; we felt in our hearts Chris would return to us. He has been through a lot these past few days, as has everyone in Hollidaysburg, but like our town...," Mary began to tear up and paused. She pulled herself together and continued, "thank God, Chris made it. We could not ask for a better Christmas gift than to have those three dear men, angels really, there to save our son, protect him, and return him to us. We are also so thankful to the residents of Hollidaysburg, Father and the Sisters of our church, our neighbors and friends, and Jimmy Bartkowski, our borough's fine young police officer.

"Donna," Susan said, "This gentleman is Father Byrne, Principal and Pastor of Immaculate Conception School and Church."

Panning the camera toward Father Byrne, the cameraman hesitated at Chris's hospital room window and the camera focused on a distant detail. Through the fourth-floor window, it depicted the entire stretch of Allegheny Street ablaze with white-lighted twinkling trees running parallel along both sides of the street. At the town center was the small festively decorated square, hosting the community's large, brightly lit, majestic pine.

Susan waited for the camera to focus on her and her interviewee, and then asked, "Father, what do you believe was responsible for Chris's safe return?"

Father Byrne cleared his throat and whispered, "Last week, Immaculate Conception lost a lamb from its flock. It was faith that returned our lamb, Chris's faith in three wonderful men who were guided to their camp in the woods by the headlights of passing locomotives. Sounds a bit crazy, doesn't it? But there were three men a couple of millennia ago who also followed a bright light for long distances for no other reason than to pay homage to a newborn baby lying in a straw-filled stable.

"I spent Christmas Day with these incredible souls. They came to Mass with me Christmas morning, but they asked that I not mention them to the congregation. They do not want their identities revealed to the media, and they are not looking for credit or reward. Now they've left our village, but not our hearts."

Sister Bernadette pressed forward and pumped a fist to show her conviction. With her rosary beads swinging from her hand, she said, "I would like to add that the Ballentine family was sustained by the charitable gifts and loving kindness of their Hollidaysburg neighbors, friends, merchants, and law enforcement officers. Immaculate Conception's very own Police Officer Bartkowski involved himself in this case from the beginning and contributed endless hours of his own holiday time relentlessly searching for our Christopher. I know Officer Bartkowski's new bride is just as proud of him as we are!"

Donna Spellman interrupted Sister's enthusiastic praise of the police officer. "Susan, Donna here. We have our legal reporter, Jonas Cutler, with Officer Bartkowski. Jonas, are you there?"

A suited man in his early thirties smiled at the viewing audience and said, "Yes, Donna, I am here with Officer Bartkowski, who has a fascinating and remarkable story. As he listened to sister sing his praises, Deputy Bartkowski said, 'Thank you, Jesus! I am going to be sleeping a lot better from now on.' Officer Bartkowski, what did you mean by that?"

Bartkowski looked surprised. "Uh, is that what you heard? I think I said everyone will be sleeping better now that Chris is home."

After a perceptible double-take, the reporter continued. "My mistake. All right then, would you describe how this ordeal unfolded?"

"It started for me when I received a call last Friday from Mrs. Ballentine informing me that Chris was missing. In all honesty, at the time, I didn't think much of it—it was the last day of school, Chris had not come home yet, and it was still early in the evening. I'm ashamed to admit it, but I just blew her off."

With damp eyes, Jimmy continued, "Sister Bernadette called me at home the following morning, and she and Sister Mary Agnes reminded me of my personal, social, and spiritual obligations, as well as my sworn oath to uphold the law and protect our citizens. Those two wonderful sisters motivated me into action, as they did when I was a recalcitrant eighth grader. Sister Bernadette chewed me a new—"

Officer Bartkowski stopped short of his graphic description, "Needless to say, Sister helped me see the light."

A broadly smiling Jonas took another tack, "So, what about these wonderful mysterious men, as Father Byrne referred to them? Where did they come from? What were they doing up on Cresson Mountain? What was their involvement with Chris and the Ballentine family?"

The rookie looked puzzled and said, "We're still trying to sort that out, but I doubt we'll ever fully understand what led the men to the Christmas miracle they were part of. These fine men asked not to have their identities made public. We're going to respect their wishes."

The police officer pulled his belt up to hike his pants a little higher on his portly belly and continued. "I can add though that the three had been riding the rails and were recently living in a camp just beyond Cresson Trestle. They saw Chris jump from the trestle, rescued him, and cared for him in their camp.

Jonas asked, "Officer Bartkowski, how is Chris's father doing? Did he survive the ordeal?"

"Yes, the doctors said because one of the men had given Joe aspirin, he had no further clotting, and his overall heart damage was minimal. The cardiologist performed a single angioplasty and inserted a stent to keep the artery open. Both the hospital and family have allowed me to announce that Joe is doing great. His condition is improving rapidly, as is Chris's health. Hopefully, without complications, Joe and Chris will both leave the hospital by the New Year."

Donna Spellman chimed in, "Jonas, please ask Officer Bartkowski about the mysterious three. Where exactly were the men living? Have you searched for them at their camp on the mountain?"

"Officer Bartkowski, did you hear Donna's questions?"

"I did. We had no legal reason to track them down other than to get a clearer understanding of what they were doing on Cresson

Mountain, but I was curious about their camp just the same. A few friends and I went up to the area where Chris described the campsite. Initially, we could find no evidence of a camp anywhere. The campsite was too secluded, and we saw no debris, no footprints, no fire pit, and no evidence whatsoever that anyone had been living in the area. We assumed the wind had blown over their tracks. However, we followed an animal trail down an incline where we had spotted a single stand of five blue spruce trees beyond the trestle, just as Chris had described the place. Inside the clearing was a fire pit, with little else in the enclosure. They had cleared the site, burned their debris, and left little behind except lots of animal footprints and a sleeping doe we spooked from beneath a low-hanging branch."

Donna Spellman again took control of the interview, and said, "Thank you, Officer Bartkowski. Back to Susan McDougal in Chris's father's hospital room. Susan, I understand Joe's wife, daughter, and son have joined him in his room. Is it correct you have a television and VCR recorder set up to play a portion of a video tape Joe Ballentine recorded as his family decorated their Christmas tree in anticipation of Chris's return home, Susan?"

"Yes, Donna, we are here with Chris and his sister and parents, along with their lovable golden retriever, Grace, who is on Joe's hospital bed with him, against hospital policy I might add."

With a wink and a smile, Susan added, "But, Donna, we won't tell anyone about Grace, will we? — Donna."

"I think after all of this, it would be very difficult to keep Grace a secret, don't you? — Susan."

Susan laughed, "You are right there, Donna! We are going to show just one small portion of the video you mentioned, which includes neighbors, friends, family, and strangers gathered in the Ballentine home last Saturday evening. These individuals came to the Ballentines' house, through deep snow and a moonless night, to offer assistance and love to a Hollidaysburg family in need of comfort. — Donna."

Donna turned to the viewers and continued, "And there you

have it, a touching story of faith, hope, charity, and yes, even Grace. A young man from our community was lost, but now is found. Add three mysterious men to the story, and you have a true Christmas miracle, unfolding right here in our own aptly named town of Hollidaysburg. What a story. Thanks to all of you who contributed to this heartwarming tale, and we owe a debt of gratitude to you, three kings of the road, who saved our middle school student, Chris Ballentine. We leave this news broadcast with the brief segment of video recorded by Chris's father during his son's absence."

"Donna? Donna, are you there?"

"Yes, Susan, we're here. Do you have something more to report?"

"Yes, we are joined in Joe Ballentine's room by a gentleman who needs no introduction. You'll recognize him by his telltale white beard and red coat, trimmed in fur."

Turning to the new arrival in Mr. Ballentine's room, Susan asked the interviewee, "Santa, you are three days into your post-Christmas vacation. What are you doing visiting the Hollidaysburg Hospital on December 28th? Isn't Mrs. Claus upset with you for being away so soon after your annual, Christmas Eve, marathon toy delivery?"

"Susan, I am a bit chagrined my team of reindeer, and I were unable to make deliveries to the injured and sick children who were in the Hollidaysburg Regional Hospital on Christmas Day. I have come today with these gifts to let those children know they were not forgotten."

"Santa, that is a wonderful idea, but it's three days past Christmas. Isn't that beyond the call of duty?"

"Christmas is never past, Susan. Christmas is in our hearts every day of the year. I am happy to be here on December 28th; I can take my vacation later."

Getting a message from her director to conclude the news segment, Susan wrapped up the interview by saying, "There you have it, Donna. Santa is working overtime to bring gifts to the children of Hollidaysburg. What a guy!"

Before Donna could respond, Santa snatched the microphone from Susan's hand. "Susan, I'd like to add that in celebration of Chris's safe return, the owner and operator of the Hollidaysburg Theatre, Mr. Tom Wasserman, asked me to announce that he will continue to show this year's Christmas movie through New Year's Day, at no cost. That's right, each evening the show is free for everyone! So, please gather your families together and celebrate Chris's safe return and the miracle men who saved Joe Ballentine's life by going to see this year's Christmas blockbuster at the Hollidaysburg Theatre, free of charge. Ho, Ho, Ho!"

Susan retrieved the microphone, held it close to her chest, and concluded, "Donna, this is quite a surprise brought to the community from Santa, who knows very well our town's favorite Christmas booster, Tom Wasserman." — Donna.

When Susan had finished speaking, the television anchor said, "This continues to be a remarkable story in every respect. Let's go next to the video recorded by Mr. Ballentine."

The television screen jerked and faltered, followed by a clear picture of a group standing, sitting, and kneeling near a lighted Christmas tree and a blazing fireplace. With mugs in their hands, the group beamed with the spirit of Christmas. A voice from outside the camera view said melodically, "one, two, three . . ." and as the group burst into song, television viewers' screens divided into a three-way split. Father Byrne, the nuns, and Chris's classmates in Chris's hospital room appeared on one portion of the screen, the middle portion showed the video recorded in the Ballentine home, with all of the folks near the fire; the third split-screen revealed Officer Bartkowski, Susan, the television reporter, Santa, and Mary and Maggie Ballentine standing to the left of Joe's bed. Joe and his son, Chris, were sitting together in bed, with Grace at their feet. Chris had his arm around his father's shoulder, with their heads touching. In the fraction of a second required to create the three-way video split, the three groups were joined together in song.

CHAPTER 21

After leaving the hospital very early Christmas morning, Father Byrne and his three guests had retreated through the deep snow and dark streets to the parish rectory. Wet, smelling of campfire and skunk, and exhausted, the men only lowered their bruised and battered bodies into Father's living room chairs and sofa because he insisted they do so. Despite their fatigue, they were too exuberant to sleep. They had found their purpose for being in Hollidaysburg for the past couple of months; they had performed their part in the unfolding drama magnificently. All that remained for them was to be on their way home. But that was yet to be. For now, the three men sat in Father's living room talking among themselves by flickering candlelight.

The priest carried into the room a tray of tuna salad sandwiches stacked three high. Around the sandwiches were pickles and cut vegetables. Father set the tray down and returned to the kitchen. Again, he entered the living room, this time with cookies, brownies, and coffee. With the food displayed before them on the coffee table like a feast, the men looked on hungrily. Leo and Hank sat together across the table from the priest on a leather sofa. Rex sat in a wing-back chair at one of the table's ends.

The priest noticed the men, seated around the food, looking a bit like vultures considering carrion on the highway. He clapped his hands together and said, "Eat up, men!"

Leo was the first to reach for a sandwich, saying, "Mmm, this is gonna taste good. It's been a while since we had anything to eat."

Father opened his hands in a gesture of offering and said, "Please, eat. There is plenty more in the refrigerator. Without electricity, it's all getting warm little by little, and we've got to eat it before it spoils. It seems the good ladies of the parish were afraid I'd starve over the holidays."

As Father poured coffee into the men's cups, Rex dug in his jeans' pocket. Curious as to what he might be seeking, Father asked, "Is there something else you need or that I can get for you, Rex?"

"No, sir, thank you very much. I got myself a little nip here, if you don't mind."

"No, by all means. I should have thought to offer you men something a little stronger than coffee. Would anyone else like some spirits, a beer, or some wine?"

Pulling a bottle of Tabasco from his pocket, Rex grinned, "This is gonna be strong enough for me, *Padre*. But I would like some of that coffee if you don't mind."

With trepidation, Hank sipped from his cup. His fears were soon relieved. Pleased that Father drank a higher quality brand of coffee than store-bought canned, Hank asked, "Father, can I ask what brand of coffee we're drinking?"

"Oh, I don't know what it is, Hank. Just some stuff I perked on the stove . . . something one of the parishioners gave me . . . he picked it up in Hawaii when his family was on vacation a couple of weeks ago. It isn't my normal store brand, but I could percolate some Maxwell House instead if you'd prefer."

Hank topped off his cup before Father Byrne could take the pot away. "Oh no, this Kona will suffice just fine, Father."

After an hour or so, when each man had unwound and was getting drowsy, Father said, "You know, I have some clothing intended for the Saint Vincent De Paul Society in here, some of which I bet would fit you three. Let's see if we can't get you guys

195

something clean to put on after your showers."

The men dug around in an assortment of eight boxes of different sizes, passing clothes back and forth between them until each man had two full sets of clothing. They showered, shaved, dressed by candlelight, and returned one at a time to the living room.

Father Byrne looked at his watch, "You guys stay up as long as you wish, but I need to get to bed. Father Mac offered Midnight Mass for me last night, but I have to be up for the eight o'clock Christmas Mass. If I am going to be anywhere near coherent, I must get some sleep."

With the priest's help, the men found places to stretch out — on the floor, the guest bed, the couch — but each of them had considerable difficulty finding sleep.

Father's alarm sounded at 6:30 a.m., and as Father showered, Leo dragged himself out of the guest bed and roused his sleeping buddies in the living room. "Hey, y'all," he whispered, "I don't know 'bout you, but I'm gonna go to church with Father. Anyone else up for a little gospel this morning?"

Yawning, Hank nodded in agreement, and Rex, without lifting his head from under the covers, held up his left hand bearing a thumbs up. The men threw their new clothes on and headed off to church with the celebrant.

Father Byrne did not mention the men during the Mass, as the men had requested, but they were moved by his Christmas homily, recognizing his indirect acknowledgement of them. Of course, this Mass was about the forever-moving story of the birth of the Christ child. But Father began a tradition that Christmas morning, one he'd maintain throughout the remainder of his years as an active priest. He paid considerable attention to the three wise men, the choice and commitment they'd made, and how on faith alone they'd walked away from their lives, followed a guiding light long distances, just to pay homage to the child born in a manger.

After Mass, Father and the three men returned to the rectory. Digging into the refrigerator and pulling eggs and ham out, Father said, "How do you men want your eggs?"

Hank replied, "Father, if you'll allow me, I'd love to see what you have in there to whip up some omelets."

"That sounds wonderful, Hank. In seminary, my fellow seminarians never allowed me to cook. I was that bad. I am certain we'd all appreciate your breakfast more than mine."

Hank jumped out of his chair, anxious to cook on a gas range again, but before he left the room, Father said, "Listen . . . isn't there someone you'd like to call this morning?"

Hank paused and then said, "Maybe later. I'll cook right now and someone else can call home."

"What about you, Leo?"

"Um, yeah, maybe later. I got some thinkin' to do before I call home."

"Rex?"

"Ah, thanks, *Padre*, but nobody's goin' to be there."

"Rex, it's early morning in Texas right now, where would your family be?"

"Oh, I don't know — church probably."

"What's with you men? Don't you want to talk to your families?"

Hank slipped into the kitchen, while Rex and Leo looked solemnly at the floor.

"All right, then. I know you men need to be on your way, and I don't want to delay you any longer. In fact, Immaculate Conception Parish would be happy to fly each of you home. I think we might be able to get you to Pittsburgh International by bus today, and then you could be out of this weather mess and on your way."

Hank spoke from the kitchen doorway, "Thank you for your very generous offer, Father. Speaking for myself, I have a credit card, and I would prefer to buy my own airline ticket. I don't want to benefit from this experience in any way other than as I have already. I've begun to get my life back. Who could ask for more?"

Leo nodded in agreement. "Father, I 'preciate your generosity too. But I got some thinkin' to do b'fore I get home, an' I was thinkin' I might just catch a Greyhound. Goin' home by bus is gonna give me the couple days I need to pull myself together."

Rex, in turn, set his coffee cup in its saucer and said, "*Padre*, I got one more thing to do before I get back to Texas, and, call me crazy if you'd like, but I want to go home the same way I came — hitchin' a ride in a boxcar. But I think all three of us would like to be on the next Greyhound to Pittsburgh, so we can start our journeys."

Father listened to the men and raised his hands in resignation. "Rex, I don't think you're crazy —"

Leo interjected, "Then you're the only one!"

Father laughed and then pressed the men a bit, "Isn't there someone you'd like to call today, given that it is Christmas morning, after all. Feel free to use the phone on the corner of the desk in my study. And please talk as long as you'd like."

Stalling, Rex replied, "Uh, *padre*. I tried to use the phone at the Ballentine's house, and it was deader than Trigger and the Lone Ranger, both."

Father Byrne slapped his knee and pointed at Rex, "That's good, but, Rex, I checked the phone just now before sitting down with you men, and I am happy to announce that, just like our savior, the local phone service has been resurrected . . . hmmm, I guess I'll have to work that into my Easter homily, won't I?"

Leo stood first, nervous about making his call, but always the first of the three to confront difficult challenges, "I guess I'll make a quick call to someone an' let her know I'm a-comin' home." Leo shuffled into the den, picked up the phone, and slowly pushed in the Georgia area code and the rest of the number. He stood with anxious anticipation waiting for the phone to be answered, and when he heard a woman's voice gleefully say, "Merry Christmas," he sat down.

Leo couldn't speak. He moved his lips, but no sound passed over them. With tears running down his dark cheeks, he heard the woman again sing into the phone, "Merry Christmas."

He tried to talk again but just couldn't. He sat with the phone to his ear, and Melvin asked in the background, "Who is it, honey?

Is it Leo?"

Leo sobbed as he heard his nephews and nieces shrieking with excitement in the background. His sister's family celebrated Christmas in his house, and everyone sounded so happy. He was just about to hang up the phone when he heard his sister say, "Leo, baby. I hear you breathin'. Are you okay? Talk to me."

Leo forced air from his belly and a weak croak emerged from his throat. The pronouncement was barely loud enough for his sister to hear, but Brenda did hear just the same. All Leo managed to utter was, "I'm a-comin' home . . ."

Before he could say any more, Brenda screamed, "Leo's comin' home!" The house erupted in celebration, making him cry even more. Leo pulled himself together enough to carry on a jagged, emotional conversation with Brenda, and after catching up for five minutes or so, she bubbled, "Wait Leo, someone wants to talk with you."

Expecting Melvin or one of his nephews or nieces, Leo cleared his throat of emotion. When the speaker got on the line, Leo recognized the gentle voice as soon as she said, "When will you get here?"

"Oh, Hey! I ain't sure. I'll be comin' in on the Greyound. Probably the 28th or maybe the 29th."

"Can I pick you up?"

Running his big hand over his bald scalp, Leo smiled and said, "If your daddy says you can?"

There was a pause on the other end, as if permission were being sought, and then, "Leo Regis! I might be the choir director for my father, but he ain't gonna tell me if I can pick you up at the bus station!

"So, you sayin' you want me to bring daddy to the bus station too?"

Leo could see how his future was going to be fast-tracked as soon as he got home, between Edna and his sister. "No, Edna, don't be bringin' your daddy to the bus station. I jus' wanna see you. I'll talk to your daddy real soon, though."

"An' what's this I hear about you buildin' a new house . . . for me?"

Smiling again, Leo said, "Edna, I ain't saying nothin' more right now. Now you put Melvin on the phone an' let me tell my brother-in-law Merry Christmas." In his softest baritone, Leo whispered, "An' I jus' want you to know I cain't wait to see you. I've missed you. Merry Christmas."

"Oh, Leo! That's so sweet. I can't wait to see you too. Okay, I'll put Melvin on the phone but please call me an' let me know when to pick you up. I can't wait! Bye now, an' Merry Christmas, Leo."

After extending Christmas wishes to Melvin and the kids, Leo joined his friends in the priest's living room. Hank stood to replace Leo at the phone, and said, "I don't know what that man heard from Georgia, but I've never seen him looking so happy. I hope my call is half as good!"

Like Leo, Hank felt trepidation about placing his call. He dialed Stan's number, not knowing what he'd say to his friend after leaving him to run the restaurant alone. When his buddy answered the phone with a groggy, "Hello," Hank remembered the time zone differences. "Oh, hey dude, what are you doing in bed? It's Christmas morning, and it's 9:30 already. Rise and shine!"

"Well, good to hear your voice too, sunshine! Merry Christmas, Hank. If you must know, I'm still in bed at this late hour because, one, it's just 6:30 here; two, I'm Jewish, and this is a day for Jews to sleep in. You Christians have closed down just about everything in town—why get up? There isn't even anything good on TV. And three, I was up late last night planning a New Year's Eve party."

"New Year's Eve Party? Save me a place. I'll be home, but I won't have a date. I'll be there, though—where is *there*, by the way?"

"What do you mean, where is there? You're co-hosting the affair. It's going to be at the restaurant. I'm closing the place New Year's Eve and New Year's Day—if you get home early enough, maybe you could help me prepare the food for this small shindig.

It's going to be just you, me, and Sandy, and forty or so of our clos- est friends. Are you sure you're up to a party, man?"

"Yes, I'm sure. The thought of seeing everyone sounds terrific. I told you that when I came home, I'd be better . . . and I am. I am real good, Stan! I've had an incredible experience. You won't be- lieve it. Becky led me on quite an adventure. I can't wait to tell you about it."

"I can't wait to hear, but, hey, your mention of Becky reminds me . . . Beck's friend Momoko Tanaka was down from San Francisco and stopped by the restaurant to see you a few days ago. She said she was just checking on how you're doing and felt lousy she hadn't seen you since the funeral . . . couldn't bear seeing you without Becky."

"That was really nice of her. She's a great girl. Almost as nice as Becky. Guess that's why they hit it off so well. It sounds like she's kind of pulled it together too. I'd like to see her and catch up and visit with some of Becky's other friends too. I'd like them to know I'm moving on, and I hope they are too. Did you get Mo's number or address?"

"No, I didn't," Hank's heart sank, "but better than that, I invited her to the party. She's not seeing anyone and didn't have plans. Said she'd be there for sure. Looks to me like you might have a date after all, old chum."

"Let's not push things, Stan, but I think Becky would be okay with me seeing Mo. We'll see. Well listen, buddy. I've gotta get go- ing. I want to get to Pittsburgh airport and get the next available plane out, and who knows when that will be, given how crazy air- ports and airlines can be over the holidays."

"You sound like a changed man, my friend. That's the best Christmas gift I've ever received, which come to think of it isn't saying much given that I don't often get Christmas gifts. Merry Christmas, Hank. I'll be waiting to pick you up."

Flushed with excitement, Hank said, "Don't worry. I'll call just as soon as I know the flight details. Merry Christmas, Stan, and be- latedly, Happy Hanukah."

After setting the cordless phone back in its cradle, Hank joined the others with the same look of glee that Leo had after placing his call. Hank pointed to Rex and said, "You're up, mate!"

Rex looked at the others and shrugged. "What do you mean, I'm up?"

"Your turn to make a call, cowboy. Now get in there and call your aunt or brother or somebody and wish them Merry Christmas."

Rex pushed on the arms of the wingback chair and reluctantly lifted himself out of his seat. He stood for a moment thinking and walked tentatively into the den. The others listened but neither conversation nor merriment could be heard in the priest's study. Leo and Hank both walked into the room to check on their friend. Rex sat at Father's desk with his head resting on his crossed arms.

Hank put his hand on his friend's shoulder, and Leo asked, "What's up, Rexter?"

The rough and tough cowboy lifted his head. Tears streaked his cheeks.

"What is it, man?" Leo asked again.

With an uncharacteristically weak voice for a macho, tough-talking Texan, Rex said to his friends, "I was a-thinkin' that as bad as I want to get home, and as much as I miss my life down in my little corner'a Texas, I'm gonna miss you guys most of all. Of all the good friends I got, none are better than you two."

Hank threw an arm around Rex's shoulder and pulled him close. Leo threw his arm around Rex's neck from the other side, and the three rugged men stood solemnly contemplating what they had been through together: how they'd met; how they'd lived together; how they'd worked seamlessly to save Chris's life; and now, how they were leaving each other to step back into their previous lives.

Leo said, "I want you guys to meet Brenda an' Melvin an' the kids an' my choir director, Edna Powell." Hank and Rex lifted their eyebrows in unison, suspecting they now knew where Leo went when he sat by the fire in silent reverie. "An' I say we gotta promise to get together once't a year, sorta like a reunion. An' I'm invitin' you both to my house for Thanksgivin' next year. What do ya say?"

"Count me in," Hank committed.

Rex concurred. "Me too, and I'd like y'all to meet my family and enjoy a Texas Thanksgivin' the next year."

"Fine by me," Hank replied, "And we'll do a California Thanksgiving the third year. It's settled then. We'll get together every Thanksgiving with each other's families, and that way we can stay in touch. Now make your call, dude. We gotta be getting to Pittsburgh."

Feeling as if a load had been lifted from his shoulders, Rex phoned his aunt, whom he knew would have all the family gathered at her place for Christmas. When she answered, he said, "Merry Christmas, Aunt Ruth. I wanted you and Uncle Bud to know that I'm a-comin' home."

"Are you bringin' that autograph I asked for?"

"I sure am—gonna pick it up on my way back. Whose autograph would you like?"

"You best get me Wayne Newton's autograph or don't bother comin' home." Then with a cackle, she said, "Well, you come home with or without Mr. Newton's autograph. We've missed you something terrible and we just want our wanderin' boy home."

"I'll be there PDQ. Give my love and Christmas wishes to the family. I'll catch up with everybody when I get home. I gotta get now, so we can catch a ride. Love ya, Aunt Ruth."

"Love you too, boy. Now git! We're gonna be waitin' for you on pins and needles."

Rex beamed as he joined the others in the living room. Grabbing another sandwich from the tray, he said, "*Padre*, we're traveling light, an' we know where the bus station is. I hope you don't mind if we eat and run, but we're anxious to get goin'."

Before the priest could respond, Hank added, "Father, back at the campsite we left the lawn chairs wrapped in what's left of our nylon tarp. We put the camping equipment, pots and pans, axe, and the like inside the one barrel still on site. The barrel is sitting upside down on the tabletop with a heavy rock on top to keep it in place, so everything should stay nice and dry. Leo's got his medical bag with him, but other than the table and things in the barrel, we burned everything else. Please tell Chris we hope he and his father will go to the campsite this summer, when the weather is good, and do some camping."

Father replied, "That's a wonderful idea, Hank. I'll be sure to pass it on."

Rex chuckled and said, "But tell the boy to be sure to check the train schedule b'fore crossin' the trestle."

CHAPTER 22

The men left Hollidaysburg by Greyhound bus, and parted ways in Pittsburgh. Leo continued on to Georgia by bus, Rex jumped a freight train carrying Hank's grip, and Hank flew home. The men traveled to their homes without incident and celebrated the New Year with loved ones.

They re-entered their lives with newfound purpose. Leo built his new house, and when it was completed, he and Edna Regis moved in. Melvin and Brenda painted their house, and Melvin and Leo farmed their land together. Hank and Momoko married, with Becky's blessings. Mo, like Becky, loved Hank's omelets and his occasional Vidalia-doctored corned beef hash, spiked with a splash of Tabasco. The restaurant business grew steadily, and Stan was both relieved and thrilled to have his partner and best friend back. Rex met a young filly while on a fishing trip to South Padre Island with his brother. Rhonda, who goes by the nickname Rusty, reeled Rex in without him even knowing she was trawling. A Texas-sized romance ensued, and like a prairie fire, their passion raged. Rex and his cowgirl married the following October, just in time to travel to Georgia for Leo's Thanksgiving celebration.

That year and every year thereafter, the three couples got together with the host family's relatives for Thanksgiving. The holiday fare always included turkey, but they learned to look forward to alternating between home-style roast turkey with cornbread or pecan stuffing, mesquite-grilled turkey, or some unique gourmet turkey repast. The couples' children became fast friends and referred to each other's parents as aunts and uncles, and to each other as cousins. Whenever the families were together, they gathered all of the children and Leo would lead the group through the verses of *Little Green Frog*. Afterward, Rex or Hank would settle the youngsters down and remind them always to do what they oughta.

Without fail, the three couples exchanged Christmas and birthday cards and occasional calls with the Ballentines. Chris and his father became close — closer than Chris had ever been with Mary's father. On occasion, to commemorate his grandparents, Chris would make his grandfather's cucumber salad, always using sour cream and a little onion. The family renewed grandpa's Christmastime tradition of walking downtown to see the Gearhart Christmas window display, followed by drinking hot chocolate at the Capitol Hotel, and then walking across the street, past the brightly lit, twenty-foot blue spruce now growing in the town square, to see Mr. Wasserman's latest Christmas blockbuster. Chris and Maggie never became too old for the tradition. Mary and Joe were forever grateful their son had been reborn as part of this Hollidaysburg miracle that changed so many lives in so many ways.

Between the influence of angels in heaven and the response of the multitude with faith on earth, the Hollidaysburg Christmas miracle, like that year's holiday weather, became an event long remembered and celebrated by the folk of the quaint village. The men's simple willingness to follow a Light and to gather where the Light called them, there to await God's plan, set the scene for a real Christmas miracle.

ACKNOWLEDGEMENTS

When the indie press that originally published The Hollidaysburg Christmas Miracle closed their doors during the Covid-19 pandemic, my book was adrift. Eventually, all printed copies of the book sold. There were no more copies, though there were frequent requests. I am grateful to Artwell LLC (artwell.ai), a Seattle-based company that creates intelligent writing tools to amplify human creativity. They shared their publishing insights and took over re-publishing the book for an eager audience. Using their Artwell Story Engine platform — which helps writers craft and refine narratives — alongside traditional publishing expertise, Artwell created a modern design, cover, and presentation, as well as navigated the convoluted path to online and paperback publication. Special thanks to Artwell for its invaluable, careful, and dedicated insights and contributions.

Thanks are due to too many family members and friends to mention. These individuals offered to read drafts of the book while I wrote it and provided useful and thoughtful commentary. My gratitude goes to two Hollidaysburg residents who read and commented on an earlier draft of the novel, Ms. Patricia Winters and Ms. Lucy Wolf. I am most appreciative of the editorial comments and support of my wife, Mary Jo Bracken, who ceaselessly encouraged me to write this holiday novel about the greater Altoona and Hollidaysburg, Pennsylvania community where she was born and raised.

Special thanks to my editors Bruce Bracken, Jr., Peter Chapman, and Sofia Starnes. Bruce encouraged me to continue this project long after the initial draft of the manuscript had been misplaced during the family move from Tennessee to Virginia. His insights into character and plot development were especially helpful as I began the project. Peter, a trusted copy editor with whom I had worked for more than twenty years on other projects, willingly took on a new fiction voice to help sharpen my message. Sofia has been a blessing since I first met her. Sofia, a former Virginia Poet Laureate and poetry editor, helped me understand the importance of conflict, tension, apprehension, sensitivity, and conveying emotion in fiction. Sofia provided the encouragement and companionship that this author needed on his solitary journey from being a well-published professional author to becoming a published fiction author.

Sincerely, thanks to you all.

Bruce Bracken

ABOUT THE AUTHOR

Bruce Bracken

Bruce Bracken obtained a Bachelor of Science degree from the College of Charleston and Master's and Doctoral degrees from the University of Georgia. He is currently a Professor Emeritus at The College of William & Mary. During his career, Bruce published more than two hundred articles, books, psychological tests, and related professional materials.

Bruce has held elected offices and chaired committees for the American Psychological Association, the International Test Commission, and the National Association of School Psychologists. He is a Fellow of the APA in two divisions, and a Charter Fellow of the American Educational Research Association. Dr. Bracken is a Diplomate and Fellow in the American Board of Assessment Psychology. Bruce received a "Senior Scientist" award from the American Psychological Association and the "Lifetime Achievement Award" from the University of Georgia.

In addition to his scholarly contributions, Bruce has flourished writing fiction, including three novels: Invisible, The Hollidaysburg Christmas Miracle, and Achilles: Feet of Clay.

211

BOOKS BY THIS AUTHOR

Achilles: Feet Of Clay

From the rubble of Beirut to the shores of Virginia Beach, one man's journey from brokenness to transcendence becomes a testament to the power of love.

Beirut, 1983. Marine Corporal Achilles Secours survives the terrorist bombing that kills over two hundred of his brothers-in-arms. Though his body heals, his heart hardens, and his spirit fractures beyond recognition.

Twenty-five years later, Achilles drifts through life — a disgraced ex-Marine living in a tool shed, surviving on odd jobs and whiskey. When a drunken night lands him in jail for a murder he didn't commit, fate intervenes in the form of Dr. Sylvia Feinstein, a court-appointed psychologist whose compassion cuts through his defenses. Under her care, Achilles confronts the ghosts that have haunted him since Beirut, discovering not only the roots of his rage but also the fragile beginnings of redemption — and love.

But when his past resurfaces in the form of betrayal, violence, and the desperate cry of a woman he once loved, Achilles must choose between vengeance and grace. In doing so, he will uncover a divine truth: that love has the power to overcome even gravity itself.

Haunted by loss, drawn toward the miraculous, Achilles Secours will learn that true healing begins only when the heart surrenders.

Achilles: Feet of Clay is a sweeping story of trauma, redemption, and transcendence—a modern myth that asks whether even the most wounded soul can rise above the weight of the world.

Invisible

A depressed Campbell Hayden nurses a few ales in a Sackets Harbor pub ten miles out of Watertown, New York. After last call, the twenty-nine-year-old leaves the bar and disappears into a whiteout blowing off Lake Ontario. Ending up in Albuquerque, New Mexico, Campbell starts a new life in a multi-hued barrio where a person can live comfortably unnoticed. Campbell settles in quickly, having spent an entire life as an invisible – "It's not that people can't see me," Campbell reveals, "mostly they just don't...While it is human nature to want to shine, or to prostrate or prostitute oneself in order to achieve notice, or even garner a glimmer of envy in the eyes of family or friends, I've accepted that such self-illuminating strivings, at least for me, are folly. I am invisible."

Campbell's otherwise ascetic life in the barrio is dramatically transformed by several incidents. In response to these affronts, Campbell devises a plan to become visible, and accepts that substantial physical, emotional, and interpersonal life-style changes will be necessary in order to be seen. Along with these personal sacrifices, Campbell bravely disregards the dangers of standing out in full view. As a stunning, larger-than-life visible, Campbell forges true love, but also creates mortal enemies. Campbell's newfound visibility, love, and enemies cannot coexist – the question is who will survive?

www.ingramcontent.com/pod-product-compliance
Lightning Source LLC
Chambersburg PA
CBHW020629110726
47899CB00002B/710